AF266290

A BONE TO PICK

MABLE MCCOY

LILIANA HART

Copyright © 2025 by Liliana Hart
All rights reserved.

Published by Silver Quill Publishing
Dallas, TX 75115

All rights reserved. This book or any portion thereof may not be reproduced or used in any manner whatsoever without the express written permission of the author except for the use of brief quotations in a book review.

This is a work of fiction. Names, characters, businesses, places, events and incidents are either the products of the author's imagination or used in a fictitious manner. Any resemblance to actual persons, living or dead, or actual events is purely coincidental.

To Scott -
You're my hero.

To Edith -
Our first granddaughter. We can't wait to meet you.

ALSO BY LILIANA HART

JJ Graves Mystery Series

Dirty Little Secrets

A Dirty Shame

Dirty Rotten Scoundrel

Down and Dirty

Dirty Deeds

Dirty Laundry

Dirty Money

A Dirty Job

Dirty Devil

Playing Dirty

Dirty Martini

Dirty Dozen

Dirty Minds

Dirty Weekend

Dirty Looks

Dirty Liars

Dirty Valentine

Addison Holmes Mystery Series

Whiskey Rebellion

Whiskey Sour

Whiskey For Breakfast

Whiskey, You're The Devil

Whiskey on the Rocks

Whiskey Tango Foxtrot

Whiskey and Gunpowder

Whiskey Lullaby

The Scarlet Chronicles

Bouncing Betty

Hand Grenade Helen

Front Line Francis

The Harley and Davidson Mystery Series

The Farmer's Slaughter

A Tisket a Casket

I Saw Mommy Killing Santa Claus

Get Your Murder Running

Deceased and Desist

Malice in Wonderland

Tequila Mockingbird

Gone With the Sin

Grime and Punishment

Blazing Rattles

A Salt and Battery

Curl Up and Dye

First Comes Death Then Comes Marriage

Box Set 1

Box Set 2

Box Set 3

The Gravediggers

The Darkest Corner

Gone to Dust

Say No More

Laurel Valley

Tribulation Pass

Redemption Road

Midnight Clear

Forgiveness River

Atonement Trail

A woman is like a tea bag—
*   you never know how strong she is until she gets in hot water.*
        ~Eleanor Roosevelt

CHAPTER
ONE

THE EVIDENCE BOX SMELLED LIKE DECADES OF MILDEW and neglect—that particular combination of damp paper and dust that made my sinuses revolt and definitely killed my appetite for lunch.

The Perfect Steep had been in my possession for exactly ten years and three months, and in all that time, I'd developed certain immutable truths about running a tea shop on Grimm Island. First, Mrs. Pinkerton would arrive at 7:15 sharp for her English Breakfast, never Ceylon, because Ceylon reminded her of her third husband who'd run off with a woman from Beaufort. Second, tourists would inevitably ask if we served sweet tea, at which point I'd have to explain that sweet tea and proper tea were entirely different creatures, like comparing a house cat to a tiger. And third, Sheriff Dashiell Beckett had started appearing at my counter with increasing frequency over the past three weeks, always ordering something different as if he were methodically working through my entire menu.

Today's visit came with a moldering evidence box that he'd placed directly between my carefully arranged displays of imported teas and this morning's batch of lemon scones.

My name is Mabel McCoy, though on Grimm Island, I was known by various other titles—Patrick's widow, that tea shop woman, the one who'd helped solve the Calvert case, and most recently (according to Mrs. Pembroke's gossiping circle), the sheriff's latest interest. The last one made me uncomfortable in ways I wasn't ready to examine, like probing a tooth that might be starting to ache.

The island itself was a peculiar place, shaped like a crooked finger pointing out into the Atlantic, thirty minutes from Charleston but a world unto itself. We had just over ten thousand permanent residents, one stoplight that nobody really obeyed, and more secrets per square mile than anywhere else in South Carolina. The Spanish moss that draped our live oaks wasn't the only thing that hung heavy here—the past clung to everything like morning fog off the marsh.

"You can't keep bringing your decomposing evidence to my place of business," I told Dash, though my protest lacked conviction. In the three weeks since we'd closed the Calvert case, he'd developed this habit of treating The Perfect Steep as his auxiliary office. Last Tuesday, he'd spread crime-scene photos across my counter during the lunch rush, causing Mrs. Wilson to faint into her oolong. Thursday, he'd brought in a box of what he swore were just old files but turned out to contain someone's collection of teeth. Human teeth, as Dottie Simmons had helpfully identified while examining them with the kind of enthusiasm usually reserved for Christmas presents.

"I brought provisions," Dash said, producing a white box from Beaumont's Bakery. "Apple turnovers. Still warm."

It was deeply unfair how quickly he'd learned my weaknesses. Apple turnovers occupied a sacred space in my personal hierarchy of pleasures, right between finding a pristine 1940s dress at an estate sale and perfectly harmonizing with Ella Fitzgerald on "Dream a Little Dream."

"Bribery is unbecoming of an officer of the law," I said, but I was already opening the box, inhaling the scent of cinnamon and buttery pastry that temporarily overwhelmed whatever was fermenting in his evidence box.

Chowder, my French bulldog and self-appointed shop mascot, lifted his head from his designated window seat to investigate. Today he wore his new sailor suit—a navy-blue number with white piping and an actual sailor's cap that I had special-ordered from a boutique pet store in Charleston. His closet now rivaled mine, filled with bow ties, vests, seasonal costumes, and formal wear for what he considered special occasions—meaning any day ending in Y.

"That's new," Dash observed, nodding at Chowder's ensemble. "The hat's a nice touch."

"He's got a photo shoot later," I said, only half joking. The *Grimm Island Gazette* had started featuring Chowder in their weekly Island Pets column, and he'd developed quite a following. Last week, a tourist had asked for a selfie with him. Chowder had obliged.

The Perfect Steep occupied a corner building that had lived more lives than a cat with good health insurance. Built in 1892 as Grimm's Pharmacy, where old Dr. Grimm (the founder's son) had dispensed remedies that were equal parts medicine and moonshine, it had evolved through various incarnations. During Prohibition, it had masqueraded as a flower shop that sold suspiciously few flowers but moved impressive amounts of Canadian whisky through its back room. In the 1950s, it had been Eloise's Dress Shop, where my grandmother had bought her wedding dress and where, according to island legend, Eloise had run a betting ring on horse races from the fitting rooms.

Now it was mine, painted the soft blue of a robin's egg in spring, with white trim that I touched up religiously every March whether it needed it or not. The interior was a careful balance of chaos and comfort—mismatched vintage tables and chairs I'd rescued from estate sales, each wall in a different pastel, and shelves lined with tea canisters from around the world. The original heart pine floors creaked in three specific spots that I'd memorized like a map, allowing me to navigate the shop in complete darkness if necessary—a skill that had come in handy during Hurricane Matthew when the power had been out for four days.

"So what fresh horror have you brought me today?" I asked, gesturing at the evidence box with a butter knife I'd been using to spread clotted cream on a scone I'd probably never get to eat.

"Cold case from 1985," Dash said, his fingers drumming against the box in that pattern I'd noticed he did when something was bothering him—three taps, pause, three taps, pause. "Double homicide. Never solved. I figured it would be perfect for you and the Silver Sleuths."

The shop's morning regulars had assumed their positions. Mrs. Pinkerton sat in the window seat she'd claimed as her own five years ago, working on another needlepoint sampler with inappropriate sayings. She liked to give them as bridal shower gifts. Most likely every married woman on Grimm Island had a needlepoint sampler from Iris Pinkerton. I had one hanging in my guest bathroom that said *Don't Be An…*and then a picture of a donkey that must have taken her hours. It was a rite of passage for new brides.

Marcus Wheeler occupied the corner table, his newspaper folded to the obituaries—not because he was morbid, but because, as he'd once explained, it was the only section of the paper that couldn't lie to you. People were either dead or they weren't. There was a simple honesty to that which appealed to him after his wife had passed three years ago. He ordered the same thing every morning—Darjeeling with one sugar, no milk—and spent exactly ninety minutes pretending to read while actually dozing behind his paper.

And then there was Dottie Simmons, one of the members of the infamous Silver Sleuths, who'd commandeered the table nearest the counter and was regaling two trapped tourists with a detailed explanation of how different types of soil affected decomposition rates. The tourists—a young couple wearing matching *I Survived Hurricane Season* T-shirts they'd definitely bought at the tourist trap on Harbor Street—looked like they were reconsidering their survival.

"Sandy soil, like we have here on the island, creates interesting conditions," Dottie was explaining, adjusting her green cat-eye glasses that had been out of style for so long they'd circled back to being almost fashionable. "The salinity acts as a natural preservative for certain tissues, while the moisture accelerates the breakdown of others. I once examined a body that had been buried in the marsh for six months, and the differential decomposition was absolutely fascinating—"

"Dottie," I called over. "You're disrupting their digestion."

"They asked what I did before retirement," she protested with the wounded innocence of someone who genuinely didn't understand why discussing putrefaction over breakfast might be considered inappropriate.

The tourists threw money on the table for a tip and fled. Dottie watched them go with the satisfaction of a cat who'd successfully defended her territory from interlopers.

"Forty years is nothing in the right conditions," she continued, seamlessly transitioning her attention to us. "I've seen tissue samples from the Civil War that were still identifiable. There was this one case in Charleston where they were renovating an old church and found—"

"The Pickering–Bailey case," Dash interrupted, before Dottie could launch into what I knew from experience would be a forty-minute dissertation on historical preservation of human remains.

The change in Dottie was immediate and dramatic. She went from animated lecturer to stone-still sentinel, her teacup frozen halfway to her lips. I'd seen that look before—it was the expression she got when someone mentioned a case that had left marks on her psyche, the kind that visited her in the small hours of the night when the world was quiet and the dead felt closer.

"You're reopening Pickering–Bailey?" Her voice had dropped an octave, losing its usual theatrical quality.

"I've been systematically reviewing all the cold cases," Dash said. "This one stands out. I want you guys to take a look at it."

"Good Lord." Dottie set down her cup with exaggerated care. "Ruby Bailey and Reverend George Pickering. Found at Turtle Point, September 16, 1985. I did both autopsies."

She stood and approached the counter with the measured stride of someone approaching a coffin. Even at seventy-eight, Dottie moved with purpose when something mattered.

"That case was wrong from the beginning," she said, peering at the box like it might contain something contagious. "Three different people confessed. All three knew details that weren't public. All three recanted within a week, claiming coercion. Evidence went missing.

Witnesses changed their stories. The whole thing stank worse than a body left in a hot car in August."

The morning light streaming through my lace curtains had taken on a different quality, like looking at the world through old glass. The usual sounds of Harbor Street—tourists chattering, seagulls arguing over stolen funnel cake, the distant toll of the marina bell—seemed muffled, as if the past was pressing in on the present, demanding attention.

"Tell me about Ruby," I said, because in my limited experience with murder, it always came back to the victims. They were the ones who mattered, whose stories needed telling, whose voices had been silenced but whose truths had a way of surfacing like bodies in the marsh—inevitable, patient, refusing to stay buried.

"Ruby Bailey was thirty-two," Dottie said, her clinical tone at odds with the emotion in her eyes. "Single mother, worked cleaning houses for the wealthy families on the island. She was pretty in that way that made certain men think they owned her, if you know what I mean. Dark hair, green eyes, a smile that could light up a room when she let it. Sang in the church choir and had a voice like an angel."

She paused, and I could see her sifting through memories like photographs in an album, each one preserved in the strange amber of professional detachment.

"The autopsy showed defensive wounds on her hands and arms. She fought hard. Multiple contusions, a fractured orbital bone, three broken ribs." Dottie's voice dropped to barely above a whisper. "Someone cut out her tongue. Postmortem, thank God, but still."

Marcus Wheeler's newspaper rustled from the corner. He'd lowered it enough to peer over the top, his weathered face pale beneath its permanent sunburn.

"You're talking about the Pickering–Bailey murders," he said. It wasn't a question.

We all turned to look at him. Marcus Wheeler, who'd been coming to my shop for three years and had never contributed more than a mumbled greeting and exact change, suddenly had our complete attention.

"My brother Tommy worked that case," he continued, his voice rough with disuse or emotion. "Deputy Thomas Wheeler. Maybe you've seen his name in the files."

Dash nodded slowly. "His reports are in here."

"Tommy died in '98. Heart attack, they said." Marcus folded his newspaper with precise creases, the same way he'd probably been folding it for fifty years. "But he was never the same after that case. Used to wake up screaming about what he'd seen. Kept saying the real killer was still out there, walking around free, probably having Sunday dinner with their family like nothing had happened."

He stood slowly, joints protesting with audible pops that sounded like punctuation marks to his story.

"Some things on this island are better left buried, Sheriff," he said, shuffling toward the door. "But if you're determined to dig them up, be careful who you trust. Forty years is a long time, but not long enough for some folks to forget. Or forgive."

The door chimed as he left, the cheerful sound at odds with the weight of his warning.

"Well," Dottie said after a moment. "That was sufficiently ominous."

"Your autopsy report," Dash said, pulling her attention back. "It mentions inconsistencies with the crime scene."

"Everything about that scene was wrong," Dottie said. "Reverend Pickering was on his knees when he died—single gunshot wound to the head execution style—the angle of the wound was clear. Ruby was shot multiple times in the chest, point-blank range. The killer was up close and personal. But the bodies were positioned. Staged. The killer moved them into a lover's embrace, so they held each other in death."

The shop had gone quiet in the way that happens when people are discussing the dead—a respectful hush, as if normal conversation might disturb them. Even the coffee maker seemed to percolate more softly, and the ceiling fan that usually squeaked on every third rotation had gone silent.

"Why would someone stage the scene like that?" I asked.

"Their relationship was a scandal," Dottie said. "Reverend Pickering was married with children. And Ruby singing in the choir every Sunday and meeting him in the cover of night. There were whispers, of course. It's hard to keep something like that quiet. You start to notice intimate looks and touches, and they weren't too careful about it. My best guess is whoever killed them wanted everyone to know what they'd been up to outside of the pulpit."

"Jealousy?" I asked. "Like the reverend's wife?"

"That's probably a good place to start," Dash said.

The door chimed again, and we all turned with the guilty startle of children caught telling ghost stories. But it was just Bea Livingston, sweeping in wearing a caftan that could have doubled as a sail for a small yacht. Today's was purple and gold with what appeared to be actual bells sewn into the hem, which announced her every movement like a one-woman parade.

"Whatever you're all discussing looks serious enough to curdle milk," she announced, making her way toward us with surprising grace for someone wearing what amounted to an entire fabric store. "Dottie's got her death face on, and the sheriff looks like someone stole his patrol car."

At eighty years of age, Bea had been married three times, widowed twice, divorced once, and was currently entertaining what she called "several gentleman callers," though most of them were confined to the assisted-living facility on the mainland and could only call on days when the shuttle was running.

"The sheriff is reviewing cold cases," I explained.

"Oh?" Bea's eyes lit up with a gleam that meant gossip receptors had been activated. "Which one? Please tell me it's juicy."

"The Pickering–Bailey murders," Dash said carefully.

The transformation in Bea was instant. Her theatrical manner dropped like a discarded costume, and for a moment, I saw the woman underneath—someone who'd lived through enough history to know which parts of it still had teeth.

"Ruby Bailey and Reverend Pickering," she said slowly, as if tasting the names after years of not speaking them. "Lord, I haven't thought about them in ages." She helped herself to one of the apple turnovers

Dash had brought, but her usual enthusiasm for pilfered pastries was absent. "Ruby cleaned my house on Thursdays. Every Thursday for three years, until…"

"You knew her?" Dash asked.

"Everyone knew Ruby, one way or another. She cleaned half the houses on the island—the big ones, the ones that belonged to the old families." Bea settled into a chair with unusual solemnity. "She was married to Jimmy Thorne for a couple of years. Long enough to have a kid with him. But he was an abusive womanizer, and she left him and moved back home with her mother. Took the kid with her."

The name fell into the conversation like a stone into still water, sending ripples through the quiet shop.

"Jimmy Thorne was rotten through and through," Bea continued. "Used to knock Ruby around when he'd been drinking, which was most nights. But he had an alibi for the murder—was sleeping it off in the county lockup. Drunk and disorderly, as usual."

Thorne. One of the old island families, the ones whose names were on streets and buildings and memorial plaques all over town. The Thornes had owned the marina before selling it to developers in the nineties, had run the ferry service before the bridge was built, had their fingers in every pie on the island until those pies started running out.

"Ruby was a beautiful woman," Bea continued. "And she wasn't afraid to use what the good Lord gave her. If it was me I would've picked someone wealthy and old enough to die and leave me all his money. But she picked George Pickering—a preacher with no money and a wife. I guess she didn't get brains to go along with her beauty."

"What was the boy's name?" Dottie asked. "I remember he had the biggest eyes I've ever seen."

"Good grief, Dottie," Bea said. "Take your B12 vitamins. How can you not remember Michael Bailey?"

"Hush up, Bea. I know who Michael Bailey is. I just couldn't remember his name for a minute. I remember the important things and that's what matters."

"Michael Bailey," I said and then looked at Dash. "He runs the funeral home."

Michael was a quiet man who'd probably buried half the island over the past twenty years, including Patrick. I remembered him from the funeral—professional, composed, with the kind of practiced sympathy that came from dealing with grief as a daily occupation.

"Poor thing was only ten when his mama died," Bea said. "Can you imagine? Growing up knowing someone did that to your mother and got away with it? I can't believe he stayed on the island. That's a hard thing to carry around your whole life—people looking at you and remembering the scandal."

I couldn't imagine. Didn't want to.

The morning was slipping away from me. The lunch crowd would start arriving soon—the ladies who ordered their Darjeeling and cucumber sandwiches—the business people grabbing quick takeout—the tourists looking for authentic island atmosphere.

"I should let you get back to work," Dash said, but he made no move to leave.

"You're leaving the box," I observed.

"I thought you might want to look through it," he said carefully. "You have a different perspective. You know the families, the connections that someone like me—someone not from here—might miss."

It was true. Being an outsider on Grimm Island was like trying to read a book where half the words were written in invisible ink. You could see the obvious story, but the real narrative, the one that mattered, was hidden in the spaces between—in the feuds that went back generations, the marriages that connected unlikely families, the secrets that everyone knew but no one discussed.

"I'll call the others," Dottie said, meaning the rest of the Silver Sleuths. Since the Calvert case, they'd considered themselves an official investigative unit. "Walt will want to know about this. He's probably got seventeen conspiracy theories about the Pickering–Bailey murders already."

"Just seventeen?" I asked. "He's slipping."

As Dash prepared to leave—he had a meeting with the mayor

about budget allocations, which sounded about as pleasant as a root canal performed by an angry dentist—he paused at the door.

"Dinner tonight?" he asked, and it was phrased as a question but felt like a foregone conclusion. We'd fallen into this rhythm without ever formally acknowledging it—three, sometimes four nights a week, he'd show up at my door with takeout from various restaurants, we'd spread case files across my dining room table, and somewhere between the sweet-and-sour chicken and the second glass of wine, we'd stop talking about murder and start talking about everything else.

"I'll cook," I offered, surprising myself. I'd been subsisting on takeout and tea shop leftovers for so long that my kitchen had started to feel more like a museum exhibit than a functional room.

"What are you making?" he asked, arching a brow.

"It's a surprise," I said, because I had no idea. I'd figure that out during the lunch rush, while making sandwiches and serving tea and pretending not to be thinking about a murder that happened when I was negative six years old.

After he left, I stood looking at the evidence box on my counter. It sat there like a portal to 1985, to a time when someone had killed two people and arranged their bodies like dolls, had cut out a woman's tongue to make a point that apparently still needed making four decades later.

Chowder waddled over, his sailor hat slightly askew, and looked up at me with those bulging eyes that somehow managed to convey both unconditional love and deep skepticism about my life choices.

"I know," I told him. "But first, we have customers to serve."

I hefted the evidence box under the counter, out of sight but decidedly not out of mind. As I turned to greet the Methodist ladies, I caught Dottie watching me from her table. She raised her teacup in a small salute—a gesture that somehow said she understood perfectly well that boxes full of old murders had to wait their turn, but that they would not, under any circumstances, be forgotten.

The lunch rush was about to descend upon The Perfect Steep like a plague of polite locusts, all wanting their specific teas prepared just so, their sandwiches cut in certain ways, their scones warmed to precise temperatures. For the next three hours, I would be Mabel McCoy, tea shop proprietor, dispenser of Earl Grey and sympathy in equal measure.

But tonight, after I'd completed whatever culinary adventure I'd promised Dash, after the dishes were done and Chowder was snoring in his bed, I would open that box. I would read about Ruby Bailey and Reverend Pickering, whose affair had scandalized the island. About two people who'd died at Turtle Point in a violence that spoke of rage and twisted love and secrets worth killing for.

The door chimed again. More customers. The lunch rush had officially begun.

Forty years was a long time for secrets to ferment, like tea left too long in the pot—growing bitter, darker, impossible to swallow. But secrets, unlike tea, couldn't simply be poured down the drain.

I smiled at the Methodist ladies and reached for my order pad, as if there weren't a box beneath my counter holding the story of two people who'd loved unwisely and died violently.

As if the truth hadn't been waiting all this time, patient as the tide, for someone to finally care enough to look.

CHAPTER
TWO

The cognac erupted into flames with an enthusiasm that Julia Child would have called "marvelous" but which I found mildly alarming. The blue fire leaped toward my kitchen ceiling with the kind of ambition usually reserved for escaping prisoners or social climbers at the yacht club.

"Julia said to let it burn off naturally," I muttered to myself, gripping the pan's handle as flames licked upward. "She did not mention ceiling height requirements."

The back door opened just as the flames reached their crescendo, and Sheriff Dash Beckett walked in to find me wielding a flaming pan like some sort of culinary Viking preparing for battle.

"Should I call the fire department?" he asked, that half smile playing at the corners of his mouth. "Or is this dinner and a show?"

"This," I said with as much dignity as one could muster while potentially setting one's kitchen ablaze, "Is a classic French technique." I smoothly slid the pan off the heat, and the flames began to subside, leaving behind the rich scent of caramelized onions, wine, and what might have been slightly singed eyebrow.

Chowder watched from his kitchen bed, wearing his Friday evening attire—a small velvet smoking jacket. He regarded the flaming pan with the kind of detached interest usually reserved for watching other people's children have tantrums in grocery stores.

"Coq au vin?" Dash asked, moving closer to inspect the pan's contents. He'd changed out of his uniform into jeans and a dark henley that made him look less like Grimm Island's sheriff and more like someone who might actually have a life outside of law enforcement. I tried not to notice how his shoulders filled out the shirt and seemed to mold to every muscle in his arms and chest. I said I tried not to notice, not that I was successful at it. Dashiell Beckett was a pleasure to look at.

"The Julia Child version," I confirmed, returning the pan to the heat at a more reasonable temperature. "I found the recipe this morning at Dr. Morrison's office, of all places. Clarissa had left last month's *Southern Living* splayed open on the wrong page—she'd been looking at 'Ten-Minute Dinners for Busy Moms' but the magazine had fallen open to Julia's four-page manifesto on proper coq au vin. Sixteen steps, each one more elaborate than the last. Step seven actually used the phrase 'a good, vigorous flame' as if flames came in varying degrees of enthusiasm."

"Sixteen steps?" Dash pulled out one of my kitchen stools, the one that had developed a personality disorder—it either squeaked like a dying mouse or sat silent, depending entirely on whether you hit the sweet spot three inches from the left edge. He found it immediately, settling into silence with the kind of precision that made me wonder what else those observant sheriff eyes had catalogued about my kitchen. About me.

"My cooking involves two steps—open container, apply heat."

"That's a lie and we both know it," I said, stirring the chicken to coat it in the now-flameless but beautifully aromatic sauce. "I saw you julienne carrots last week. That's skilled knife work."

"YouTube University," he admitted. "Amazing what you can learn at two in the morning when you can't sleep."

I wanted to ask what kept him awake—was it the job, the adjustment to island life, or something deeper that had driven him from whatever life he'd lived before Grimm Island? But I'd learned that

Dash revealed things in his own time, like a cat deciding when it wanted affection. Push too hard and he'd retreat behind that professional façade that fit him like armor.

Instead, I poured two glasses of the wine I'd opened for the recipe —a decent Burgundy that Patrick had laid down years ago. I'd finally started working through his wine collection this year, each bottle a small goodbye I hadn't been ready to say until recently.

"Needs forty minutes to finish properly," I said, handing him a glass. "Julia was very specific about the timing."

"To Julia, then," Dash said, raising his glass. "And to flames that don't require fire departments."

We were just settling into the comfortable rhythm of conversation —he was telling me about Lois Goodacre's latest complaint about her neighbor's wind chimes being "aggressively musical"—when his radio crackled to life.

"Sheriff, we've got a situation at the harbor." The dispatcher's voice carried the tone of someone trying to maintain professional calm while dealing with the absurd. "Multiple calls about something huge in the water."

Dash set down his wine glass with the resignation of someone who'd learned that Grimm Island's definition of emergency could range from actual danger to Mr. Fredericks losing his emotional-support iguana again.

"Define 'huge,'" he said into the radio.

"Caller says bigger than a boat. Another says it's moving. Harbor patrol is requesting backup because we've got about thirty people gathering and Eugene Bradshaw is threatening to swim out with his— hold on, I'm getting the exact words—therapeutic intervention equipment."

I snorted. Eugene ran the crystal shop on Third Street and firmly believed that every problem, from arthritis to failing marriages, could be solved with the right combination of crystals and positive thinking. Last month he'd tried to heal the pothole on Harbor Street with sage smudging, whatever that was.

"On my way," Dash said, then looked at me. "Want to come? Your coq needs another forty minutes anyway, and I might need someone who actually knows all these people."

"You want me to be your local guide to crazy?"

"I prefer the term cultural liaison," he said, already heading for the door.

I turned the heat down to the lowest simmer, the kind that would let the flavors meld slowly without any risk of burning. I grabbed my light cardigan. The evening had turned cool with a suddenness that made me think fall would be coming early this year.

Dash's SUV still smelled new, the combination of leather and electronics that suggested a vehicle more accustomed to city streets than sandy island roads. But sand had already begun its inevitable invasion—grains in the cup holders, a fine dust on the dashboard that would never fully disappear no matter how much one cleaned.

"So what do you think it actually is?" I asked as we drove down Harbor Street, passing The Perfect Steep with its windows dark except for the small light I always left on, the one that made the teacups on the shelf glint like small moons.

"Last week someone called about a sea monster that turned out to be Georgia Bellington's pool float," Dash said, taking the turn toward the marina with practiced ease. "If you can imagine a chartreuse dragon the size of a small car, complete with silver wings that caught the wind like sails and googly eyes that somehow made it look both ridiculous and vaguely menacing. The storm had lifted it clean over her fence—we found security footage later—and it had sailed three miles across the island to traumatize a group of early morning kayakers who thought they were witnessing the return of something prehistoric."

"Georgia was convinced the Clemmons twins had orchestrated the whole thing," I said, remembering her standing in The Perfect Steep, vibrating with righteous indignation while clutching a manila folder she claimed contained evidence of their delinquency dating back to kindergarten. "Even after Tom Clemmons showed her the security footage of the storm launching it like a medieval siege weapon."

Dash's mouth twitched and his eyes gleamed with humor. It was the same expression he'd worn when Eugene Bradshaw had reported his meditation crystals stolen, only to find them in his other pants. "She came to the station yesterday with a notebook full of YouTube screenshots. Apparently the twins have been watching videos about weather patterns. She wanted to know if that constituted probable cause for a search warrant. She was completely serious."

"Well, you traded in excitement for island life, so..."

"Yeah, yeah," he said, grinning.

The harbor came into view, and even from a distance, I could see the crowd gathered on the main dock. The setting sun painted the water copper and gold, and silhouetted against it were enough people that whatever was happening had drawn serious attention.

We parked and made our way through the crowd, Dash's presence creating a natural path as people stepped aside like water around a stone. I recognized most of them—Howard from the bookstore with his phone held high, determined to document history in the making, the Methodist youth group kids in their usual uniform of ripped jeans and hoodies (even though it was May and entirely too hot to wear a hoodie), and Vivian Lockwood clutching the pearl necklace she wore religiously, running the beads through her fingers like worry stones. The pearls had belonged to her grandmother, who'd reportedly won them in a poker game from a Charleston madam in 1923—a story Vivian neither confirmed nor denied but told through the knowing arch of her left eyebrow whenever anyone asked.

"There!" someone shouted, pointing at the water about fifty yards out.

Something large and dark broke the surface, water streaming off it in sheets that caught the dying light. It wasn't moving like debris. It rolled slightly, and I caught a glimpse of what looked like a massive flipper.

"Is that a whale?" I breathed, hardly believing what I was seeing.

Whales occasionally passed by Grimm Island during migration, but they stayed in deep water, visible only as distant spouts on clear days. This one was close enough that I could see barnacles on its hide when it surfaced again.

"Everyone stay back from the edge," Dash called out, his sheriff voice cutting through the excited chatter. "Harbor patrol is en route."

"It's a sign!" Eugene Bradshaw pushed through the crowd, carrying what appeared to be a set of Tibetan singing bowls. His flowing white shirt and numerous crystal necklaces made him look like a new-age prophet, or someone who'd gotten lost on the way to Woodstock and decided to just stay lost. "The universe is sending us a message!"

"The universe needs to send that message from deeper water," Dash muttered, then he said louder, "Mr. Bradshaw, please don't—"

But Eugene was already settling himself at the dock's edge, arranging his bowls with the reverence of a priest preparing communion. He began to play them, the haunting tones drifting across the water.

Eugene's singing bowls had reached a particularly ethereal note when Margaret Calhoun leaned toward her bridge club companion, her voice carrying that special island talent for whispered commentary that somehow reached everyone within a ten-foot radius. "He's either harmonizing with the whale's chakras or giving the poor creature a migraine. With Eugene, the line between spiritual healing and acoustic assault is remarkably thin."

Her companion—Dolores Whitmore, Deidre's cousin who ran the antique shop—nodded sagely. "Last month he tried to cure my sciatica with a tuning fork. I couldn't hear properly out of my left ear for three days, and my back still hurt."

The whale—and it was definitely a whale, I could see that now—continued its slow, confused circles. It would disappear for thirty seconds, maybe a minute, then surface again with an explosive exhale that sent spray twenty feet into the air. Each time it appeared, the crowd would gasp collectively, phone cameras clicking like a swarm of digital crickets.

"Somebody needs to help it!" This from Tommy Morrison, sixteen years old and possessor of more courage than sense. He was already moving toward his surfboard when Dash's voice cut through the evening air with the kind of authority that could stop a charging bull.

"Morrison. Stand down."

The command had the effect of freezing not just Tommy but every teenager within earshot. Dash had already positioned himself between the kids and the water, his presence somehow expanding to fill the space in that way certain people could—making themselves into an immovable wall through sheer force of will.

"But Sheriff—" Tommy started.

"Harbor patrol is three minutes out," Dash said, his voice calm but carrying an authority that suggested arguing would be spectacularly unwise. "They have the proper equipment and training. You have a surfboard and a death wish. Which one do you think the whale needs?"

One of the Clemmons twins—the one with the questionable mohawk—made a move toward the paddleboard rental stand. Dash didn't even turn his head. "Jake Clemmons, if your hand touches that board, you'll be spending your weekends cleaning barnacles off the harbor patrol boats until you graduate. Your brother too, just for genetic proximity."

The twin's hand retreated as if the paddleboards had suddenly developed teeth.

The teenagers stood in a frustrated cluster, their heroic impulses thoroughly leashed by Dash's calm authority. He hadn't raised his voice once past that initial command, hadn't needed to. He simply stood there, hands relaxed at his sides, watching the whale with the same steady attention he was somehow simultaneously giving to every teenager on the dock.

The next twenty minutes were controlled chaos. I found myself deputized as crowd control, which mostly meant using my local knowledge to assign tasks that made people feel helpful while keeping them from doing anything spectacularly stupid.

The crowd had swelled to nearly fifty people now, all jostling for the best view and creating the kind of chaos that could quickly turn dangerous on a narrow dock. Dash was handling the teenagers, but the adults were developing their own unhelpful ideas.

"Someone needs to organize these people before they push each other into the harbor," I said, surveying the scene.

I intercepted Margaret Calhoun, who was inexplicably carrying a fishing net she'd grabbed from somewhere. "Margaret, would you mind going to the tea shop and making thermoses of hot tea? You know where the extra key is. The harbor patrol crew will need something warm when they're done." It was busywork, but it made her feel useful and, more importantly, got her and her fishing net away from the whale.

Howard needed no direction—he'd appointed himself official documentarian and was providing running commentary to his phone about witnessing maritime history in the making.

The Methodist youth group had begun an enthusiastic rendition of "Wade in the Water," which, while thematically appropriate, was only adding to the chaos. Their youth leader looked grateful when I suggested they might better serve the situation with silent prayer at the foot of the dock—safely away from both the edge and the increasingly agitated whale.

"You're good at this," Dash said, materializing at my elbow just as the marine biologist—a woman named Dr. Battle who'd arrived moments earlier in a spray of gravel and barely contained scientific euphoria—arrived.

"I run a tea shop," I said. "Half my job is managing people who think they're being helpful."

The whale chose that precise moment to demonstrate what Dr. Battle had been so excited about. Its massive head rose from the water —slow, deliberate, impossibly large. For one suspended heartbeat, an eye the size of a dinner plate regarded us all with what seemed like ancient patience. It was the sort of eye that had seen the ocean floor and remembered when the world was younger, and finding it here in our shallow harbor felt like discovering a cathedral in someone's back garden—magnificent and entirely wrong.

"Juvenile humpback," Dash said, though I hadn't seen him leave or return from consulting with Dr. Battle. He had a talent for moving through crowds without seeming to move at all, appearing and disappearing like smoke. "Separated from its pod. Dr. Battle thinks it might be sick—that's why it came so close to shore."

Eugene's singing bowls continued their ethereal drone. Someone had brought him a microphone and a small amplifier, because why not? The whale didn't seem bothered by it, but then again, the whale didn't seem specifically bothered by anything.

"When I took this job," Dash said, settling beside me on the hood of his SUV where we could watch the entire scene, "I thought I'd be dealing with normal crime. Theft, vandalism, the occasional domestic dispute."

"And instead you get whales and emotional-support iguanas."

"Don't forget the lighthouse incident last week."

"That wasn't an incident," I said. "That was Gerald Fitzgerald forgetting his glasses and trying to break into what he thought was his own shed. For three hours."

"He was very committed to that lock," Dash said, and I could hear the smile in his voice. "Even after I showed him his actual house across the street. That man has terrible eyesight."

Margaret materialized through the thinning crowd like a ship emerging from fog, bearing a tray of my familiar to-go cups with the determined expression of someone who'd fought a minor war and emerged victorious. Wisps of silver hair had escaped her usually immaculate bun.

"I commandeered your apple spice tea," she announced, as if confessing to a minor crime. "The one you keep hidden in the back like contraband. It smells like Christmas morning, and frankly, we could all use a bit of magic right now, even if it's only the caffeinated kind."

I accepted a cup with the resignation of someone watching their profit margins evaporate into steam. That particular tea cost more per ounce than some people's car payments, which was precisely why I kept it hidden behind the everyday Earl Grey like a miser's gold. But Margaret was right—it did smell like Christmas, all cinnamon and clove and the warmth that made you believe, if only for a moment, that everything might turn out all right.

"The ladies are putting your shop back together," Margaret continued, brushing invisible dust from her cardigan with the efficiency of someone who organized charity auctions for sport. "We've left it better than we found it, which admittedly wasn't difficult given that we found it with your counter covered in police evidence and what appeared to be someone's collection of teeth."

"Thank you, Margaret," I said, making a mental note to warn Carly that "better than we found it" in Margaret's vocabulary could mean anything from military precision to complete reorganization according to a system only Margaret understood.

She bustled off to distribute tea to the harbor patrol, leaving Dash and me standing in the strange quiet that follows chaos—the kind of silence that feels louder than noise because it's so unexpected.

"Tell me something," Dash said, his voice cutting through my thoughts. "Why do you stay here?"

The question caught me off guard. "What do you mean?"

"You're young, talented, you could run a tea shop anywhere. Why Grimm Island?"

I thought about it, watching the whale surface again, its massive body ghostly in the fading light. "After Patrick died, I thought about leaving. His insurance money could have taken me anywhere. But this place...it's like that whale. Sometimes you end up where you don't belong because you're lost or hurting, and then you discover that's exactly where you need to be."

"Even with Eugene and his singing bowls?"

"Especially with Eugene and his singing bowls." I took another sip of tea. "What about you? What makes someone leave undercover work for...this?" I gestured at the scene—generations of Grimm Islanders, Eugene now standing and swaying with his bowls, the crowd taking selfies with the whale in the background.

"Would you believe me if I said it was the emotional-support iguanas?" he asked.

"Not even a little bit."

He was quiet for a moment, and I thought he wouldn't answer.

"I got tired of being someone else. Undercover work, it's like...you put on these personalities like clothes, and after a while, you forget which one is really you. Here, I'm just the sheriff. It's simple."

"Simple," I repeated, thinking of the evidence box under my counter, of cold cases and old murders and secrets that fermented for decades. "Right."

The whale was finally moving toward open water, guided by the coast guard boats that had arrived with spotlights and the kind of equipment actually designed for marine mammal emergencies.

The whale was barely a distant shadow when the claiming began—that peculiarly human need to own a miracle by proximity.

Eugene stood at the dock's edge like a prophet who'd just parted the Red Sea with tuning forks, his crystal necklaces catching the last light as he explained to a growing audience how the whale had responded to the sacred frequencies he'd channeled. His hands moved through the air, conducting an invisible orchestra of cosmic connection that only he could hear.

Twenty feet away, the Methodist youth group had formed a prayer circle, hands clasped, heads bowed, their voices rising in genuine gratitude. There was something moving about their absolute faith—these teenagers who'd witnessed an extraordinary event and turned instinctively to prayer, believing with the kind of certainty that adults rarely managed anymore.

Tommy Morrison, meanwhile, had gathered his own congregation of teenagers, his voice cracking with the intensity of his conviction: "I'm telling you, when it looked at me—right at me—it was like it knew, you know? Like we understood each other." His hands gestured wildly, recreating the moment for his audience, the whale growing larger and more mystical with each retelling.

"Everyone needs to be the hero of their own story," Dash observed, but there was something in his voice that suggested he understood this human failing intimately—the need to matter, to be the protagonist rather than merely another face in the crowd watching someone else's drama unfold.

"What's ours?" I asked without thinking, then felt heat creep up my neck.

But Dash just smiled, that rare full smile that made my stomach do complicated things. "Haven't figured that out yet. But it probably involves your coq au vin burning."

"Oh no!" I checked my phone. We'd been gone almost two hours. "Julia will never forgive me."

But when we got back to my house, the kitchen smelled like heaven—wine and herbs and butter all melded into something that suggested French countryside kitchens and long, leisurely dinners. The coq au vin had achieved that perfect state where the sauce had reduced to glossy perfection and the chicken was falling-off-the-bone tender.

"Julia knows her business," I said, plating the dish with the kind of care usually reserved for tea ceremonies or neurosurgery.

We ate at my kitchen island rather than the formal dining room, Chowder watching hopefully from his bed, still wearing his smoking jacket, which was now slightly askew, giving him the appearance of a gentleman who'd had one too many at the club.

"This is incredible," Dash said, and there was something reverent in the way he savored each bite, as if he understood that good food was about more than mere consumption.

"It's more elaborate than what I usually bother with," I admitted. Over three weeks of dinners, I'd defaulted to the kind of simple, efficient meals that someone who cooked professionally all day would make—quick stir-fries, perfect omelets, the occasional pasta. Nothing that required sixteen steps and setting things on fire. "After spending all day making scones and assembling sandwiches, I usually don't have the energy for anything more complex."

"But tonight you channeled Julia Child?"

"Tonight I had time, and frankly, I was showing off." I gestured at the perfectly caramelized chicken, the sauce that had reduced to exactly the right consistency. "You've been bringing increasingly sophisticated takeout—that Thai place from Charleston last week, the French bistro before that. My professional pride couldn't let that stand."

"So this is a competition?" He was trying not to smile.

"This is me reminding you that I can do more than brew a perfect Earl Grey." Though the truth was more complicated—that cooking for him felt different than cooking for customers, that I'd wanted to create something memorable, something that might linger in his mind the way his presence had started lingering in mine.

We fell into the comfortable rhythm of conversation that had become our pattern—comparing our mutual horror of reality television (except *The Great British Bake Off*, which we both watched religiously). He revealed his collection of historical fiction first editions. I confessed my abandoned dream of singing jazz.

"You sing all the time," he pointed out. "I've heard you. You hum when you're making tea, sing when you're nervous."

"That's different. That's just...sound. Performing is about being seen."

"And you don't want to be seen?"

It was a loaded question, one that hung in the air between us like the lingering scent of cognac and caramelized onions. I thought about the past ten years, how I'd wrapped widowhood around myself like armor, visible but untouchable, playing a role that had become so familiar I'd forgotten it was a performance.

"I'm working on it," I said finally.

We did the dishes together, moving through my small kitchen with the kind of synchronization that usually takes years to develop. He washed, I dried, our movements creating a rhythm that felt both entirely new and impossibly familiar, as if my kitchen had been waiting for exactly this—for someone who knew instinctively that the good plates went on the second shelf, never the third, and that the dishcloth needed to be folded precisely in thirds or it wouldn't fit in its designated spot by the sink.

"I should go," Dash said finally, when the last spoon had been polished and there was no excuse left for lingering except the truth neither of us was ready to speak aloud.

At the door, he paused. "Thanks for tonight. For coming with me. I needed someone who knew the people."

"You needed someone to assign tasks so they'd feel important," I corrected. "It's a very specific skill set."

"One of many, apparently." He leaned in and kissed me—gentle, familiar, the kind of kiss that spoke of affection rather than passion. We'd been doing this dance for weeks now, comfortable but careful, neither of us quite ready to push for more. "Good night, Mabel."

The door closed softly behind him, and I stood there wondering how long we could keep this up—the careful kisses, the unspoken boundaries, the elephant in the room neither of us wanted to name.

That's when I noticed his watch on the counter—a black tactical watch with a sturdy rubber strap, the kind designed to survive whatever chaos law enforcement might encounter, its face slightly scratched from real use.

It sat among my things like a foreign ambassador—masculine where my kitchen was decidedly feminine, practical among my collection of vintage curiosities. The leather still held the warmth of his wrist, and when I picked it up, I could smell the scent that was uniquely his—cedar soap and something indefinable that made my stomach perform a slow, complicated somersault.

I could return it tomorrow. Text him right now, even—*your watch is here, forgot to mention it.* Simple. Practical. Safe.

Instead, I set it carefully next to my tea canisters, where morning light would catch the crystal face, where I would see it every day until he came back for it. Or until I gathered the courage to return it. Or until it simply became part of my kitchen's landscape, like the widow's grief I'd been slowly, carefully, setting aside.

Chowder waddled over, his smoking jacket now twisted at such an angle that he looked like a Victorian gentleman who'd lost a fight with his own wardrobe.

"Don't look at me like that," I told him. "Nothing happened."

He produced the kind of snort that only French bulldogs can manage—part disapproval, part disbelief, wholly judgmental. He knew, as I knew, that something had shifted tonight.

Outside, Grimm Island settled into its evening rhythm—waves against sand, wind through Spanish moss, the distant call of something wild in the marsh. Somewhere in deeper waters, a whale was finding its way back to where it belonged, guided by instincts older than memory.

I picked up Dash's watch again, running my thumb across its worn face. Sometimes the things we think are lost—whales, hearts, the ability to want something beyond safety—aren't lost at all. They're just waiting, patient as time itself, for someone brave enough to guide them home.

CHAPTER
THREE

Saturday morning on Grimm Island possessed a quality of light that made even mundane objects appear blessed—as if God had finally found the correct Instagram filter and decided to leave it on permanently. The May sunshine streamed through my bedroom curtains with the enthusiasm of a golden retriever, promising a day that would be hot enough to make everyone question their life choices by noon.

I stood before my closet, contemplating what one wore to examine forty-year-old murder evidence. After considerable deliberation, I selected a 1950s day dress in sage green with tiny pearl buttons down the front—the sort of dress that suggested I might be equally comfortable at a garden party or a crime scene, which seemed appropriate for Grimm Island, where social events and scandals were often indistinguishable.

My house stood at the end of Harbor Street like a beautiful dowager who'd aged gracefully despite witnessing more than her share of drama. The white Charleston single façade caught the morning light in a way that made it glow like the inside of an oyster shell—luminous and slightly mysterious. Three stories of traditional architecture that had sheltered generations of island secrets, each room holding memories like pressed flowers in a book.

Patrick had given me this house as a wedding gift, this grand corner property where the camellias we'd planted had just finished their spring blooming. The wraparound piazza faced the harbor, its columns wound with jasmine that was already beginning its summer campaign to seduce everyone within a three-block radius with its perfume.

But it was always the sycamore that caught my eye—the one Patrick had planted our first year here, promising shade that would cool our bedroom when we were old and gray, when we had grandchildren to push on the swing he'd planned to hang from its branches. The tree towered over the house now, finally casting the shadows he'd promised, its leaves whispering secrets to the wind about all the futures that would never be.

Chowder emerged from the mudroom in his Saturday attire—a Hawaiian shirt featuring pineapples wearing sunglasses, because even fruit needed eye protection on Grimm Island. He conducted his morning patrol with the solemnity of a palace guard, if palace guards were shaped like overstuffed sausages and occasionally got distracted by butterflies.

"You're looking very festive today," I told him. "Though you might need to lay off the treats if you want your shirt to button the next time you wear it."

Chowder sniffed disapprovingly at my criticism and waited for me to open the door to the backyard.

His first stop was the hydrangea bush where Mr. Henderson's tabby sometimes conducted surveillance operations. Chowder sniffed thoroughly, gathering intelligence that only he could interpret. His second stop was the sacred spot by the garden gate where he'd once discovered a ham sandwich, a miracle of such magnitude that he still checked daily for its second coming. Finally, the ceremonial marking of the sycamore, because some traditions transcended fashion choices.

Back inside, I stood at my kitchen counter making coffee, humming "Blue Moon" as the morning light illuminated my collection of vintage tea canisters. Dash's tactical watch sat among them where he'd left it the night before—this aggressively practical thing amid my delicate porcelain, like finding a hammer in a jewelry box. Its presence made me smile. It was such an obvious excuse to return, and yet somehow that made it more charming, not less.

The evidence box squatted beside it, managing to look both ominous and slightly embarrassed, as if it knew it didn't belong in such a cheerful kitchen. I decided to move it to the formal dining room only because the table was large enough to display all the photos and documents. And maybe because it was one of the only rooms in the house that didn't get a lot of use. I usually ate at the kitchen island so I could look out at flowers I paid someone else to plant and tend to because I had a black thumb.

The doorbell rang at precisely nine o'clock. Through the peephole, Walt Garrison stood on my porch, checking his watch with the concentration of someone defusing a bomb. His Saturday uniform was pristine—khakis with creases that could slice bread, navy polo shirt that had never known the indignity of a wrinkle, veterans cap positioned at the exact angle that suggested he'd measured it with a protractor.

"Good morning, Walt," I said. "It's 9 in the morning."

"Oh-nine-hundred hours." He was already pushing past me, drawn to the evidence box like a moth to a flame. "Prime operational time. Only wastrels and vagabonds are still slothing about at this hour. I heard you had the Pickering–Bailey files."

Before I could ask how he'd heard—though on Grimm Island, asking how anyone knew anything was like asking how fish learned to swim—he was already pulling latex gloves from his pocket.

Within twenty minutes, my dining room had been colonized by the Silver Sleuths. They'd arrived with the inevitability of high tide, each bringing their expertise and breakfast contribution. Deidre Whitmore had brought apple fritters from Beaumont's, the bakery that charged enough to make you reconsider your commitment to pastry. Hank Hardeman wore cargo shorts that had been ironed within an inch of their life and a fishing vest with pockets organized according to a system only he understood. Dottie carried her old medical bag, the leather worn soft as butter from decades of use. And finally, Bea Livingston swept in wearing purple silk that moved like liquid money and earrings that could double as wind chimes in an emergency.

"Right," Walt announced, assuming command with natural authority. "Let's see what we're dealing with."

The evidence box released its contents reluctantly, each document crackling with age and resentment.

"Case number 85-09-116," Walt read from the official report, his voice taking on the measured cadence of military briefings. "Double homicide. Victims—Ruby Theresa Bailey, age thirty-two, and George Norris Pickering, age forty-five. Date of discovery: Monday, September 16, 1985, approximately 6:15 a.m. Location: Turtle Point, eastern shore of Grimm Island."

Turtle Point was one of those places on Grimm Island that tourists photographed for its wild beauty—a curved stretch of beach where the trees grew right down to the sand, their roots creating shadowy caves where teenagers went to do things their parents preferred not to know about. At night, it transformed into something else entirely, a place where the sound of waves could mask almost anything.

"Discovered by Samuel Morrison during his morning jog," Walt continued. "Bodies found positioned in embrace near tree line. Morrison reported the victims were unclothed and appeared to be sleeping together until he noticed the blood."

"That's Tommy Morrison's father," I said, recognizing the name. Tommy, who just last night had been ready to swim out to save a whale, came from a family that had its own tragic history with the island's violence.

"I remember they were killed the weekend before the Seafood Festival," Bea inserted, picking apart a fritter between crimson nails. "Really put a whole damper on the thing. I tell you one thing, any man who had a sidepiece was thinking twice about paying her a visit. No one wanted to end up with their goods hanging out in the wind and a bullet in their head."

The Seafood Festival—Grimm Island's annual celebration of all things that could be caught, fried, and served with cocktail sauce. Even murder, apparently, worked around the island's social calendar.

"So crass, Bea," Deidre said, clucking her tongue.

"These are excellent fritters," Hank piped in. "Beaumont's really has a light hand with their pastries. Reminds me of the time Eleanor dragged me to Paris. Stood in line for hours to see the *Mona Lisa*—I wasn't impressed, let me tell you. And then we shuffled through the halls and Eleanor assured me it was okay to look at the paintings of naked women because it was art."

"Maybe if we could focus on the mission," Walt interrupted, before Hank could prolong his story.

Walt spread the crime-scene photos across the table. They were in color, though faded to the peculiar sepia of 1980s photography. Ruby Bailey lay on her side in the sand, her dark hair spread like seaweed around her face. Three bullet wounds were visible on her chest. Reverend Pickering was positioned behind her, his arm draped over her body as if protecting her even in death.

"Same weapon," Dottie said, consulting her notes from the original autopsy. "A .38 caliber for both victims. Three shots to Ruby's chest, one to Pickering's head. All close range."

"So someone let them get close," Hank said. "Maybe someone they knew."

"The positioning," Dottie continued, pointing to specific details in the photos. "They were arranged immediately after death, while the bodies were still pliable. By the time they were found, rigor mortis had set in. The responding officers had difficulty separating them for transport. Someone wanted them found this way—embracing, like lovers."

"A statement," Hank said. "The killer was making a point."

"But what point?" I asked, humming nervously—a few bars of "Blue Skies" escaping before I caught myself.

"That's the question," Walt said, creating a timeline on my dining room wall with index cards and string. "Let's trace their last day. We'll put it on the murder board. I must say, Mabel, the new computer and printer you bought is very helpful. You just scan the papers and they print right out. Like magic."

Deidre rolled her eyes. Since she was the only one of the Silver Sleuths who actually knew how to work any kind of technology, she'd been designated with the task of getting the items from the evidence box scanned and printed so we could put them on the whiteboard that had somehow taken up permanent residence in my dining room over the last several weeks. Walt had it delivered, and he was so excited about the possibility of our next cold case that I didn't have the heart to tell him it didn't match my décor.

Walt pulled out witness statements, yellowed with age. "Ruby Bailey's movements the day of her murder: She was seen singing in the choir at the Methodist church that morning, and she and her son left around 11:30 that morning. Then she cleaned two houses that afternoon. The Carver house, from noon to 3 p.m. And the Watson estate, from 3:30 to 6 p.m. Her son said she didn't come home that night, but he was used to doing for himself since she worked so much."

"Old money, the Watsons," Bea said, studying the timeline. "Cotton fortune from before the war—and when I say the war, I mean the one where we lost but still insist on calling it the War of Northern Aggression at garden club meetings."

"Ruby was seen leaving the Watson property at 6 p.m. by the gardener, James Mitchell," Walt continued. "That's the last confirmed sighting."

"Her car?" Hank asked.

"Found at her apartment complex. A 1972 Mercury Cougar."

"Now on to Pickering," Walt said. "Friday schedule: He arrived at the church at 7 to pray and do final preparations for the sermon. His wife said he had pot roast for lunch at home, and then he had a counseling session with a parishioner back at the church. There was a youth group meeting from 3 to 5 p.m.—twelve teenagers present, all later interviewed. He told his wife he had church business to attend to that evening. He left the parsonage at 7 p.m. and didn't return."

"His car?"

"1983 Buick, found about a half a mile from where his body was found." Walt produced pictures of the vehicle and where it had been located. "Wallet was in glove compartment, ninety-three dollars cash."

"That was a lot of money back then," Dottie said. "Especially for a preacher."

I studied the photographs after Deidre scanned them and started printing the pictures. "He didn't want anyone to see his car," I said. "Parked behind some trees."

"Yes, ahh, well," Walt said, and then cleared his throat before shoving the report across the table to me. "You can see there…"

I arched a brow, wondering if Walt was actually blushing.

"Oh, for Pete's sake, Walt," Dottie said, shaking her head. "You're eighty years old. You know what people do in the back seats of cars. You probably did it yourself."

Bea snickered. "Not straightlaced Walt. Margaret probably had to schedule sex with his secretary to make sure it got on the calendar."

Walt bristled, his posture straightening more than it already was. "I'll have you know that I've always been a very creative partner in the bedroom. And sometimes out of the bedroom."

"Oooh," Bea, Dottie and Deidre said in unison.

"Do give details, Walt," Bea added.

His lips pinched together and he said, "A gentleman never tells."

"There was no DNA back then," Dottie said, "But I remember they took samples from the back of the car. Who knows what happened to them. If I remember right there was a blanket laid out. You know how big those back seats are in a Buick. Might as well have been a bed. And there were obvious signs of dallying."

"So Pickering picks up Ruby at her apartment," Hank said. "They drive out to Turtle Point, get down to business, and then someone shows up. They were found without clothes on, so it makes sense they were interrupted. Or at least occupied to the point they didn't see another car or person approach."

"Not much you can do when you're naked and someone pulls a gun on you," Bea added.

"Why does that sound like a personal story?" Deidre asked.

"I'm going to write about it in my memoirs," Bea said. "I don't want to spoil it now."

"You've been writing those memoirs for twenty years," Dottie said. "We'll all be dead by the time you finish them."

Bea just smiled and said, "We're talking about the reverend. Let's focus on their affair." She settled into what was clearly her favorite subject—other people's scandals. "Everyone knew about Ruby and the reverend. It was the worst-kept secret on the island." She paused for dramatic effect, her earrings tinkling like tiny silver bells. "Betty Mae at the Flamingo Motel told me years later that they had a standing reservation. Room twelve, every Tuesday and Thursday afternoon. Always paid cash."

"The Flamingo Motel," Deidre said with the kind of delicate shudder that suggested she'd rather not think about what went on there. The Flamingo had been Grimm Island's worst-kept secret—everyone knew what it was for, but everyone pretended they didn't, like a shameful relative at a family reunion that nobody acknowledged but couldn't quite ban from attending.

"But here's what's interesting," Bea continued, leaning forward conspiratorially. "Ruby wasn't stupid. She knew Pickering would never leave his wife—June Pickering's family had some money, and George liked being comfortable. Ruby was practical about it. She was saving money, planned to move to Charleston with Michael once she had enough. The affair with Pickering? He was helping her financially, slipping her extra cash."

"Transactional," Dottie said without judgment.

"Survival," Bea corrected. "Ruby had a ten-year-old son and an ex-husband who drank away every penny he ever earned. She was doing what she had to do."

"Speaking of the ex-husband," Walt said, pulling out another report. "Jimmy Thorne. Mean drunk who used to beat Ruby when he was in his cups. But he was in the county lockup that night—picked up for drunk and disorderly at 8 p.m., held until Monday morning."

"Convenient alibi," Hank noted.

"Or deliberately arranged," Walt suggested. "Get yourself locked up the night your ex-wife is murdered?"

"Let's look at the confessions," Hank said, arranging three separate documents. "This is what really makes this case unusual. Three different people confessed within a week of the murders." Then he looked at me and asked, "Mabel, do you have anything besides coffee? You know I can't drink it after ten o'clock or it messes with my digestive system."

"I have iced tea," I said. "Or lemonade."

"Iced tea is fine."

I nodded and hurried into the kitchen, not wanting to miss the information about the confessions. But my southern hospitality wouldn't let me just get the tea pitcher and slap it on the table. I got out my big wooden tray, set out the pitcher, goblets, and a plate of tea cookies, along with napkins, and I hurried back into the dining room and set the tray in the center of the table.

"Lovely, dear," Deidre said. "What tea is that?"

"Hibiscus," I said.

"Very refreshing. Just what we need after those fritters."

"Did I miss anything?" I asked.

"No," Walt said. "Hank was just about to read the statements, but he couldn't find his glasses. They were on top of his head."

"They're very light," Hank said. "Just like the optometrist said. Featherweight."

Hank adjusted his glasses and then read the document in front of him. "Samuel Ricker, age forty-one, transient laborer. Confessed September 18. Claimed he killed both victims after Ruby refused his advances. Knew about the positioning of bodies and the weapon used."

"Perfect patsy," Bea said. "A drifter no one would miss or believe."

"Recanted September 25," Hank continued, "Claiming Sheriff Roy Milton coerced him with threats of worse charges."

"Good old Milton," Dottie said. "His sins are likely to follow us into every investigation we look into. May he rot in prison."

"Hear, hear," Walt said, raising his goblet in a mock toast.

"Moving on," Hank said. "Betty Mae Hutchins, age twenty-eight, worked at the Flamingo Motel. Confessed September 20. Claimed she killed them in a jealous rage after discovering Pickering had been cheating on her with multiple women, including Ruby. A classic case of jealous lover scorned."

"Was Pickering seeing other women?" I asked.

"Not according to Betty Mae when she recanted," Bea said. "She later told me Milton threatened to charge her with prostitution if she didn't confess. She was scared, alone, and did what he said."

"Prison really isn't good enough for that man," I said, thinking of all the lives Roy ruined in his quest for money and power.

The third confession was the most elaborate. "Tommy Garrett, age nineteen. Son of Councilman William Garrett. Confessed September 19. Claimed the murders were drug related, that he was Pickering's dealer."

"There were no signs of drugs or alcohol in Pickering's system," Dottie said.

"Recanted September 21 after Daddy hired a Charleston lawyer," Walt finished.

"Three false confessions," Hank summarized. "Each designed to muddy the waters, each easily discredited. Someone was managing this investigation from the start."

"Roy Milton?" I asked.

Bea shrugged. "We certainly know Roy could be bought for the right price. But it could have just as easily been he was getting pressure to solve the case, and Roy being Roy, went about it however he saw fit. It wouldn't matter to him if whoever he arrested was guilty or innocent."

Walt pulled out a manila envelope marked *Confidential*. "This was sealed. Never opened."

"Why would Milton seal something and never open it?" I asked. "What good would that do?"

"Why would he be a low-down dirty snake in the grass?" Dottie said. "These are all questions we ask ourselves."

We watched as Walt carefully slit the aged envelope. Inside was a single witness statement.

"Statement of Elsie Crawford, September 20, 1985," Walt read. "'I was walking my dog at Turtle Point around 9 p.m. on September 15. I saw Reverend Pickering near the tree line. He was with a woman, but it wasn't Ruby Bailey. The woman was white, blond hair, wearing a white nurse's uniform.'"

The room went silent.

"A witness at the actual murder scene," Dottie breathed. "And Milton buried it."

"Look at his note," Walt said, pointing to scrawled handwriting at the bottom. "'Witness unreliable. History of mental illness. Statement disregarded.'"

"Elsie Crawford," Bea said slowly, searching her memory. "She had what they called nervous episodes. Today we'd call it anxiety. But she wasn't crazy. Wonder why she was out there so late at night. Sounds like a busy area. Maybe George should've picked another place for his trysts."

"A blond woman in a nurse's uniform," I said. "At the murder scene."

"If Elsie saw this woman with Pickering at 9," Hank said, working through the timeline, "And the murders happened between 10 and 2..."

"The blond woman could be our killer," Walt finished.

"Or a witness who never came forward," Dottie suggested.

"In 1985, who would have been wearing a nurse's uniform?" I asked.

"Someone from the medical center," Dottie said. "Or someone pretending to be a nurse. Uniforms aren't hard to acquire."

"I've done it myself when I needed to go undercover for a story," Bea said, referring to her days as a reporter.

Walt added this to our murder board, which was beginning to look like the fever dream of someone who'd watched too much true crime television. Colored strings connected victims to witnesses to suspects, creating a web that somehow made the case both clearer and more confusing.

"June Pickering picked up and left town a few weeks after the murder," Bea said. "Took the kids and moved to Charleston with her sister. The parsonage belonged to the church and whoever they hired to replace George, so she was out on her keister. I heard through the grapevine that there were a couple of members of the church board who blamed June because if she was fulfilling her wifely duties then George wouldn't have strayed elsewhere."

"What a bunch of hooey," Deidre said. "June could've presented herself like a Thanksgiving turkey and George still would've gone somewhere else for dinner. He had a wandering eye from the start."

"That talk of turkey is making me hungry," Hank said.

"You're always hungry, dear," Dottie said and patted him on the shoulder.

I raised my brow at the ease of the show of affection. I'd had an inkling that something had been going on between Hank and Dottie for a few weeks now, but they'd always been very discreet.

Outside, Grimm Island was waking to its Saturday routines—tourists heading for beach rentals, locals walking dogs, the eternal rhythm of a place that had learned to carry its secrets as easily as the tide carried shells.

"We need to find Elsie Crawford," Walt declared, breaking the spell. "If she's still alive."

"And identify the blond woman," Hank added.

"And talk to Michael Bailey," I said. "Ruby's son."

"He's a strange one," Deidre said.

"He stayed, though," Dottie observed. "That takes either courage or..." She trailed off.

"Or what?" I asked.

"Or a reason," she finished quietly.

Chowder wandered in then, his Hawaiian shirt slightly askew from his morning adventures. He surveyed our work with the patience of a dog who recognized the signs of human obsession, then settled at

Bea's feet with a dramatic sigh that suggested we were all making things unnecessarily complicated.

"Monday," Walt announced, as if declaring war. "We start interviews Monday. Everyone takes the weekend to review their assignments."

As they prepared to leave, carefully packing their notes and evidence copies, I stood before our murder board. Ruby Bailey and George Pickering stared back from their photographs—two people who'd found each other in a place that didn't approve, who'd carved out their small rebellion in room twelve of the Flamingo Motel, who'd died together on a beach while someone watched, someone who might still be walking these streets, sitting in these churches, shopping at the Piggly Wiggly like any other resident of Grimm Island.

"We'll find out what happened," I told their photos, then found myself humming "Amazing Grace"—for Ruby who'd sung in the choir, for Pickering who'd preached redemption but couldn't find it for himself, for all the secrets Grimm Island held like pearls in tightly closed oysters, waiting for someone brave enough to pry them open.

CHAPTER
FOUR

Sunday morning descended upon Grimm Island with the reverence of a benediction, golden light filtering through the live oaks like heaven's own approval of our small corner of creation. I stood before my wardrobe contemplating the eternal question of what one wore to investigate a murder after worship—a dilemma that Emily Post had inexplicably failed to address in her etiquette guides.

I selected a dove-gray dress with ivory piping along the collar and cuffs, the sort of dress that suggested I took both God and fashion seriously but not to the point of ostentation. The pearl buttons caught the morning light, and the full skirt moved with the kind of grace that made walking feel like floating—essential for maintaining dignity during the post-service social gauntlet.

The doorbell rang at precisely 9:15, as it had every Sunday for the past three weeks. Through the peephole, Dash stood on my porch in his navy suit—not his first-day-in-court suit or his meeting-with-the-mayor suit, but what I'd come to think of as his Sunday suit, the one that made him look like he'd stepped out of a Graham Greene novel about complicated men with complicated pasts.

"Morning," he said when I opened the door, his eyes taking in my dress with an appreciation that made my stomach perform acrobatics.

"Good morning," I replied, collecting my purse and Bible. "Fair warning—we're going Methodist today."

His eyebrow rose fractionally. "Changing denominations? Should I alert the press?"

"Reverend Sutton was George Pickering's associate pastor back in 1985," I explained, locking my door with the brass key that had worn smooth from years of use. "He worked under him for three years before Pickering was killed. I thought he might have some insight."

"So we're combining worship with witness interrogation?"

"We're multitasking," I corrected. "It's very modern of us."

First Methodist Church of Grimm Island stood at the corner of Church and Broad like a dignified matron who'd seen everything but was too well-bred to gossip about it. Where St. James Baptist proclaimed its faith with enthusiasm and white clapboard that needed painting every other year, the Methodist church whispered its devotion through red brick and stained glass that had survived three hurricanes and countless scandals.

The parking lot was already filling with sensible sedans and the occasional Cadillac that suggested someone's grandmother had died and left them something substantial. I recognized Dr. Morrison's ancient Mercedes, held together by rust and stubbornness, and Georgia Bellington's new Tesla, which she drove with the aggressive confusion of someone who wasn't ready to give up the control of the wheel to a computer.

"Ready for the Methodist experience?" I asked Dash as we approached the arched doorway.

"How different can it be?"

"Oh, honey," I said, affecting my best Southern belle drawl. "You're about to find out."

The sanctuary smelled of furniture polish and old hymnals, a combination of reverence and resignation. The pews were actual wood —none of those padded numbers the Baptists had installed after the great back pain uprising of 2003. These were pews that demanded good posture and better behavior.

We found seats halfway back on the left side—close enough to seem engaged but not so close as to suggest we were gunning for a committee position. Margaret Calhoun sat three rows ahead, her hat a conservative black number with just enough veil to suggest mourning without actually committing to grief. The Silver Sleuths had claimed their territory: Walt positioned for optimal exit surveillance, Dottie near enough to the front to catch every word, Bea in a turquoise ensemble that somehow managed to be both inappropriate and magnificent.

Reverend Douglas Sutton took the pulpit with the measured grace of someone who'd been doing this for decades and had learned that rushing only led to perspiration and misquoted scripture. He was thin in that way that suggested worry had been his primary food group for decades, with silver hair that caught the light through the stained glass, creating a halo effect that was either divine providence or excellent positioning.

"Good morning," he said, his voice warm but not overly familiar, welcoming but maintaining appropriate boundaries.

The congregation responded with their measured "Good morning," nothing like the enthusiastic call-and-response of the Baptists. This was worship as choreographed dance, everyone knowing their steps and keeping to them.

"Today's scripture comes from the book of James," Reverend Sutton announced, and I felt Dash shift beside me. "Chapter five, verse sixteen. Therefore confess your sins to each other and pray for each other so that you may be healed."

The coincidence was too pointed to be anything but providence or perversity—I wasn't sure which.

"Confession," Reverend Sutton continued, his pale eyes scanning the congregation, "is not simply admitting wrongdoing. It's the act of bringing darkness into light, of refusing to let secrets fester in shadow."

I thought of George Pickering, standing at this very pulpit, carrying the weight of his affair with Ruby Bailey while preaching righteousness to his flock. Had he felt the hypocrisy burning in his throat like acid? Or had he compartmentalized so thoroughly that Sunday

George and Tuesday-at-the-Flamingo George were entirely different people?

The sermon continued with Methodist precision—three points, each with subpoints, a poem by Charles Wesley, and exactly two personal anecdotes that illustrated the theme without revealing anything actually personal. Reverend Sutton was a master of the form.

"Some of you," he said, his voice dropping to that register that made everyone lean forward slightly, "are carrying secrets that are eating you alive. You think you're protecting others, but you're only protecting the darkness."

I felt Dash go rigid beside me, his whole body tensing like someone had pressed a blade to his spine. His breathing changed—subtle, controlled, but I'd spent enough time with him to recognize when something hit too close to home. His jaw tightened, that muscle jumping the way it did when he was processing something he didn't want to think about.

His hand rested on the pew between us, and I watched his fingers curl slightly, knuckles going white with the pressure of whatever memory Sutton's words had summoned. Without thinking, I shifted my hand until my pinky finger just barely touched his. The contact was minimal, deniable, but I felt it like electricity, making me acutely aware of every breath, every small movement.

He didn't pull away. If anything, he seemed to lean into that tiny point of connection, like it was anchoring him to the present instead of whatever darkness Sutton's words had dragged up. His finger relaxed slightly, pressing back against mine with deliberate intention.

I wanted to look at him, to read what was written on his face, but I kept my eyes forward. Whatever ghosts were haunting Dash Beckett, they weren't mine to exorcise in the middle of service. But I could offer this—this small, secret touch that said *I'm here* without demanding explanations he wasn't ready to give.

After the service—which ended at exactly noon because Methodists believed that God himself observed proper mealtimes—we lingered as the congregation filed out with dignified efficiency.

Reverend Sutton stood at the door, shaking hands with friendly familiarity.

"Reverend Sutton," I said when we reached him. "I'm Mabel McCoy, and this is Sheriff Beckett. We were hoping we might speak with you for a moment?"

His pale eyes sharpened with interest. "Mrs. McCoy. I know who you are—the tea shop on Harbor Street. And Sheriff, of course. What can I do for you?"

"It's about George Pickering," I said quietly.

Something flickered across his face—not surprise exactly, but a kind of weary recognition, as if he'd been waiting a long time for someone to ask.

"I wondered when someone would come," he said. "My office, if you don't mind? I'd prefer not to discuss this where others might overhear."

His office was exactly what you'd expect—dark wood, theological volumes, and a window overlooking the cemetery. He gestured for us to sit in the worn leather chairs across from his desk.

"You're investigating the murders."

The words hung in the air like incense, heavy with the weight of decades of silence.

"We're reviewing cold cases," Dash said carefully.

Sutton moved to the desk, running his fingers along the worn wood. "George worked here for fifteen years. Every sermon, every wedding, every funeral planned at this desk." He paused, looking at the wall that separated this office from the next. "George spent hours in that office. I could hear him through the heating vent, practicing his sermons over and over. Same passages, different inflections, trying to find just the right tone of righteousness."

He moved to a filing cabinet that might have been here since Wesley himself walked the earth, its brass handles worn smooth by generations of searching hands. "He was meticulous about some things, careless about others. Which is why I have this.

"George Pickering was my mentor." He drew out a composition book, the kind children use for spelling tests, its marbled cover faded to the color of weak tea. "Brilliant preacher. Complicated man. Terrible at keeping the confidences he'd been entrusted with."

The notebook felt fragile in my hands, as if the secrets inside had weight enough to crumble the pages to dust. Sutton watched me hold it with the expression of someone handing over a loaded weapon.

"I found this tucked behind his commentary on Romans—ironic, considering what Paul had to say about judgment." His laugh was dry as communion wafers. "I've kept it all these years, like a splinter under the skin. Too deep to dig out, too painful to ignore."

The pages whispered against each other as I opened it, releasing the ghost of Pickering's cologne—something pine scented and aggressive, the kind of aftershave that announced a man before he entered a room. His handwriting cramped across the pages like ants at a picnic, organized and relentless.

"He collected secrets," Sutton said. "The way other men collect stamps or coins. Every confession, every whispered shame, every sin that walked through his office door—he wrote it all down."

The entries read like a catalog of human frailty.

Margaret C. keeps a bank account in Charleston. Her husband thinks she's visiting her sister. She's visiting her husband's brother. The Whitmore boy isn't theirs by blood. Bought from a girl in Savannah, fifteen years ago. Cash transaction. They burned the real birth certificate. Judge Prioleau takes bribes. Not money—favors. Has a ledger of who owes what. Keeps it in his mother's Bible.

Each entry was dated, annotated, cross-referenced. George Pickering had been building a map of Grimm Island's sins, and everyone was marked on it.

"Good Lord," I breathed, then caught myself. "Sorry. It's just—"

"Appalling?" Sutton supplied. "George confused knowledge with power, and power with godliness. He thought holding these secrets made him indispensable. Instead, it made him dangerous. I wouldn't normally turn these over because as pastors, we do hear things from congregants that are kept in strictest of confidence. But there are certain things we would be obligated to report on if there were murder or child abuse for instance. I figured after so many years have passed that most of these people are gone and the stakes aren't quite so high. I trust you'll keep this in confidence?"

"Confidence is the nature of my business too," Dash assured him. "But this will give us a good place to start. The investigators didn't have this information back then."

"Well, with Milton in charge it probably wouldn't have mattered," Sutton said. "Maybe I was meant to keep it all these years for exactly this moment."

An entry from late August caught my eye, the handwriting more erratic, pressing so hard the pen had torn through in places.

Ruby knows about this journal. Saw me writing in it. Now she's scared—not of me, but FOR me. Says I'm playing with fire, that some secrets on this island have teeth and claws. She wants us to leave, start over somewhere else, but I could never leave June. It would ruin me. She would ruin me. God help me, I don't know what to do anymore.

The final entry was scrawled like a confession of its own, dated September 14, 1985—the day before they died.

I can't shake the feeling I'm being watched. Ruby feels it too. She's terrified, keeps looking over her shoulder. Says she saw someone following her home from work yesterday, but when she turned around no one was there. We're meeting at Turtle Point tomorrow night. She says we need to talk about leaving, about disappearing before it's too late. Maybe she's right. Maybe I've been playing God for too long, collecting sins like baseball cards. Maybe it's time to run.

"He was paranoid at the end," Dash observed.

Sutton nodded slowly. "George had made so many enemies with this journal. Any one of the people he'd documented would have had motive to silence him. And Ruby—poor Ruby knew about the journal. That knowledge alone made her a target."

As we prepared to leave, Sutton caught my arm with fingers that felt like bird bones.

"There was a witness," he said quietly. "At Turtle Point the night they died. Elsie Crawford—chronic insomniac, walked her dog at ungodly hours. She saw something that night, told the police, but Milton dismissed her testimony. Said she was unreliable, prone to fantasies."

He wrote down an address in Charleston, his penmanship as precise as his sermons. "She's at Magnolia Gardens now—the assisted-living place. Her mind wanders sometimes, gets lost in the past. But when she's clear, she remembers that night like it was yesterday. Says what she saw is burned into her memory."

"What did she see?" I asked.

Sutton shook his head. "I only know what she told me years later —that she saw George and Ruby at Turtle Point, and that someone else was there too. But Milton buried her statement, never followed up. You'll have to ask her yourself.

"George wasn't entirely evil," he said, and there was pleading in his voice. "He genuinely loved God, loved his congregation. He just... he confused being needed with being loved. And that confusion killed him."

Outside, the afternoon had ripened into something overripe, the humidity so thick you could practically see it shimmer between the tombstones in the cemetery. The dead lay in neat rows, their secrets safely buried, unlike George Pickering's, which were about to be dragged into the light whether they wanted to be or not.

"Your house?" Dash suggested. "I should get my watch. And we need to process what we just learned."

"I was going to make lunch," I offered. "We can plan our next move."

The walk back took us through Sunday afternoon Grimm Island— families heading home from church, teenagers escaping to the beach before their parents could assign chores. Eugene Bradshaw had set up his crystal healing station in the park for those interested in an alternative to church.

In my kitchen, I moved through the familiar ritual of sandwich-making while Dash sat at the counter, reading Pickering's notebook more carefully.

"He mentions the Flamingo Motel repeatedly," Dash observed. "Not just for his meetings with Ruby. He saw something there, or someone."

"The blond woman," I said, slicing tomatoes with perhaps more force than necessary. "She keeps appearing in the narrative but never quite comes into focus."

I retrieved his watch from its place among my tea canisters. "Your watch," I said, handing it to him.

He took it but caught my hand before I could withdraw it. "Mabel," he said, and something in his tone made my pulse skip.

"We should talk to Michael Bailey tomorrow," I said quickly. "Ruby's son. He would have been ten when she died."

"Old enough to remember things," Dash agreed, but his thumb was tracing circles on my wrist, and I found myself humming nervously—a few bars of "Blue Moon."

"You hum when you're nervous," he observed softly.

"Bad habit," I managed.

"I like it," he said, finally releasing my hand. "I should go. Tomorrow's going to be complicated."

At the door, he paused. "Be careful, Mabel. Someone killed two people to protect these secrets. Maybe more, if Pickering was right about—"

"Stay."

The word escaped before I could think better of it, hanging in the air between us like a challenge.

He turned slowly, his expression unreadable. "Mabel..."

"Not for... I mean..." I took a breath, trying to gather words that kept scattering like startled birds. "We could just...be normal for an afternoon. Watch a movie. Order Chinese food. Pretend we're not investigating a murder."

"That's a bad idea," he said softly, but he hadn't moved toward the door.

"Why?"

He stepped closer, and I could smell his cologne—cedar and something darker, like smoke. His thumb was still tracing those maddening circles on my wrist, each pass sending heat spiraling up my arm.

"Because," he said, his voice dropping to that register that made my stomach perform complicated acrobatics, "you're already driving me half crazy, Mabel McCoy. Every time you start singing, every time you wear one of these dresses that make you look like you stepped out of a different era, every time you look at me like you're looking at me right now." His thumb stilled against my pulse point, which was racing like I'd run a marathon. "If I stay…"

"We'll watch a movie," I said firmly, though my voice came out breathier than intended. "Something with explosions. Or car chases. Very unsexy car chases."

He laughed—a real laugh that transformed his face. "Unsexy car chases?"

"The unsexiest. Maybe with Nicolas Cage."

"You're negotiating my staying with the promise of Nicolas Cage movies?"

"Is it working?"

He studied me for a long moment, and I could see him weighing something, making calculations I couldn't follow. Then his shoulders relaxed, decision made.

"One condition," he said.

"What?"

"Phones off. If we're pretending to be normal, we're committing to it. No case calls, no Silver Sleuths dropping by, no investigating."

I reached for my phone and powered it down, the screen going dark with finality. "Done."

He pulled his out, hesitated for just a moment—the sheriff in him warring with the man—then turned it off too.

"So," I said, suddenly aware that we were alone in my house with no murder to investigate, no evidence to examine, no excuse for the proximity we'd been dancing around for weeks. "Nicolas Cage?"

"God help me," he said, but he was smiling. "Yes. Nicolas Cage."

We ended up on my couch, watching *Con Air* because it was the perfect combination of ridiculous and distracting. Dash had removed his suit jacket and rolled up his shirtsleeves, revealing forearms that I tried very hard not to stare at. I'd kicked off my heels and tucked my feet under me, the skirt of my church dress spreading across the couch between us like a fence made of fabric and good intentions.

"This movie makes no sense," I said, stealing a piece of sesame chicken from his container. "Why would they put all these dangerous criminals on the same plane?"

"Because Nicolas Cage needed something to do," he replied, his arm stretched across the back of the couch, not quite touching my shoulders but close enough that I could feel the heat of him. "Also, stop analyzing. You promised unsexy car chases and explosions."

"There haven't been any car chases yet. Just plane...hijacking."

"Patience."

On screen, Nicolas Cage was saying something about putting the bunny back in the box, and I found myself laughing at the absurdity of it all—the movie, this afternoon, the way Dash's fingers had somehow found their way to playing with the ends of my hair, so gently I might have been imagining it.

"Your hair smells like vanilla," he murmured, and when I turned to look at him, his face was closer than I'd expected.

"It's the shampoo," I said stupidly, my voice barely above a whisper.

"Mabel." The way he said my name made it sound like a prayer and a curse all at once.

"Very unsexy movie," I reminded him, though my eyes had dropped to his mouth. "Nicolas Cage. Explosions."

"Right," he agreed, but neither of us looked back at the screen.

The afternoon stretched between us like taffy, sweet and pulling tighter with each passing moment. The sun had shifted to that golden hour light that made everything look like a painting. We'd migrated closer somehow, my head on his shoulder, his arm around me, both of us pretending this was casual, normal, not a careful negotiation of boundaries we weren't quite ready to cross.

By the time the credits rolled, I'd somehow ended up tucked against his side, his arm around me, both of us pretending this was casual. Normal. Just two people watching a movie.

Except my heart was racing, and I was acutely aware of every place our bodies touched, and this didn't feel casual at all.

"I should go," he said quietly, but neither of us moved.

"Probably," I agreed.

When he finally stood, the absence of his warmth felt like loss. At the door, he kissed me good night—warm, lingering, familiar. The kind of kiss that felt like a promise without specifying what was being promised.

"Lock your doors," he said against my hair.

"Always do."

After he left, I stood there for a moment, my lips still tingling, my heart doing complicated things in my chest. Then I picked up my phone and turned it back on to find six missed calls from Dottie.

I called her back immediately.

"We need to meet," I said. "All of us. Tomorrow morning, before the shop opens. We have new information about the case."

"What kind of information? And why haven't you been answering your phone? I was about to send Walt over there."

I looked at Pickering's notebook on my counter, then thought about the afternoon I'd just spent pretending murders didn't exist. "The kind of information that suggests Ruby and Pickering weren't the only victims. This goes deeper than we thought."

Through my window, Grimm Island basked in its evening peace. But somewhere out there, someone had successfully hidden the truth for years. Tomorrow, we would start pulling at threads that might unravel everything.

Some secrets, I was learning, were patient. They could even wait for a Sunday afternoon to end.

The question was whether we were brave enough—whether I was brave enough—to drag them into the light while also navigating whatever was happening between Dash and me.

Because that was becoming a mystery all its own.

THE PRE-DAWN DARKNESS OF MONDAY MORNING WRAPPED around The Perfect Steep like a wool blanket—heavy, familiar, and slightly scratchy around the edges. I'd been awake since four, unable to sleep with George Pickering's confessions swimming through my mind like poisonous fish in a polluted pond. Each secret he'd recorded felt like a small stone dropped into still water, and I couldn't stop imagining the ripples spreading outward, touching everything, everyone.

I'd selected a 1940s tea dress in navy blue with tiny white polka dots, the kind of dress that suggested I meant business but wouldn't let murder interfere with proper presentation. The fabric whispered against my stockings as I moved through my kitchen, and I found myself singing softly while measuring out coffee—*"I get along without you very well, of course I do…"* The Hoagy Carmichael melody felt appropriate, given what we were about to unearth. Lies we told ourselves about being fine, about moving forward, about not needing closure.

"What do you think, Chowder?" I asked, watching him waddle into the kitchen wearing his Monday ensemble—a crisp bow tie in brown tweed and a matching vest he'd selected himself from his wardrobe. He had exquisite taste for a French bulldog, suggesting he understood the importance of making an entrance. He'd taken to Mondays with the grim determination of someone who understood that weekends were too short and bills came too often.

"Don't forget your tweed cap," I reminded him. "You'll look just like Sherlock Holmes. Very appropriate for our current case."

He snorted his opinion of early mornings and positioned himself by his food bowl with the patience of a saint awaiting martyrdom.

"I know, I know. Your breakfast is three minutes late. How ever will you survive such deprivation?" I filled his bowl with the fresh chicken and rice package from the fridge that cost as much as a human meal. "We're solving a murder today. Possibly multiple murders, if Pickering's journal is any indication. But yes, your gastrointestinal needs take precedence."

Chowder ignored my sarcasm with considered practice, attacking his breakfast like it might escape if he didn't pin it down immediately.

After he'd finished and conducted his morning ritual in the back garden—a process that involved extensive sniffing and the careful selection of exactly the right spot—we set out for The Perfect Steep on foot. The walk was only six blocks, a pleasant morning constitutional that Chowder had come to expect as part of our routine.

Harbor Street at 5:30 in the morning possessed a quality of light that made even the most ordinary things appear touched by grace. The Spanish moss hanging from the live oaks caught the early sun like silver lace, swaying in the salt-tinged breeze that rolled in from the harbor. The street itself was brick—old brick, laid sometime in the 1890s, uneven enough to require attention but charming enough to make tourists stop and take photographs.

We passed the Grimm Island Public Library first, a narrow building painted Charleston green with black shutters, its windows displaying this month's featured books and a poster for the summer reading program. Deidre would be arriving there later—even in retirement, she volunteered three mornings a week, unable to fully let go of her decades organizing the island's collection. Then came Whitmore's Antiques, housed in a restored 1920s storefront with beveled glass windows that caught the morning light. The shop's displays showcased carefully curated pieces—Victorian mourning jewelry, Depression glass, fine porcelain that had once graced Charleston drawing rooms. Deidre's cousin Dolores ran the place with an impeccable eye for quality.

Beaumont's Bakery occupied a corner building with French doors that would open onto the sidewalk once the day warmed. Through the windows, I could see Clarence Beaumont pulling trays from the oven with practiced efficiency. The bakery had been featured in *Southern Living* twice—once for their croissants, once for their bourbon pecan tarts worth every penny of what he charged.

Chowder paused to investigate the lamppost outside Nature's Remedy—Eugene Bradshaw's crystal and wellness shop, painted in soft sage with cream trim. The window display featured an artful arrangement of amethyst clusters and rose quartz on white linen, looking more like a gallery installation than a retail display. Eugene might believe in the metaphysical properties of crystals, but he had the marketing sense of someone who understood his wealthy clientele.

The harbor itself stretched out to our left, visible between buildings, the water painted copper and gold by the rising sun. A few boats were already heading out—sleek fishing vessels and the occasional yacht, their silhouettes dark against the brightening sky. The smell of salt and expensive cologne from the men's boutique mixed with the sweetness from the bakery, creating the low-country perfume that meant home.

We passed Harborside Gallery, its windows showcasing local artists whose work commanded serious prices. Next was The Copper Pot, a farm-to-table restaurant that had waiting lists stretching weeks in advance during tourist season. Then Bella Boutique, where tourists bought linen dresses that cost more than some people's mortgage payments.

The Perfect Steep sat on its corner like a grande dame hosting morning court. Even from half a block away, I could see the robin's egg blue paint catching the light, the white trim crisp and clean from my March touch-up. The vintage sign—wrought iron with gold lettering—creaked slightly in the breeze, a sound so familiar I'd have noticed its absence more than its presence.

I unlocked the back door—the one that opened directly into my commercial kitchen—and was immediately enveloped by the smell of home. Tea leaves and lemon oil I used on the heart pine floors, underlaid with the ghost of yesterday's scones. The pre-dawn quiet made every sound feel amplified—the creak of floorboards in their familiar spots, the tick of the vintage clock above the register, the soft hum of the refrigerator that occasionally sounded like it was trying to communicate in Morse code.

Chowder made his way to his designated spot by the window, where early morning sun would shortly arrive to warm his cushion. He settled in with a sigh that suggested walking six blocks had exhausted him beyond measure, though I'd seen him chase butterflies for twice that distance when properly motivated.

I moved through my opening routine with the muscle memory of years of practice. First, the ovens—preheated to exactly 375 degrees for the scones that would be my first batch of the day. While they warmed, I pulled out my industrial mixer and began assembling ingredients for lemon scones with lavender glaze, measuring flour and sugar with precision. Baking was chemistry, not art, and chemistry required exactitude.

The dough came together under my hands—butter worked into dry ingredients until it resembled coarse sand, then cream and eggs folded in until just combined. I shaped it into rounds and slid the trays into the oven, setting my timer for eighteen minutes. Eighteen, never twenty. Twenty made them dry.

Next came the chalkboard—a massive slate board that took up most of the wall behind the counter. I wiped away yesterday's specials with a damp cloth and began writing in my careful script.

Monday's Offerings:

Lemon Lavender Scones—$4.50

Cucumber & Mint Tea Sandwiches—$8.00

Featured Teas: Silver Needle White Tea, Darjeeling First Flush, Chamomile Citrus

Soup of the Day: Tomato Basil Bisque

I arranged the featured tea canisters on the counter display—the delicate silver needle with its fuzzy white buds, the Darjeeling in its elegant tin with hand-painted peacocks, and the chamomile citrus blend I'd created myself, bright with dried orange peel and lemon verbena. Each canister was positioned just so, labels facing out, part of the carefully curated aesthetic that made The Perfect Steep feel less like a business and more like stepping into someone's (admittedly eccentric) living room.

The timer chimed. I pulled the scones from the oven—golden brown, perfectly risen, filling the shop with that combination of citrus and butter that would draw customers in like moths to flame. While they cooled, I mixed the lavender glaze, thinning it to just the right consistency before drizzling it across the tops in elegant zigzags.

Only then, with everything ready for the day's business, did I allow myself to think about murder.

I'd set up the back room for our meeting—the space I usually reserved for private tea parties and the occasional book club that devolved into wine and gossip. The large farmhouse table could accommodate all the Silver Sleuths, and more importantly, it was away from the front windows where curious passersby might catch a glimpse of what we were doing. Grimm Island had enough gossip without adding me and the geriatric detective squad to the morning's conversation starters.

Genevieve would be arriving at 7 to help with the morning rush before heading to her classes at the community college. She was reliable, efficient, and had learned my systems well enough that I could leave the front of the shop in her capable hands while I dealt with murder in the back room. The juxtaposition felt absurd—serving lattes and scones while discussing forty-year-old homicides—but that was becoming my new normal.

Pickering's journal sat in the center of the table, its marbled cover innocuous enough to be mistaken for a child's school notebook. I'd spent two hours last night scanning and printing every page. Now those pages were organized in neat stacks, each one a small grenade of information that might explode in someone's face.

The back door opened at precisely 6:30—Walt's arrival announced by his trademark three sharp knocks before entering, as if storming the beaches of Normandy required proper door etiquette.

"Oh-six-thirty hours," he announced, though we could all see the clock. He wore his investigation uniform: pressed khakis that could stand up by themselves, a crisp white oxford shirt, and his veterans cap positioned with mathematical precision. "I brought my notes and the tactical timeline I've been working on."

"Coffee's ready," I said, gesturing to the industrial-sized carafe I'd prepared. "Fair warning—it's strong enough to wake the dead, which seems appropriate given the circumstances."

"Gallows humor," Walt approved, pouring himself a cup. "Sign of a sound tactical mind."

Dottie arrived next, her oversized tote bag slung over her shoulder, looking purposeful despite the early hour. Today's cat-eye glasses were purple, matching her silk blouse, and her jet-black bob was styled with the kind of precision that suggested she'd been to the salon recently. The bag clinked slightly as she set it down—probably the tin of home-made cookies she inevitably brought to share.

"I called in a favor at Charleston Medical," she announced, settling into her chair with the authority of someone who'd autopsied half the low country. "Got the staff records from 1985. Every nurse who worked there that year is documented, along with their schedules and specialties." She patted her bag. "Cross-referencing them against our blond woman in white is going to be tedious, but I've performed worse miracles. Once identified a body from a single molar and three inches of femur."

"Do we want to know the story behind that?" I asked, pouring her coffee.

"Absolutely not," she said cheerfully. "But I'm happy to tell it if you're interested. The decomposition patterns alone were fascinating—"

"Let's save that for after breakfast," I interrupted, knowing from experience that Dottie's forensic anecdotes could curdle milk at thirty paces.

Bea swept in at 6:45, today's caftan a swirl of emerald green and gold that shimmered like peacock feathers in motion. Instead of her usual chandelier earrings, she wore elaborate jade drop earrings that swayed with each step, and her dyed red hair was swept up in a style that somehow managed to look both elegant and slightly chaotic— very Bea.

"I've been up since four," she announced dramatically, accepting the coffee I offered like it was holy communion. "Couldn't sleep. Kept thinking about Ruby Bailey and that reverend." She settled into her chair with a rustle of silk. "You know, I covered the story when it happened. I was still at the *Gazette* then, working the society beat, but murder trumps charity galas every time. The whole island was buzzing for months."

Deidre arrived moments later, her canvas tote bag bulging with what I knew would be meticulously organized research materials. Her silver hair was pinned back in a neat bun, and she wore sensible khaki pants and a lavender cardigan—her research uniform.

"Sorry I'm a bit late," she said, though she was still seven minutes early. "I was at the library since opening, pulling old newspaper articles from the microfiche. The *Gazette*'s archives from 1985 are fascinating." She pulled out a folder thick with photocopies. "I've got every article they ran about the murders, plus society pages from the months leading up to it. You'd be amazed what you can learn from who attended which garden parties."

"That's why we keep you around," Bea said with a wink. "Your obsessive organizational skills."

"I prefer thorough," Deidre corrected, but she was smiling as she settled into her chair.

Hank arrived last, at 6:52, apologizing for being late though he was still eight minutes early by normal human standards. He wore his investigation vest—the fishing one with seventeen pockets, each containing something he'd deemed essential. Today's cargo shorts had been ironed to within an inch of their life, the creases sharp enough to cut paper.

"I brought my notes," he explained, pulling out a leather notebook that looked like it had survived several wars and possibly the sinking of the *Titanic*. "Figured if I'm going to play detective at my age, I should at least document it properly."

"How very Nancy Drew of you," Bea said, but her tone was fond. Hank had always been thorough, the kind of man who organized his spice rack alphabetically and kept detailed records of everything from his blood pressure to his golf scores.

I hadn't heard him arrive, but suddenly Dash stood in the doorway, looking every inch the professional lawman despite the early hour. His sheriff's uniform was pressed to perfection, the light blue shirt crisp and the dark pants showing their usual razor-sharp crease. His hair was slightly damp, suggesting a recent shower, and I caught myself wondering what his morning routine looked like before forcing my attention back to the matter at hand.

"Morning," he said. "Hope I'm not late."

"Seven on the dot," Walt confirmed, frowning with disapproval. In Walt's book, on time was as good as being late.

"Coffee?" I offered, already reaching for a cup.

"Please," he said, settling into the empty chair at the head of the table. "Black, two sugars."

I poured his coffee, acutely aware of how domestic the gesture felt, how easily we'd fallen into these small rituals over the past few weeks. When I set the cup in front of him, our fingers brushed, and I felt that familiar spark of electricity that made me want to both step closer and retreat to a safe distance.

"So," Dash said, accepting the coffee with a nod of thanks. "Let's see what Pickering was hiding."

With everyone assembled, I distributed the copied pages from Pickering's journal.

"Goodness gravy," Bea breathed after a moment, her eyes wide behind her reading glasses. "I knew Margaret Calhoun had secrets, but an affair with her husband's brother? And she's still married to Harold after all these years?"

"Maybe she recommitted to her marriage," I said.

"Or maybe Harold never found out," Walt said grimly. "Some secrets stay buried because everyone involved works very hard at the burying."

"Here's one about the Rutledge family," I said, reading aloud. "'Thomas Rutledge isn't actually a Rutledge by blood. His mother, Catherine, had an affair with the family's groundskeeper—a man named Samuel Price. When she got pregnant in 1968, the family paid Samuel fifty thousand dollars to leave South Carolina and never come back. They told everyone the baby was premature. Thomas has his real father's eyes, but nobody dares say it out loud. Catherine keeps a photograph of Samuel hidden in her Bible.'"

The room went silent. The Rutledges were one of the oldest families on Grimm Island—their ancestors had signed the state constitution.

"Thomas Rutledge is a judge now," Hank said quietly. "Circuit court. Very respected."

Bea had found another entry, her expression darkening as she read. "Oh, this is ugly. 'Dr. Laurens Middleton has been writing fraudulent prescriptions for opioids for five years. Sells them to a dealer in Charleston for cash. His wife, Marie, thinks the extra money comes from his investment portfolio. She has no idea her Lexus was bought with drug money.'"

"Middleton still practices," Walt said, his jaw tightening. "Has an office on Harbor Street. My cardiologist refers patients to him."

"Here's the Prioleau scandal," Deidre said. "Judge Benjamin Prioleau took bribes from developers for favorable rulings. Twenty thousand per case, paid through his law partner's consulting firm. His son James knows—helped set up the shell company. The Prioleau family legacy isn't old money, it's dirty money wrapped in a bow tie."

"Judge Prioleau retired in 1990," Hank said, his expression grim. "But James Prioleau is the attorney who handles most of the island's real estate closings. Everyone uses him."

I flipped to another page, this one making my stomach turn. "Listen to this: 'Eleanor Ravenel's daughter didn't die in that car accident in 1974. Eleanor was driving drunk, hit a tree on River Road. The girl survived but was brain damaged. Eleanor and her husband Phillip put her in a facility in Georgia, told everyone she'd died, even had a funeral with an empty casket. They visit her twice a year and pay cash so there's no paper trail. The girl's name is still Sarah, but she doesn't know who she is anymore.'"

"Dear God," Dottie breathed. "I remember hearing about that funeral. Everyone on the island mourned that poor child."

"Eleanor Ravenel is the garden club president," Bea said, her voice hollow. "She gives out a scholarship every year in her daughter's memory. Lord have mercy."

"There's more," Dash said, holding up another page. "The Lowndes family—Pickering documented an affair and what looks like embezzlement from a family trust. And here's one about the Pinckneys covering up their son's involvement in a hit-and-run by paying off the victim's family."

We continued reading in horrified silence, each entry more damning than the last. The morning light streaming through the windows seemed to lose its warmth as we catalogued Grimm Island's sins—adultery, embezzlement, blackmail, abuse. Pickering had been thorough in his documentation through 1985, noting dates, amounts, specific details that could only have come from confession or careful observation.

"Some of these people are still alive," Walt said grimly. "Living right here on the island. And some of them have children and grandchildren who've inherited their secrets along with their money."

"I can attest to that," Bea said.

"We've identified seventeen entries that mention people still living on Grimm Island or their direct descendants," Walt announced finally, having made a list as we read. "Each one represents a potential motive for murder."

We couldn't investigate seventeen different scandals simultaneously, much as the Silver Sleuths might enjoy trying. We needed to focus on the murders themselves, on the blond woman in white who kept appearing in the narrative like a ghost that refused to be exorcised.

I pulled out the diary entry from late September, the one that had made my skin crawl when I first read it. "'Someone is watching me. I feel eyes everywhere now, like God finally got tired of waiting for me to confess and sent an avenging angel to hurry things along. Ruby's scared too. More scared than I've ever seen her. She knows something she won't tell me, something about why we're being watched. Tomorrow night at Turtle Point. Ruby says we need to talk about leaving, about starting over somewhere safe. Maybe she's right. Maybe I've been playing God for too long, collecting sins like baseball cards. Maybe it's time to run.'"

The silence that followed was profound, broken only by Chowder's snoring from his bed in the corner. He'd positioned himself in the early morning sunlight streaming through the window, his bow tie slightly askew, completely unconcerned with human drama.

"He never made it to 'starting over,'" Dottie said softly. "Neither of them did."

"There's only one other mention of feeling watched," Dash said, flipping through his notes. "An entry from two weeks before this one. Pickering wrote that he thought someone had been in his office, that his desk had been disturbed. But he wasn't sure if it was real or paranoia."

"That's it?" Walt asked. "Just two entries about surveillance?"

"The rest of the journal is all about documenting other people's sins," Dash confirmed. "These two entries about feeling watched stand out because they're personal. They're about his own fear."

"So we don't actually know who was watching them," Hank said thoughtfully. "Or if anyone was. Could have been paranoia from a guilty conscience."

"Except they ended up dead," Bea pointed out. "So someone was definitely paying attention to them."

"We need to talk to Elsie Crawford," Dash said. "According to Reverend Sutton, she was at Turtle Point that night walking her dog.

Saw something. But Milton dismissed her as an unreliable witness and buried her statement."

"Convenient," Walt muttered. "Milton had a habit of burying inconvenient truths."

"The staging bothers me," Dottie said, tapping her fingers against the table. "Someone took the time to arrange them like that—in an embrace—after killing them. That's not rage. That's not panic. That's deliberate."

"A message," Bea said. "About their affair. About sin and punishment."

"Or mockery," Hank suggested. "Making a spectacle of what they'd tried to keep hidden."

"Either way," Dash said, "It tells us something about the killer's state of mind. They weren't just eliminating a problem. They were making a statement."

"Which brings us back to motive," Walt said, consulting his notes. "Who benefits from their deaths? Who had the most to lose if Pickering or Ruby talked?"

"It would have taken some physical effort to move two bodies and position them," Dottie said.

"So we're looking for someone with strength," Walt noted. "Or possibly more than one person involved."

"That complicates things," Hank said.

Bea had been unusually quiet. Her crimson nails tapped against the paper—a nervous gesture I'd rarely seen from her.

"What is it?" I asked.

She looked up, and there was something sharp in her eyes, the look she got when a story was coming together. "This entry from mid-July: 'A reporter from the *Gazette* has been asking questions around the church. Wants to know about our finances, about donations and where the money goes. June told me the woman came to the house, very polite, very professional, asking about the new community center fund. I told June to say nothing, but she's never been good at keeping secrets. The reporter's name is Sutherland—blond, efficient, always dressed in white. She smells like trouble.'"

The room went quiet.

"Sutherland," Dash repeated. "That name mean anything to anyone?"

"Jane Sutherland," Bea said, and now her voice carried recognition. "I knew her. She worked at the *Gazette* from '84 to '86. I was still doing the society column then, but Jane—she was investigative from day one. Charleston girl, had worked at the *Post* and *Courier* before moving here."

"What was she investigating?" Hank asked.

"Church finances," Bea said slowly, piecing it together. "There'd been whispers about some of the churches on the island—money going missing, building funds that never quite added up. Jane thought she had a corruption story. Methodist, Baptist, Presbyterian—she was looking at all of them."

"And Pickering's church specifically?" Dash pressed.

"First Methodist had the biggest budget," Bea confirmed. "Wealthiest congregation on the island. If there was financial impropriety happening, that's where the money would be."

"So she wasn't interested in Ruby at all," I said. "She was after Pickering."

"Or whoever was embezzling from the church," Walt added. "Pickering might have just been collateral damage."

"She wore white," Dottie observed. "Always white, you said?"

Bea nodded. "It was her trademark. White suits, white blouses. Very Diane Sawyer. She thought it made her look more credible, more trustworthy. People would open up to her."

"And she left town right after the murders," Dash said.

"Disappeared," Bea corrected. "I came in one Monday morning—this would have been the week after they found the bodies—and her desk was cleaned out. Editor said she'd resigned, effective immediately. No forwarding address, no explanation. We all thought it was strange, but..." She shrugged. "Journalists move around. It happens."

"Except it's awfully convenient timing," Hank said.

"I can track her down," Bea offered. "I still have contacts at papers throughout the region. If Jane Sutherland is still in journalism, someone will know where."

"And if she's not?" Dottie asked.

"Then we find out why she left the profession," Dash said. "People don't just walk away from investigative journalism without a reason."

"Especially not when they're onto a good story," Bea added darkly. "Jane was ambitious. Tenacious. The kind of reporter who wouldn't let go until she had answers. If she ran, something scared her badly enough to make her quit everything."

"Or someone paid her to disappear," Walt suggested. "Cover-up payment."

"Either way," Dash said, "We need to find her."

"I'll check property records," Walt added. "See if she owned anything on the island, if she left any paper trail we can follow."

The conversation continued, plans forming and reforming like clouds before a storm. We divided tasks with the efficiency of people who'd learned to work together through our investigation of the Calvert case. Dottie would track down the medical center nurses from 1985. Hank would research the Flamingo Motel's employee records. Walt would handle the official documents and property records. Bea would hunt for Jane Sutherland through her network of journalism contacts.

And Dash and I would visit Michael Bailey at the funeral home.

By the time the Silver Sleuths dispersed, the sun had fully risen, painting Harbor Street in shades of gold and possibility. Genevieve had arrived and was handling the morning customers up front while I tidied the back room.

"Two o'clock," Dash said as he prepared to leave. "I'll pick you up here."

"A funeral home." I wiped down the table. "Very romantic."

His mouth quirked. "I live to impress."

He stepped closer, reaching past me for Pickering's journal. His arm brushed mine—deliberate, warm.

"Be careful," he said quietly.

"Always am."

He held my gaze a moment, then left.

I finished cleaning, humming an old folk song my grandmother used to sing while tending graves. Dark and minor key, about secrets that wouldn't stay buried.

"Oh, dig my grave both wide and deep, place a marble stone at my head and feet..."

Appropriate for where we were headed.

Somewhere on this island, someone had gotten away with murder.

And we were about to dig it all up.

CHAPTER
SIX

MONDAY'S LUNCH SERVICE AT THE PERFECT STEEP PROVED, as Monday lunch services always did, to be a trial of patience and precision. The tourists—a harried-looking couple with matching visors—were studying the chalkboard menu as though it contained secrets of the Illuminati, while the business crowd hurried in and out with the brisk efficiency of people who had Somewhere Important to Be. I served tea, plated sandwiches, and smiled at customers, all while my brain refused to cooperate with the task at hand. Instead, it insisted on circling endlessly around blond nurses in white uniforms, missing church funds, and reporters who'd fled the island—as though thinking about murder hard enough might somehow solve it.

Marcus Wheeler came in around noon, ordering his Darjeeling with one sugar, settling into his corner table with his newspaper. But instead of turning to the obituaries like normal, he just sat there staring at the folded newsprint like it contained the secrets of the universe.

When I brought his tea, he looked up at me with an expression I couldn't quite read. "I remembered something last night," he said quietly. "About Tommy. About someone he trusted."

I slid into the chair across from him, the lunch crowd humming around us but giving us privacy the way islanders did when conversations turned serious.

"There was a deputy who worked with Tommy back then," Marcus continued, his weathered fingers wrapping around the teacup like it could warm something deeper than just his hands. "Name was Frank Holloway. Good cop, honest, the kind who actually believed in serving and protecting. He and Tommy were partners for a few years."

"What happened to him?" I asked.

"He quit." Marcus took a slow sip of his tea. "About six months after the Pickering–Bailey murders. Just turned in his badge one day and left the island. Tommy said Frank couldn't stomach what Milton was doing anymore—the cover-ups, the looking the other way, the way evidence would disappear or witnesses would suddenly change their stories."

My pulse quickened. "Did Frank know something specific about the murders?"

"Tommy thought so. They'd talk sometimes, late at night when they were on patrol together. Frank would say things like 'this whole case stinks' or 'someone's pulling strings we can't see.' But he never said anything concrete, at least not that Tommy told me about." Marcus paused and rubbed at his temple. "After Frank left, Tommy tried to keep in touch with him. Called him a few times, but Frank wouldn't talk about it. Said he'd put Grimm Island behind him and wanted to keep it there."

"Do you know where he went?"

"Last I heard, he was living in Beaufort. Opened a hardware store. Got out of law enforcement completely." Marcus looked up at me, his eyes sharp despite his years. "If anyone knows what really happened with that investigation, it would be Frank Holloway. He was there, he saw things, and he got out because he wasn't willing to be part of whatever Milton was running."

"Would he talk to us?" I asked.

Marcus shrugged slowly. "That's the question, isn't it? Man doesn't quit his career and leave town because he wants to chat about old times. But Tommy always said Frank was a good man at heart.

Maybe if you approached him right, told him you were trying to give Ruby Bailey and that preacher justice after all these years…" He trailed off. "Maybe he'd finally tell what he knows."

He stood slowly, leaving exact change plus his usual generous tip. "Frank Holloway. Beaufort. That's all I can give you. What you do with it is up to you and your sheriff."

After he left, I stood holding his teacup, staring at the dregs as if they might reveal something useful. The old tradition of reading tea leaves had always seemed like wishful thinking to me, seeing patterns in random distribution. But maybe that's exactly what we were doing with this case—trying to find meaning in chaos, patterns in violence, sense in something that might just be senseless.

At 1:55, I checked with Carly to make sure she was good handling the shop alone for the afternoon. The lunch crowd had thinned to just a few tables—Mrs. Pinkerton with her needlepoint, a couple of tourists lingering over their tea, nothing Carly couldn't manage with her eyes closed.

"Take your time," she said, already wiping down the counter with practiced efficiency. "I've got this."

I grabbed my cardigan and found Chowder waiting by the back door with his leash in his mouth. He'd somehow sensed we were going somewhere and had positioned himself with the determination of a French bulldog who would not be left behind.

"You want to come investigate a murder?" I asked him, fastening his walking harness and straightening his bow tie.

He snorted his affirmative, his expression suggesting that obviously he should come—who else would provide the necessary gravitas?

Dash arrived at precisely two o'clock, and his face lit up when he saw Chowder ready to go. "There's my guy," he said, crouching down to Chowder's level. "Looking very dapper today. Is that a new bow tie? Very Sherlock Holmes. You here to help us solve a murder?"

Chowder's entire rear end wiggled with pleasure at being addressed properly.

"Of course he's coming," Dash said to me, standing back up. "Look at him. He's dressed for detective work."

"The tweed cap really completes the look," I agreed, adjusting said cap on Chowder's head.

"Elementary, my dear Chowder," Dash said seriously to the dog, and I caught the full smile that transformed his face.

We walked rather than drove—the funeral home was only four blocks away, and the afternoon had turned beautiful in the way May afternoons sometimes do in the low country, when the heat hasn't yet become oppressive and the humidity sits at that perfect threshold between comfortable and sweltering. The kind of weather that makes you forget July is coming, when breathing feels like work and the air conditioner becomes your best friend.

Harbor Street was busy with the lunch crowd dispersing and the afternoon shoppers arriving. We passed Beaumont's Bakery first, where the smell of fresh bread and butter made my stomach remind me I'd forgotten lunch. Through the French doors, I could see Clarence Beaumont arranging pastries in the display case with the precision of someone creating art rather than merely selling baked goods.

"You ever wonder why he charges so much for an éclair?" Dash asked.

"Because tourists will pay it," I said. "And because they're genuinely that good. I've tried to replicate his technique—it's the ratio of butter to flour in the pâte à choux. He won't tell anyone the exact measurement."

"Trade secrets?"

"Baking secrets," I corrected. "Which on Grimm Island are taken as seriously as state secrets."

Next came Nature's Remedy, where Eugene Bradshaw was arranging crystals in his window display with the concentration of someone defusing a bomb. Today's arrangement appeared to be organized by color—amethyst fading into rose quartz, which melted into citrine, creating a rainbow effect that was admittedly beautiful even if you didn't believe in crystal healing.

"You think crystals actually do anything?" Dash asked.

"I think Eugene's crystals work about as well as his attempt to heal that pothole on Harbor Street with sage smudging," I said. "The pothole's still there. It's just spiritually aligned now."

"He tried to heal a pothole?"

"With crystals and incense. The town council had to physically remove him so the road crew could actually fix it. He kept insisting the pavement needed to 'release its trauma' first." I shook my head. "Last month he told Bea Livingston that her aura was blocked and tried to sell her a crystal the size of a grapefruit for two hundred dollars. She told him the only thing blocking her aura was his prices."

Dash laughed—that real laugh that made his whole face change. "What happened?"

"She bought it anyway. Uses it as a doorstop."

Chowder stopped to investigate a lamppost outside The Copper Pot, where the lunch crowd was visible through the windows—well-dressed tourists and locals mixing in that careful way Grimm Islanders had perfected, separate but cordial. The restaurant's herb garden spilled over into the sidewalk, rosemary and thyme and basil creating a small oasis of green that smelled like Provence and summer dinners.

"This island," Dash said, watching the careful choreography of people maintaining their social boundaries. "It's like everyone knows exactly where they stand in relation to everyone else. There's a hierarchy nobody talks about but everyone follows."

"Old families, new money, locals, transplants, tourists," I ticked off. "Everyone has their place. It's very feudal, actually. The DuBoses and the Conroys and the Whitakers—they're practically royalty. Patrick's family on his mother's side, the DuBoses, are one of the founding families. Then there are middle-class families who've been here for generations but aren't quite old money. And then everyone else—people like me, whose parents moved here for work. My dad was military, so we moved around a lot before settling here when I was a teenager. I'll always be an outsider, even after marrying Patrick."

"Where do I fall?" he asked.

"Law enforcement occupies a strange middle ground," I said.

"Powerful but not necessarily respected unless you have a last name that predates the Civil War. You have authority, but you'll never be invited to certain dinner parties."

"That's pretty typical for cops," he said. "There's a reason they only hang out with each other. It can be a lonely job."

"Grimm Island specializes in certain kinds of loneliness," I said, then immediately wished I hadn't. It felt too revealing, like I'd exposed something raw.

But Dash just nodded, his hand brushing mine as we walked—brief, warm, possibly accidental. "It's always lonely at the top," he said quietly. "That's something they don't tell you when you're working your way up through the ranks. You think making detective will be different, then sergeant, then lieutenant. You keep thinking the next promotion will change things, that you'll finally be part of something." He paused, watching a tourist family cross the street. "But the higher you climb, the more isolated you become. Can't be friends with your subordinates—blurs the lines, compromises authority. Can't talk about cases with civilians. Can't let anyone see what the job does to you, because that's weakness, and weakness gets people killed."

His voice had gone flat, professional, but I heard something underneath it—years of holding things in, of carrying weight alone.

"So you learn to keep your private life private and your thoughts close to the vest," he continued. "You become really good at being alone. Sometimes too good at it." He glanced at me, something vulnerable flickering across his face before he shuttered it. "This island's not that different from anywhere else I've been. The names change, the scenery changes, but the loneliness is pretty much the same."

"Yeah," I said softly, understanding more than he'd probably meant to reveal. "It is."

We walked in silence for a moment, Chowder trotting between us, and I realized we'd just shared something—not just information, but the weight of carrying things alone. Of being isolated even in the middle of community.

Maybe that's what drew us together. Two people who'd learned to be self-sufficient, who'd built walls so high we'd forgotten what it felt like to let anyone in.

We turned onto Broad Street, where the houses got larger and the gardens more elaborate. Old Charleston singles and Greek revivals, their piazzas facing south to catch the breeze, their gardens bursting with camellias and perfume of summer roses.

The Whitmore house sprawled behind an elaborate wrought-iron fence, its garden a testament to what unlimited money and good gardeners could accomplish. The Rutledge place sat directly across, equally impressive, equally maintained—two old families staring at each other across the street for generations, probably knowing each other's secrets but keeping them out of some unspoken agreement.

"Patrick's funeral was the worst day of my life," I said suddenly, surprising myself. We'd been walking in comfortable silence, but the words came out anyway, pulled by the proximity to where we were going. "But Michael somehow made it feel less like an ending and more like...I don't know. Like Patrick was still part of things, just in a different way."

I hummed a few bars of "Someone to Watch Over Me" without quite meaning to, the melody slipping out the way it always did when I was nervous or processing something difficult.

"That's a gift," Dash said quietly. "Making people feel like death isn't the end of connection."

"A terrible gift to have," I agreed. "Having to be everyone's comfort when you're carrying your own grief. Can you imagine? Every funeral he conducts, he's probably thinking about his mother. About how he never got closure. About how the person who killed her just...walked away."

Grimm Island Funeral Home materialized at the corner of Broad and Meeting—a Victorian mansion painted in shades of gray that managed to be both elegant and slightly oppressive, like a beautiful woman in mourning clothes. The gardens were immaculate, azaleas and camellias arranged with the kind of precision that suggested someone spent serious time and money on keeping death beautiful.

Crepe myrtles lined the walkway, their bark smooth and pale as bone, their branches reaching up like supplicants.

A brass sign beside the door read *Grimm Island Funeral Home—Serving The Community Since 1952*. Below it, in smaller letters: *Michael P. Bailey, Director.*

Chowder paused at the gate, sniffing the air with intensity. His ears perked forward, and he looked up at me with those bulging eyes that somehow conveyed both alertness and judgment.

"You sense death?" I asked him. "Very atmospheric of you."

He snorted and proceeded forward, his bow tie bobbing with each step.

"Michael inherited this place from his grandparents," I said as we approached the door. "Ruby's parents. Must be strange, preparing bodies for burial when your own mother's murder was never solved. Seeing death professionally while carrying that personal loss."

The front door opened before we could knock, as if Michael Bailey had been watching for us. He was tall—nearly six feet—with the kind of thin frame that suggested he forgot to eat when he was focused on work. His dark hair was graying at the temples in that distinguished way that some men achieved and others just looked old attempting. He had his mother's striking green eyes—I'd seen photos of Ruby in the case file—and they held a sadness that comes from intimate acquaintance with grief, the professional sorrow of someone who guides others through loss while carrying his own.

It was like looking at a mirror—I recognized that expression because I'd worn it myself for years after Patrick died.

He wore a dark suit, impeccably tailored, with a burgundy tie that was the only splash of color in his otherwise monochromatic presentation. His hands were long-fingered and careful, the hands of someone who handles fragile things for a living—bodies, grief, the delicate art of making death presentable.

"Sheriff Beckett," he said, his voice measured and soft, the kind of voice that could comfort the bereaved without ever actually promising that anything would get better. It was a voice that had been trained to absorb pain without reflecting it back. "Mrs. McCoy." His gaze dropped to Chowder, and something in his expression softened. "And guest."

"I hope you don't mind," I said. "He's very well behaved."

"I like dogs," Michael said simply. "They understand grief better than most humans. They don't try to fix it or talk you out of it. They just...sit with you in it." He stepped back, gesturing us inside. "Please, come in."

The interior of Grimm Island Funeral Home smelled like furniture polish and lilies, with an underlying chemical scent that I recognized from Patrick's funeral—formaldehyde, disguised but never quite eliminated. No matter how much air freshener or how many flowers, that smell always lurked underneath, a reminder of what the business actually involved. The entry hall was all dark wood and thick carpeting that absorbed sound, making every footstep feel muffled and somehow guilty, like we were intruding on sacred space.

Chowder's nails clicked against the hardwood in the foyer before we moved onto carpet, each click echoing in the high-ceilinged space. Victorian furniture lined the walls—uncomfortable-looking chairs that probably cost a fortune, side tables with elaborate flower arrangements, paintings of peaceful landscapes that were meant to be soothing but somehow just emphasized the unnaturalness of the whole enterprise.

Michael led us past the viewing rooms—doors discreetly closed, but I knew what lay beyond them from my own experience. Rooms set up to look like living rooms, as if the dead person had just decided to take a nap in their best clothes. The elaborate fiction we constructed around death, pretending it was sleep or peace or any number of euphemisms that avoided the stark reality of cessation.

His office was at the back of the building, overlooking the gardens through tall windows that let in afternoon light. It was a room lined with leather-bound volumes about grief and loss, grief counseling, the psychology of mourning, books with titles like *Understanding Bereavement* and *The Art of Funeral Direction*. A massive mahogany desk dominated the space, probably weighing more than my car, its surface clear except for a single photograph and a leather desk pad.

Family photos covered one wall—black-and-white images of Baileys going back generations, all wearing the same expression of professional sympathy. It was like looking at a timeline of grief—Grandfather Bailey in his 1950s suit, Grandmother Bailey in her proper dress, Father Bailey (who I realized must have been Ruby's father), all of them with that same carefully neutral expression that said *I'm here for you* without promising anything more.

One photograph stood apart from the others—a color picture, slightly faded with that particular quality of 1980s photography, of a young woman with dark hair, laughing at something outside the frame. She wore a simple yellow dress, and she held a small boy's hand. Both of them looked radiantly, impossibly happy, caught in one of those perfect moments that you don't recognize as perfect until they're over.

"That's the only picture I have where she's truly smiling," Michael said, catching me looking. His voice had gone soft, almost reverent. "Most photos from back then, she looks tired. Worn down. Like the world was pressing on her and she was too polite to complain. This was taken at my eighth birthday party, two years before she died. She'd gotten a raise that week—Mrs. Watson had given her an extra fifty dollars for doing such good work—and Mama said we were going to celebrate properly. We went to the Dairy Queen in Charleston, got banana splits, stayed until they closed."

He gestured for us to sit in the chairs across from his desk—comfortable leather that had been broken in by generations of grieving families, the kind of chairs that absorbed tears and pain and all the complicated emotions that came with planning funerals. I sank into mine, feeling the weight of all that accumulated sorrow pressing down like humidity. Chowder settled at my feet with a dramatic sigh that suggested he found funeral homes exhausting, which was fair—I found them exhausting too.

Dash remained standing for a moment, studying the family photographs, his cop eyes cataloguing everything, looking for patterns and connections that might not be immediately obvious.

"You want to talk about my mother's murder," Michael said, not making it a question. He settled into his chair behind the desk with the heaviness of someone who'd been carrying weight for so long he'd forgotten what it felt like to be unburdened.

I must have looked shocked at his prescient statement because he said, "Sheriff Beckett called yesterday, said you were reviewing the case. I've been waiting a long time for someone to ask the right questions."

"What are the right questions?" Dash asked, sitting in the leather chair across from the desk.

Michael was quiet for a moment, his fingers drumming against his desk in an odd pattern. Maybe grief had its own language, its own Morse code that only the bereaved could interpret.

"Everyone always asked about Reverend Pickering," Michael said finally. "About their affair, about the scandal, about whether my mother loved him or was using him. No one ever asked the right questions." Michael's voice had gone soft, thoughtful, like someone sorting through memories that had been carefully packed away for decades. "Like who else knew about them. Who had the most to lose if it all came out."

The room went quiet except for the tick of the antique clock on Michael's desk—a steady, patient sound that marked the seconds like a metronome counting down the decades. Outside, a mockingbird called from the azaleas, its song bright and careless, utterly unaware of the weight of what was being discussed in this room where so many people had come to say their final goodbyes.

Chowder, who'd been dozing at my feet, lifted his head and made a small sound—not quite a whine, more like a question. He could always sense when something important was happening, when the air in a room changed texture.

Michael stood and moved to the window, his movements slow and deliberate, like someone walking through water. He looked out at his carefully maintained gardens where azaleas bloomed in shades of pink and white—colors chosen for their ability to soothe, to comfort, to make death seem like just another gentle transition. Everything was ordered and beautiful out there, precisely because dead things were kept carefully hidden underground, their decay transformed into nourishment for living beauty. There was a metaphor in that, I thought. A lesson about how we bury our secrets and pray they'll feed something better than what they were.

When Michael spoke again, his voice had shed years, decades falling away until I could hear the ghost of the ten-year-old boy who'd lost everything. "Mama was scared those last few weeks. Not the kind of scared you get from a spider or a scary movie. The real kind. The kind that makes your hands shake when you think no one's looking." He pressed his palm against the window glass, and I watched his breath fog the pane. "She kept talking about leaving the island, about starting over somewhere else. She'd been looking at apartments in Charleston, even took me to see one on a Sunday afternoon. It was small—just two bedrooms in a building that smelled like someone else's cooking—but Mama talked about it like it was a palace. Said we'd be safer there."

"Safer from what?" Dash asked, his voice gentle but insistent, the way you'd coax a frightened animal out of hiding.

"She never said. Not exactly." Michael turned back to face us, and the afternoon light caught him in profile, highlighting the lines around his eyes, the gray at his temples, the weight of the past carried in the set of his shoulders. He had his mother's bone structure—I could see it in the crime-scene photos I'd memorized, in the shape of his jaw, the angle of his cheekbones. Ruby Bailey looking out at me through her son's face, still asking to be heard after all this time. "But I knew she meant safer from someone here. Someone on Grimm Island."

The funeral home seemed to press closer around us, all that carefully maintained peace suddenly feeling oppressive, like the calm before a storm when the air gets so heavy you can taste electricity on your tongue.

"Did she mention anyone specifically?" Dash asked. He was listening with his whole body, the way good investigators do, absorbing not just words but tone, body language, the spaces between what was said.

"Elder Matthias Crenshaw." The name fell into the room like a stone into still water, sending ripples through the quiet. Michael's hands gripped the back of his chair hard enough that his knuckles went white, tendons standing out like cables under skin. "He was on the church board—one of the senior elders. Handled a lot of the church business, made decisions about money and property and who got to do what. Very powerful man, the kind who thought his position in the church gave him authority over everyone's lives."

I'd heard that name before, somewhere in the background noise of Grimm Island life. Crenshaw. One of those old families that had roots going back to before the Civil War, the kind of people who considered themselves the island's guardians, its moral arbiters.

"What happened with Elder Crenshaw?" I asked softly.

Michael moved back to his desk. "Mama said he'd caught her and Reverend Pickering together one evening at the church. They weren't doing anything wrong—not then, anyway. Just talking in Reverend Pickering's office after choir practice. But Elder Crenshaw knew. He made it very clear he knew what was going on between them."

The office felt smaller suddenly, the walls closer, as if the past was pressing in on the present, demanding space. The lilies on Michael's desk seemed too fragrant, their scent cloying, making it hard to breathe properly.

"What did he say to them?" Dash's voice had gone very quiet, very still, the way water looks before it freezes.

"I don't know exactly. I wasn't supposed to know about any of it." Michael's hands gripped the back of his chair. "I was ten. Mama never talked to me about Reverend Pickering, never explained what was going on. I just knew he came to the house sometimes. He'd bring her flowers or money because we didn't have much, and sometimes they'd talk on the back porch while I did homework. I thought they were friends."

He moved back to his desk, that careful funeral director's walk that suggested he'd learned long ago how to move through rooms without disturbing the grief that lived in them.

"Then one day I left school early—told the teacher I was sick so I could skip the afternoon. It was spring, nice weather, and I wanted to go to the beach with some friends." A ghost of a smile crossed his face. "Mama was at work cleaning houses, wasn't supposed to be home until after 5. So I figured I could get away with it, be back before she knew I'd skipped."

He paused, and the smile disappeared.

"Our house was small—just a few rooms in the part of town people didn't talk about much. You know the area, down past the fish processing plant where the paint peels off the houses and the yards are more weeds than grass. The kind of neighborhood where people minded their own business because everyone had something they didn't want looked at too closely." He paused. "You could hear everything through those thin walls. When I came in the back door, I heard voices coming from Mama's bedroom. The door was open just a crack. I saw them." His voice had gone flat, emotionless, the way people sound when they're describing something they've spent years trying not to think about. "I was ten years old and I saw more than a ten-year-old should see, and I knew—even then, even without understanding what I was looking at—I knew it was wrong."

The office felt too quiet, too still, like the air had stopped moving.

"I left," Michael continued. "Went outside, sat on the back steps for maybe twenty minutes until I heard Reverend Pickering's car leave. Then I came back in and Mama was in the kitchen making dinner like nothing had happened. She smiled at me, asked how my day had gone. And I never said a word about it. Not to her, not to anyone."

I could see it so clearly—a little boy carrying that knowledge like a stone in his pocket, too heavy to hold but impossible to put down.

"After that, I paid more attention. Noticed things. The way people at church would whisper when Mama walked by. The way other mothers would pull their kids away from me at Sunday school, like whatever sin Mama was committing might be contagious. The way Mama would get dressed up on certain evenings, put on perfume, tell me she had to run errands even though the stores were closed."

"She wasn't hiding it," I said softly, understanding. This was the Ruby Bailey from the case file—the one who sang in the choir every

Sunday with Pickering watching her, who didn't care what people thought, who wore the affair like armor.

"No," Michael agreed. "She wasn't. I think that's what made Elder Crenshaw so angry. A few weeks before she died, I woke up one night and heard her on the phone. She was in the kitchen talking to someone, and her voice was different. Not scared exactly. More like…defiant. Angry."

"What did she say?" Dash asked.

"She said something like, 'You can threaten me all you want, but I'm not going anywhere. George and I have every right to be together.'" Michael's eyes were distant. "And then she got quiet, listening. Then she said, 'You think I care what the congregation thinks? They're a bunch of hypocrites anyway. At least I'm honest about what I'm doing.'"

That sounded more like the Ruby Bailey I'd been piecing together —bold, unashamed, almost reckless in her refusal to hide.

"Did she say who she was talking to?" I asked.

"I assumed it was Elder Crenshaw, based on what happened next. A few days later, I was playing in the yard after school when I saw him pull up. He didn't come to the door—just sat in his car at the curb. Mama went out to talk to him. I couldn't hear what they said, but I could see Mama's body language. She had her arms crossed, chin up, that look she got when she was being stubborn."

Michael stared at the photograph of his mother. "Elder Crenshaw was pointing his finger at her, jabbing it toward her face. She didn't back down. Just stood there taking it. Then he drove off and Mama came back inside. She saw me watching and told me to stay away from Elder Crenshaw, that he was a mean old man who liked to stick his nose where it didn't belong."

"And then?" Dash prompted.

"About a week later, I heard her on the phone with Reverend Pickering. It was late, maybe ten o'clock. I'd gotten up to get water." Michael's voice went quieter. "She was pacing in the kitchen, and I heard her say 'I know where you're getting the money, George. Don't think I haven't figured it out.' She was quiet for a minute, then she said, 'We need to talk about this in person. Not here. Not at the church. Somewhere private.'"

The funeral home's air-conditioning hummed steadily, a counterpoint to the silence.

"That was the last time I heard her voice," Michael said. "She left Friday evening, told me to heat up the casserole in the fridge for dinner, that she'd be home late. She kissed the top of my head and walked out the door." His hands were shaking now. "The next morning, the police came to tell me she was dead."

The mockingbird called again outside, its song unchanged, cheerful, oblivious. Life going on while we sat here excavating death.

"Is Elder Crenshaw still alive?" Dash asked, making a note.

"I think so," Michael said. "He'd be in his eighties now. Last I heard, he moved to one of those retirement communities on the mainland after his wife died. Sea Pines or Oak Grove or one of those places with *pleasant* in the name that's supposed to make you forget you're waiting to die."

Beside me, Chowder shifted, his bow tie slightly askew, his expression thoughtful in that way French bulldogs sometimes get when they're processing something important. Or possibly gas. With Chowder, it was hard to tell.

"Did your mother ever mention anyone else who worried her?" Dash pressed gently, still watching Michael with that focused attention that missed nothing.

"Not that I can think of," he said.

"Did you tell the police any of this?" I asked, though I already knew the answer. I could see it in the guilt that lived in his eyes.

"I was ten years old," Michael said. "The detectives who interviewed me were scary—these big men in uniforms with guns on their hips and voices that sounded like they were used to people doing what they said. They kept asking if Mama had been happy, if she'd been sad, if there had been arguments at home. They'd already decided what they thought happened—scandalous affair, crime of passion, maybe my dad did it, maybe it was a mugging gone wrong."

He stood abruptly, pacing to the window again like he couldn't bear to sit still under the weight of memory. "I tried to tell them about Elder Crenshaw, about the phone call I'd heard, but they weren't really listening. They were just checking boxes, going through motions, waiting to move on to whatever case was next."

"And Sheriff Milton?" Dash asked, and something in his voice had gone hard, cold, like steel left out in winter.

"He came to see me about a month after Mama died. I was living with my grandparents by then, trying to figure out how to be a kid again when I felt like I'd aged a hundred years."

Michael turned from the window, and his eyes held memories ancient and painful. "Milton came to my grandparents' house about a month after Mama died. Sat in their living room with his hat in his lap, same patient expression, same concerned voice asking the same questions everyone had already asked. And when I tried to tell him about Elder Crenshaw confronting Mama, about the phone call where she said she knew where Reverend Pickering was getting money, he patted my head like I was a dog who'd done a trick."

The bitterness in his voice was sharp enough to cut.

"He said I was confused. That grief was making me remember things wrong, mixing up what really happened with what I'd seen on TV or heard adults talking about. He said the investigation was over, that they knew what had happened, and I needed to stop telling stories or I'd make things harder for everyone. He said the best thing I could do for my mama's memory was to let her rest in peace and move on with my life.

"I became a funeral director because of her," Michael said quietly, staring at the photograph of Ruby in her yellow dress, young and happy and impossibly alive. "Because I wanted to give other families the closure I never got. I wanted to help people say goodbye properly, with dignity, with certainty. Every body I prepare, every service I conduct, every family I guide through their grief—it's my way of making up for not being able to help my mother when she needed it. For being too young, too small, too powerless to save her."

Tears had started tracking down his face, cutting paths through his carefully maintained composure. He made no move to wipe them away, and I realized this might be the first time he'd cried about this in decades. Some grief gets buried so deep it fossilizes, becomes part of your bones.

I felt my own throat tighten with emotion. How many times had I conducted this same internal autopsy of my own grief? How many times had I cataloged all the things I should have done differently before Patrick died, all the signs I'd missed, all the moments I'd let slip away because I'd thought we had infinite time? The what-ifs that haunted you in the small hours of the morning, the guilt that wrapped around your ribs like barbed wire, making it hard to breathe, hard to move, hard to live.

"You were a child," I said firmly, leaning forward in my chair, making sure he heard me, really heard me. "Traumatized and alone. The failure wasn't yours—it belonged to every adult who should have asked better questions, who should have listened more carefully, who should have protected you instead of telling you to forget. It belonged to Roy Milton, who dismissed what you said because it was inconvenient for whatever narrative he was constructing. It belonged to every person who knew something was wrong with that investigation and stayed silent anyway."

Michael looked at me with gratitude in his red-rimmed eyes.

Chowder, who'd been remarkably patient through all of this, waddled over to Michael's desk and looked up at him with those bulging, impossibly earnest eyes. There was something about a French bulldog's gaze that could convey profound sympathy while simultaneously suggesting that what you really needed was a snack and a nap. It was a gift.

Michael actually smiled—just a small one, but real. "Nice dog," he said.

"He's exceptional," I agreed.

Dash was quiet for a moment, letting the weight of everything Michael had shared settle between us. Then he leaned forward slightly. "Thank you, Michael. This has been incredibly helpful. We'll look into Elder Crenshaw, see if we can track him down for an interview."

"There's one more thing," Michael said, and his voice had changed, become steadier, like he'd made a decision. "After Mama died, my grandparents gave me a box of her things. Nothing valuable—just photos and letters, a few pieces of jewelry, her Bible. I've kept it all these years, couldn't bring myself to go through it. It's still in my attic, sealed up just like they gave it to me." He pulled a card from his desk drawer, wrote something on the back in careful script. "My home address. If you want to come by sometime, look through it, you're welcome to. Maybe there's something in there that could help. Maybe she left some clue I was too young to understand."

Dash took the card carefully, like it was precious. "We'll be in touch."

Michael stood, and we did too, Chowder rousing himself from his dignified repose at my feet. At the door, Michael paused, looking back at the photograph of Ruby.

"My mother was a complicated woman. And she didn't always do the right thing. But she was my mother. And she deserves justice," he said quietly. "Even now. Especially now."

"We'll do everything we can," I promised.

The afternoon sunlight hit us as we stepped outside, bright and warm and somehow heavier than before. The funeral home's door closed behind us with a soft click that felt final.

Chowder's tweed cap had gone askew, his bow tie crooked from an hour of sitting still. He looked up at me with an expression that clearly said his work here was done, and he'd like his compensation in the form of treats.

Dash and I stood on the front steps for a moment, neither of us speaking, both of us processing what we'd just heard. A ten-year-old boy who'd carried guilt that wasn't his. A mother who'd tried to protect her son and paid for it with her life. A box of belongings that had waited decades to tell their story.

But secrets didn't stay buried forever. Ruby Bailey had known that. And George Pickering had learned it too late.

The walk back to The Perfect Steep felt longer than four blocks, as if the weight of what Michael Bailey had shared had somehow altered the geography of Grimm Island, stretching the familiar streets into something foreign and heavy. The afternoon sun painted everything in shades of gold and amber, but the beauty felt wrong somehow—too bright, too cheerful, like wearing a ball gown to a funeral.

Chowder trotted between us with the satisfied air of a dog who'd conducted important business and deserved recognition for his contributions to justice. His tweed cap sat at a jaunty angle, and every few steps he'd look up at me with those bulging eyes that somehow conveyed both wisdom and the desperate need for a snack.

"Elder Matthias Crenshaw," Dash said finally, breaking the silence that had wrapped around us like Spanish moss. "That's our first real lead. Someone who confronted Ruby directly, who had power in the church, who could have been involved in whatever financial impropriety Pickering was hiding."

I hummed a few bars of "All of Me." The Ella Fitzgerald version, not the Billie Holiday one, because somehow Ella's voice felt more appropriate for this particular moment.

"You do that when you're worried," Dash observed, glancing at me with that half smile that made my stomach perform complicated gymnastics.

"Do what?"

"Hum. Sing. Whatever that was. I've noticed you have a whole catalog of songs for different emotions. Happy Mabel sings Frank Sinatra. Nervous Mabel goes for blues standards and Ella. Contemplative Mabel brings out Billie Holiday and Jo Stafford.

"I wasn't aware I was such an open book," I said, though I wasn't actually annoyed. There was something intimate about being noticed that way, about someone paying attention to the small details of your existence.

"Occupational hazard," he said, but his tone was gentle. "Cops notice patterns. And you, Mabel McCoy, are a walking anthology of the American songbook."

We passed Beaumont's Bakery again, where the afternoon crowd was thinning and Clarence was already starting his end-of-day cleanup. Through the windows, I could see him wiping down the display cases with methodical precision. There was comfort in that kind of repetition, in knowing exactly what came next.

"My grandmother taught me to sing," I said, surprising myself with the confession. "She said music was how you made sense of things that didn't make sense any other way. When words weren't enough, you could always find a song that said it better."

"Sounds like a wise woman."

"She was. She died when I was sixteen, right after we moved to the island. Heart attack while she was hanging laundry." I could still see it—the white sheets billowing in the breeze, her body crumpled beneath them like she'd just decided to take a nap in the grass. "She'd been singing—I heard her from my bedroom window. The wind had carried her voice—*It is well, it is well with my soul*—then silence. Just…silence. Like someone had turned off the music of the world."

Dash's hand found mine, his fingers tangling with my own in a gesture that felt both natural and revolutionary. We'd held hands before—brief touches, those maddening almost-kisses—but this felt different. More deliberate. More like a decision than an accident.

"After Patrick died," I continued, not quite sure why I was telling him this except that Michael Bailey's grief had cracked something open in me, some sealed compartment where I'd been storing my own losses, "I couldn't sing for almost a year. Not even humming. It was like the music had died with him, like whatever part of me that could make sound had just…stopped working."

"What brought it back?"

"Chowder, actually." I looked down at my French bulldog, who had paused to investigate a promising scent near the curb. "I got him about eight months after Patrick died. Deidre insisted I needed company, said I was spending too much time alone in that big house talking to the ghost of my dead husband. Which was true, but I didn't appreciate her saying it out loud."

Dash laughed, that real laugh that transformed his whole face.

"Anyway, Chowder was this ridiculous puppy—all wrinkles and snorts and stubborn determination. And one morning I woke up and he was staring at me with those eyes, waiting for breakfast, and I just started singing without thinking about it. Some silly thing about how much is that doggie in the window. And suddenly I could breathe again."

We'd reached The Perfect Steep, the pale blue paint glowing in the afternoon light. Through the windows, I could see Genevieve handling the last of the afternoon customers with her usual efficient grace.

"The Silver Sleuths are reconvening at 6 at my place to share what they've found. Should be interesting, if nothing else. Want to join us?"

"Wouldn't miss it," Dash said. "Besides, someone needs to make sure Walt doesn't try to organize a military assault on a retirement home."

"That's a very real possibility," I agreed.

Inside, The Perfect Steep smelled like home—lemon and lavender and the ghost of this morning's scones. Genevieve looked up from where she was wiping down tables, her expression relieved.

"Thank goodness you're back," she said. "Mrs. Pembroke has

called three times asking if you're planning to attend the garden club meeting on Wednesday. I told her I didn't have access to your social calendar, but she seems to think I'm lying to protect you from her."

"That's because you are lying to protect me from her," I said. "And I appreciate it more than you know. Garden club meetings are four hours of passive-aggressive arguments about hydrangeas disguised as civic duty."

"Should I tell her you'll be there?"

"Tell her I have a prior commitment. Investigating a murder is a prior commitment, right?"

"I feel like that should definitely count," Genevieve agreed. "Also, Dottie called. Said to tell you she has news and you're going to want to hear it before tonight's meeting."

I glanced at the clock—4:47. I had just over an hour before the Silver Sleuths descended on my house en masse. Time enough to change out of my funeral-visiting dress and into something more appropriate for detective work. Maybe brew a fresh batch of tea. Definitely feed Chowder before he staged a hunger strike.

"I'm going to head home and change," I told Dash. "Get some snacks and drinks ready. Detective work makes you hungry."

"I need to check in at the station," he said. "Make sure nothing's burned down in my absence. Though on Grimm Island, that's a legitimate concern. I'll see you at six."

At the door, Dash caught my hand, his thumb tracing circles on my palm—a gesture that had become familiar over the past weeks.

"Michael's story got to you," he observed quietly.

"Ten-year-old boy watching his mother prepare for a date that would end with her murder," I said. "Of course it got to me."

He stepped closer, his free hand coming up to tuck a strand of hair behind my ear. The tenderness of the gesture made my throat tight.

He kissed me then—warm and slow, the kind of kiss that felt like coming home. When he pulled back, he rested his forehead against mine for a moment.

"See you tonight."

After he left, I stood at the door for a long moment, my fingers touching my lips. Chowder appeared at my feet with a judgmental snort.

"Don't look at me like that," I told him. "Maybe you need to meet a nice lady and mind your business."

———

My house welcomed me back with the silence of a place that knew it was empty too often. The afternoon light streamed through the windows, painting everything in shades of gold, catching on the crystal doorknobs Patrick had installed, the vintage tea canisters I collected, the framed photographs of a life that felt both intimately familiar and increasingly distant.

I fed Chowder first—his dinner of chicken and rice from the fancy pet store on King Street. He attacked it with the enthusiasm of someone who hadn't eaten in weeks rather than hours.

Then I stood in front of my closet contemplating what one wore to a murder investigation strategy session. After considerable deliberation, I selected a 1940s blouse in cream silk with mother-of-pearl buttons, paired with high-waisted navy trousers that made me feel like Katharine Hepburn in *The Philadelphia Story*. Confident. Capable. Ready to ask hard questions and demand real answers.

I was pinning back my hair with a vintage comb when my phone rang. Dottie's name flashed on the screen.

"I found her," she said without preamble. "The blond nurse. Well, I found three possibles, but one of them is very interesting."

"Tell me," I said, putting her on speaker while I finished with my hair.

"Stephanie Michelle Chester, twenty-six years old in 1985, worked at Charleston Medical Center as an OR nurse. Blond, five foot seven, athletic build. Here's where it gets interesting—she married Matthias Crenshaw Jr. in 1987, two years after the murders."

The hair comb slipped from my fingers, clattering against the vanity.

"Elder Crenshaw's son?"

"The very same," Dottie confirmed, and I could hear the satisfaction in her voice. "She's Stephanie Donaldson now. She divorced Crenshaw about seven years into the marriage. But she lives right here on Grimm Island and has for thirty-eight years. You've probably seen her around town."

My mind was racing, connecting dots that suddenly felt blindingly obvious. "Elder Crenshaw confronts Ruby Bailey. His son's girlfriend—or future wife—is a blond nurse. Elsie Crawford sees a blond woman in a nurse's uniform at Turtle Point the night of the murders."

"It's circumstantial," Dottie cautioned. "But it's a heck of a coincidence."

"We need to talk to her and see if we can pin her down," I said.

"She works at the medical center three days a week. Pediatrics now, not OR. Married to a surgeon. Pillar of the community type."

"Can you get me her address?"

"Already have it," Dottie said. "I'll bring everything to the meeting tonight. Along with information on the other two possibles, though neither of them has the same interesting family connections."

After we hung up, I sat at my vanity staring at my reflection. The former Stephanie Crenshaw. I checked the time. The Silver Sleuths would be arriving in forty-five minutes, and I still needed to prepare refreshments and give Chowder his evening constitutional.

"Come on, boy," I called, reaching for his leash. "Let's get some air before the chaos descends."

Chowder waddled over with the enthusiasm of a dog who knew that evening walks sometimes involved interesting smells and the possibility of running into Mr. Henderson's cat. I clipped on his leash and grabbed my cardigan from the hook by the door.

My house sat on the harbor side of Harbor Street, the kind of prime real estate that came with both prestige and property taxes that made my accountant wince. But the view was worth every penny—straight across the street, beyond the seawall, the harbor stretched out in all its moody glory, painted now in shades of peach and lavender as the sun began its descent.

We crossed Harbor Street carefully—Chowder had strong opinions about cars that didn't properly respect his right of way—and made our way to the public seawall that ran along the water's edge. The walkway was wide enough for joggers, dog walkers, and tourists taking sunset photos, all of them navigating around each other with the practiced choreography of people who'd learned to share limited space.

Chowder sniffed every section of the seawall with the intensity of a detective gathering evidence. The evening air smelled of salt and mud and the faint sweetness of honeysuckle from someone's garden. The tide was coming in, the water lapping gently against the stones with a sound like whispered secrets.

"Mabel! Yoo-hoo!"

I turned to see Eleanor Grantham waving from her back porch next door, her silver hair perfectly coiffed despite the hour. She wore a silk caftan in shades of coral, and she clutched a martini glass like it was a religious artifact.

"Evening, Eleanor," I called back, trying not to sound as reluctant as I felt. Eleanor was harmless but relentlessly curious, the kind of neighbor who noticed everything and forgot nothing.

"I saw the sheriff's vehicle at your house last night," she said, not even pretending she hadn't been watching. "And then again last week. Twice, if memory serves. Which it always does." She took a delicate sip of her martini. "Things progressing nicely in that department?"

Heat crept up my neck. "We're working on a case together."

"Mmm-hmm." Eleanor's smile suggested she wasn't buying what I was selling. "That's what they're calling it these days, is it? Working on a case?" She leaned against her porch railing, settling in for what she clearly hoped would be a lengthy gossip session. "You know, Audrey Morrison saw you two at church together yesterday. Said the way he looked at you during the sermon was positively smoldering."

"Audrey Morrison needs stronger glasses," I said, though my traitorous heart did a little flip at the thought of Dash looking at me during church.

"And my bridge club met yesterday afternoon—you know we play at Vivian's house every other Sunday—and Vivian mentioned she'd seen his car parked outside your place past midnight on Friday. Of course, we all agreed it was perfectly innocent. Police business and all that. Though Constance did point out that police business at midnight usually involves criminals, not widows in their nightgowns."

"I was not in my nightgown," I said, which was technically true—I'd been in my vintage silk robe, which was entirely different and somehow worse.

"Oh, honey." Eleanor's expression softened with something that might have been genuine affection. "I'm just giving you grief because you're easy. Patrick's been gone a long time. If the sheriff makes you smile—and don't think I haven't noticed you've been smiling more lately—then good. You deserve some happiness. Lord knows this island could use some romance that doesn't end in somebody's prenup being violated."

Chowder, having finished his inspection of a palm tree, tugged on his leash with the insistence of a dog who had more important things to investigate. I took the excuse gratefully.

"I really should get back," I said. "I have guests coming."

"More police business?" Eleanor called after me, her tone suggesting she knew exactly what kind of business it was.

"Something like that," I replied, already heading back toward the house.

Inside, I unclipped Chowder's leash and went straight to the kitchen. The Silver Sleuths would expect refreshments—not a full meal, but something substantial enough to keep them fueled through what would likely be hours of discussion and debate.

I pulled out my serving platters—vintage Haviland china that had been Patrick's grandmother's, delicate pink roses on cream porcelain. From the refrigerator I retrieved the cheese board I'd prepared that morning—aged cheddar, creamy brie, gouda with herbs, arranged with water crackers and grapes. I added a selection of tea sandwiches I'd brought home from the shop—cucumber and cream cheese, chicken salad, tomato and basil.

For drinks, I set out my beverage station on the sideboard in the dining room. Sweet tea in a crystal pitcher, ice water with lemon slices, and—because I knew Bea would want it—all the fixings for sidecars. I arranged glasses in neat rows, added small plates and linen napkins, and stepped back to survey my work.

The dining room looked ready for company, though the murder board on the wall and the evidence spread across the table gave it a decidedly unconventional atmosphere. It wasn't every day you hosted a gathering where the centerpiece was a double homicide.

By six o'clock, the Silver Sleuths had taken over my house with their usual efficiency. Walt had claimed the head of the table, his laptop open and timeline materials spread in precise rows. Dottie's bourbon oatmeal cookies sat in the center—still warm, their scent competing with the smell of cognac as Bea mixed sidecars at my sideboard, her turquoise caftan catching the evening light. Hank and Dottie had arrived together (again), and Hank was already flipping through his leather notebook with the satisfaction of someone who had information to share.

"I have news about the Flamingo Motel," Hank announced, settling deeper into his chair. "Tracked down Betty Mae Hutchins—she worked the front desk for more than thirty years. Still lives in Charleston, works at a hotel near the Battery. I called her this afternoon."

"You didn't," Dottie breathed.

"I absolutely did. Told her I was writing a book about the history of Grimm Island and wanted to interview people who remembered significant events. She was very chatty once I got her talking."

"And?" Walt demanded.

"She remembers Ruby Bailey and Reverend Pickering. Said they had a standing reservation every Tuesday and Thursday afternoon, 2 to 5 p.m., paid cash, never caused problems. But here's the interesting part—about a month before the murders, someone else started asking questions about them."

The room went silent except for the hum of the refrigerator in the kitchen.

"Who?" I asked.

"Betty Mae didn't know her name, but the description matches

Jane Sutherland. Blond, dressed in a white suit, professional manner. Claimed she was with the insurance company, asked to see the registration records for room twelve."

"Insurance company," Walt repeated flatly. "That's a lie if I've ever heard one."

"Betty Mae thought so too," Hank continued. "Said she wouldn't have given her the information, but the woman offered her two hundred dollars cash. Which in 1985 was serious money."

"So Jane Sutherland was tracking Ruby and Pickering's affair," Dash said. He'd arrived during Hank's story, leaning against the doorframe with his arms crossed, every inch the cop processing information. "She knew about the Flamingo Motel, knew their schedule. She was building a case."

"But for what story?" I asked. "A small-town affair isn't exactly Pulitzer material."

"Unless the affair was connected to something bigger," Deidre suggested. She'd spread out her research materials on the table—photocopies of newspaper articles, property records, society page clippings from the *Grimm Island Gazette*. "I found something interesting in the church financial records. They weren't easy to get—churches don't have to file with the IRS like regular nonprofits—but many churches publish annual reports for their congregations. I managed to track down copies from the church archives and the historical society."

She pulled out a spreadsheet that looked like it had been copied from microfiche. "First Methodist's building fund in 1985 showed donations of nearly two hundred thousand dollars—significant money for a church of that size. But here's what's strange. The new community center they were supposedly building? Never got built. The project was canceled in late 1985, right after the murders, citing unforeseen complications."

"Where did the money go?" Dash asked, moving closer to examine the documents.

"That," Deidre said with the satisfaction of a librarian who'd found the missing book, "Is the two-hundred-thousand-dollar question. The financial records after 1985 show the money being reallocated to various church expenses. But it's vague. No specific line items, no clear accounting."

"Elder Crenshaw was on the finance committee," Walt said, checking his notes. "He would have had access to all the accounts, all the records."

"And George Pickering as head pastor would have been the one signing checks," Dottie added.

"So maybe that's what Ruby Bailey figured out," I said slowly, the pieces arranging themselves in my mind like a jigsaw puzzle. "That Pickering was involved in embezzling church funds. Maybe with Elder Crenshaw. She was cleaning houses for all these wealthy families, probably heard things, saw things. Maybe that's what she meant on the phone when she told Pickering she knew where he was getting the money."

"And if she knew," Dash continued, "She was a liability. Someone who could expose the whole scheme."

"Same with Pickering," Hank said. "If he was planning to run away with Ruby like Michael suggested, that meant leaving the church. Leaving behind the money. Or maybe he was planning to take it with him. Either way, someone couldn't allow that."

Bea had been uncharacteristically quiet, but now she set down her highball glass with a soft click. "I found Jane Sutherland," she said. "Took some digging, but I have contacts everywhere in this business. She left journalism completely after she left the island. Married a lawyer, moved to Atlanta, became a stay-at-home mother. Very suburban, very conventional. Nothing like the ambitious reporter I remember."

"Did you talk to her?" I asked.

"Briefly. She didn't want to discuss Grimm Island or anything about her time here. But she wasn't hostile exactly. More like…scared. She said some stories aren't worth telling if the cost is too high. When I pressed her about the Pickering–Bailey case, she hung up."

"So whatever she uncovered scared her enough to leave her entire career," Walt said grimly.

"Or someone paid her to disappear," Dash suggested. "Gave her enough money to start over somewhere else, on the condition that she never published what she'd found."

Dottie cleared her throat, commanding attention with authority. "I have the file on our blond nurse." She pulled out a folder thick with documents, the kind of satisfying weight that suggested hours of meticulous research, and spread photographs across the table with the reverence of someone laying out tarot cards that might divine our future.

A young woman with blond hair and a professional smile looked out at us from 1985, frozen in her hospital ID. She was pretty in that wholesome way—the kind of woman you'd trust with your children, with your secrets, with your life. The kind of pretty that opened doors and disarmed suspicions.

"Stephanie Chester in 1985," Dottie said, her crimson nail tapping the photograph with decisive precision. "Now Stephanie Donaldson. And as I told Mabel earlier, she was married to Matthias Crenshaw Jr. for a short time. Two years after the murders—just long enough for the scandal to fade but not long enough for the connection to be coincidence."

"Elder Crenshaw's son," Dash said, leaning forward to study the photograph.

"The very same," Dottie confirmed. "Worked in the OR at Charleston Medical back then, had access to uniforms from every department. Could walk into any wing of that hospital and nobody would question her presence."

"I called Sea Pines Retirement Community," Walt said, pulling out his notes with military precision. "Elder Matthias Crenshaw is a resident there. Eighty-six years old, lives in the assisted-living wing. The woman I spoke with said he's mentally sharp most days, though he has some mobility issues. She also said he doesn't get many visitors."

"We need to talk to him," Dash said. "Tomorrow if possible."

"And Stephanie Donaldson," I added. "We need to know where she was the night of the murders."

"Don't forget Elsie Crawford," Deidre said. "Did anyone follow up on getting her address at Magnolia Gardens?"

"I did," I said. "Reverend Sutton gave it to me. She's in the memory-care unit, but he said she has good days and bad days. On her good days, she remembers that night clearly."

The table had transformed into a war room—documents and photographs spread across every surface. Walt's timeline stretched across one wall, each entry color-coded by importance and reliability. Red for confirmed facts. Yellow for likely but unverified. Green for speculation.

In the center of it all—two photographs. Ruby Bailey, laughter in her eyes. And George Pickering in his clerical collar, looking stern and righteous and utterly unaware that someone would put a bullet in his head on a September night in 1985.

"So here's what we have," Dash said, standing to survey the organized chaos. "Elder Crenshaw confronted Ruby Bailey about the affair. His son's girlfriend—Stephanie Chester—was a blond nurse who later became his wife. Jane Sutherland was investigating the church's finances and tracking Ruby's and Pickering's movements. Michael Bailey heard his mother say she knew where Pickering was getting money. Two hundred thousand dollars disappeared from the church building fund around the time of the murders. And Roy Milton buried every piece of evidence that might have led somewhere uncomfortable."

"Don't forget Frank Holloway," I said. "The deputy who quit six months after the murders because he couldn't stomach what Milton was doing."

"He's in Beaufort," Walt said. "Owns a hardware store on Bay Street. I found the address this afternoon. Holloway's Hardware—been there since 1986."

"So our priorities," Dash said, moving into command mode, "Are Elder Crenshaw, Stephanie Donaldson, Elsie Crawford, and Frank Holloway. Four interviews that could break this case open or send us in entirely new directions."

"I'll go with you to talk to Elder Crenshaw," I said to Dash. "And Stephanie—we should approach her carefully. She's a respected member of the community now. Married to a surgeon, works in pediatrics. We can't just accuse her of murder without proof."

"Proof," Bea said darkly. "That's what Jane Sutherland was looking for. And look what happened to her. She ran away and never looked back."

"Maybe Jane Sutherland was smarter than we're giving her credit for," Dottie said. "Maybe she realized that some secrets on Grimm Island have teeth and claws, and the smart money was on getting out while she could."

The weight of that settled over us like a blanket. Decades might have passed, but whoever had killed Ruby Bailey and George Pickering might still be walking these streets. Might still have power, connections, the ability to make things—or people—disappear.

"We need to be careful," Dash said quietly. "Milton's gone, but that doesn't mean everyone who was involved in covering this up is dead or powerless. Someone has been keeping this secret for four decades. They're not going to appreciate us digging it up."

"Let them try to stop us," Walt said with conviction. "We've faced worse than some geriatric church elder and his former daughter-in-law."

"Have we though?" Hank asked mildly. "Because last time we investigated a murder, Mabel was kidnapped and tied up in a boathouse. I'd say we're escalating, not improving our safety record."

"Details." Walt waved dismissively. "The point is, she survived. And we'll all survive this too."

Bea poured more sidecars, and even Walt accepted a glass, which suggested he was more worried than he was letting on. We sat there for another hour, refining plans, assigning tasks, trying to anticipate what we might find when we started pulling at these threads.

"Tomorrow," Dash said, "Mabel and I will drive to Sea Pines to talk to Elder Crenshaw. Then we'll head to Magnolia Gardens—it's only about twenty minutes away. If Elsie Crawford is having one of her good days, we might get lucky."

"And Holloway?" Walt asked.

Dash frowned. "That's the problem. An ex-deputy who quit

because he couldn't stomach Milton's corruption isn't going to trust another sheriff. He'll see the badge and shut down."

"So we go without you," Dottie said.

"You want to drive to Beaufort alone?" he asked.

"Not alone," I said. "Dottie, Hank, and I will go. A retired medical examiner, a retired judge, and a tea shop owner aren't exactly threatening. He's more likely to talk to us than to you."

"Especially law enforcement from Grimm Island," Hank added. "He left for a reason."

Dash didn't look happy about it, but he nodded. "Fair point. Just— be careful. Call me when you're done."

Bea leaned forward. "So while you're all running around the low country, what am I supposed to do?"

"Work on Jane Sutherland," I said. "You're both journalists. Appeal to that. Tell her we're not trying to ruin her life—we just want to know what scared her badly enough to run."

"And if she won't talk?"

"Then we know she's still scared," Dash said. "Which tells us something on its own."

Walt nodded, already making notes. "Dottie researches Stephanie Donaldson. I coordinate from here. Bea pursues Sutherland. Teams deploy for interviews."

"It's three conversations," Hank said mildly.

"Exactly," Walt agreed. "Precision operation."

By the time the Silver Sleuths dispersed, full darkness had descended upon Grimm Island like a velvet curtain. The last of them— Bea, naturally—swept out in a rustle of turquoise silk and tinkling silver earrings, leaving behind the faint scent of her expensive perfume and the promise to track down Jane Sutherland by whatever means necessary.

Dash lingered in my dining room, surveying the murder board with the air of a general contemplating battle plans. The whiteboard had transformed over the course of the evening into something that looked rather like a spider's web—strings connecting suspects to victims, dates to locations, secrets to lies. It was both beautiful and terrible in its complexity.

"I should help you clean up," he said, though he made no move toward the table still littered with evidence folders and half-empty glasses.

"You should," I agreed, equally immobile.

The thing was, neither of us seemed particularly motivated to end the evening. It hung between us, this moment, heavy with unspoken things and the weight of what tomorrow might bring. Tomorrow we would confront Elder Crenshaw. Tomorrow we would ask questions that had been buried for a long time. Tomorrow, someone might decide we were getting too close to truths that were meant to stay hidden.

But that was tomorrow.

Chowder, who had been dozing in his bed with the satisfied air of a dog who had supervised important detective work, lifted his head and regarded us with what could only be described as profound judgment. His bow tie had gone thoroughly askew during the evening's proceedings, and he looked rather like a tiny, wrinkled professor who had fallen asleep during his own lecture.

"Don't look at me like that," I told him.

He snorted—a sound that conveyed volumes about what he thought of humans who couldn't sort out their own romantic entanglements—and settled back down with a dramatic sigh.

Dash smiled at this exchange, and the expression transformed his entire face. The severe lines softened, the wariness in his dark eyes giving way to something warmer, more human. It occurred to me, not for the first time, that Sheriff Dashiell Beckett wore his authority like armor, carefully constructed to keep the world at a safe distance.

"Tomorrow's going to be complicated," he said finally, turning from the murder board to face me properly.

"Most tomorrows are," I replied, aiming for lightness and achieving something closer to breathlessness. The dining room, which had felt spacious enough for seven people moments ago, seemed to have shrunk considerably now that we were alone.

"And potentially dangerous." His voice dropped lower. "We're about to confront people who may have killed to protect these secrets. People with money and power and practice at keeping things hidden."

"I know," I said quietly.

He crossed the room then—three strides that eliminated the careful distance we'd been maintaining—and suddenly he was close enough that I could see the faint scar along his jawline, could smell the cedar scent of his cologne mixed with coffee and the peculiar smell of old paper that clung to anyone who'd spent hours poring over evidence files.

"I need you to promise me something," he said, and there was something almost fierce in the way he looked at me, as if he could anchor me to safety through sheer force of will.

"What?"

"When you go to Beaufort tomorrow with Hank and Dottie to interview Frank Holloway—" He paused, his jaw tightening. "I don't like you going without me. We're stirring up a forty-year-old murder, confronting people with money and power who've spent decades keeping secrets buried. Someone killed Ruby Bailey and George Pickering. Someone may have killed to protect those secrets before, and they might not hesitate to do it again."

His hands found my arms, warm and solid, his thumbs tracing small circles that sent shivers down my spine. "If anything feels wrong —anywhere, at any point during the day—you call me immediately. You don't try to handle it yourself. You don't play detective without backup. You get somewhere safe and you call. Do you understand?"

The intensity of it should have frightened me—this protectiveness that bordered on possession, this concern that felt personal rather than professional. But I'd spent a decade being careful, being safe, being the widow who didn't make waves or cause trouble. And it had gotten me exactly nowhere.

"I promise," I said, and meant it.

"Mabel," he said, my name a question and a statement and possibly a prayer.

Something in his expression shifted then—relief, perhaps, or maybe something deeper. His dark eyes held mine with an intensity that made my breath catch, and I watched his gaze drop to my lips, linger there for a long moment that stretched like taffy. The air between us felt charged, electric, like the moment before lightning strikes.

I thought he was going to kiss me. Every nerve in my body was waiting for it, anticipating the feel of his mouth on mine. But instead, he drew in a slow breath and said, very quietly, "We're going to need to talk soon, Mabel. About this. About us."

"Us," I repeated, the word feeling both terrifying and wonderful on my tongue.

"I'm finding it extremely difficult to leave you at the end of the night." His thumb traced my jawline with maddening gentleness. "You're consuming my thoughts—during the day when I should be focused on evidence and timelines, at night when I should be sleeping. I think about you when I'm drinking my morning coffee, when I'm reviewing case files, when I'm supposed to be listening to the mayor drone on about budget allocations."

A smile tugged at the corner of his mouth, self-deprecating and utterly disarming. "I've never been very good at this—at letting someone in. My work has always been easier than people, safer than caring. But you…" He paused, seeming to search for the right words. "You've gotten under my skin, Mabel McCoy. And I need to know if I'm alone in this, or if you're feeling even a fraction of what I am."

"You're not alone," I managed, my voice barely above a whisper.

His expression softened, something almost vulnerable flickering across his face before he leaned down and pressed his lips to my forehead in a kiss so tender, so achingly gentle, that I felt it reverberate through my entire body. It was somehow more intimate than any passionate embrace, this simple gesture that spoke of protection and promise and something that looked remarkably like devotion.

"Soon," he murmured against my skin. "When we're not chasing murders and confronting people who may have killed to keep secrets. When I can think clearly enough to say everything I want to say without worrying about keeping you safe. We'll talk about where this is going. Because Mabel—" He pulled back just enough to meet my eyes again. "I very much want it to be going somewhere."

"Me too," I whispered.

He stepped back then, breaking the contact between us with visible reluctance. "Lock your door. All of them. And turn on your alarm—the actual alarm system."

Despite everything, I smiled. "I promise."

After he left, I stood in my dining room for a long moment, my pulse gradually slowing.

Chowder appeared at my feet, looking up at me with an expression of profound exasperation.

"You wouldn't be so judgmental if you'd been in my situation," I told him. "Maybe you need a girlfriend."

He made a sound that was half snort, half sigh, and waddled toward the stairs.

I followed him up, checking locks and setting the alarm like I'd promised. Through my bedroom window, I could see the harbor stretching out toward Turtle Point, dark water reflecting scattered lights.

Ruby Bailey had cleaned houses and sung in the church choir. She'd loved her son and planned for a better future in Charleston. And someone had decided she didn't deserve to see it.

I turned away from the window and climbed into bed. Tomorrow, Elder Crenshaw would answer for what he knew.

The teakettle's whistle cut through the pre-dawn silence of my kitchen with the insistence of an alarm clock that refused to be ignored. I'd been awake since 4:30, unable to sleep past the point where anxiety and anticipation tangled themselves into a knot behind my ribs that no amount of deep breathing could untangle.

Outside my kitchen window, Grimm Island was still draped in that peculiar darkness that comes just before sunrise—not quite black anymore, but not yet willing to commit to gray. The harbor was invisible beyond the seawall, though I could hear the water moving against the stones, patient and eternal and utterly indifferent to the questions we planned to ask today.

I poured boiling water over loose Earl Grey leaves in my Brown Betty teapot—the one with the chip on the spout that Patrick had always meant to replace but never did. The bergamot scent rose with the steam, sharp and citrusy, cutting through the fog in my brain that three hours of restless sleep had left behind.

Chowder materialized in the doorway, naked as the day he was born except for his collar, and gave me a look that clearly indicated he expected me to remedy this situation immediately.

I surveyed his wardrobe options with the seriousness the day demanded. After some deliberation, I selected a navy blazer with gold buttons—the kind that made him look like a tiny yacht club commodore who'd taken a wrong turn into journalism. I added a red-and-white striped bow tie that gave the whole ensemble a patriotic flair, as if he were ready to break the next Watergate scandal while also possibly running for office.

"Very Woodward and Bernstein," I told him, fastening the bow tie and straightening his blazer. "Though I'm not sure which one you're supposed to be."

He snorted his opinion of the comparison and positioned himself expectantly by his food bowl, clearly prioritizing breakfast over investigative journalism.

I filled his bowl with the chicken and rice mixture, watching as he attacked it with the dedication of someone breaking a Pulitzer-worthy story.

I carried my tea upstairs to contemplate the morning's sartorial challenge. What did one wear to interrogate an elderly church elder about embezzlement and possible murder? After standing before my wardrobe for longer than strictly necessary, I selected a 1950s day dress in dove gray with three-quarter sleeves and a full skirt that would photograph beautifully if we ended up on the front page of the *Gazette*. The white Peter Pan collar added just enough innocence to make me look trustworthy while still maintaining the gravitas the situation required.

I finished my tea and collected my things, the morning already pressing against the windows with insistent golden light. Chowder waited by the door in his blazer and bow tie, projecting an air of professional readiness that would have been more convincing if he hadn't been eyeing the treat jar with naked longing.

"Work first, treats later," I told him, clipping on his leash.

The drive to The Perfect Steep took me through a Grimm Island just beginning to wake—Clarence Beaumont's truck already parked outside his bakery, the smell of fresh bread drifting through my open window. Harbor Street wore its early morning face, the one tourists never saw, when the island belonged to the people who actually lived here rather than those passing through in search of low-country charm and overpriced souvenirs.

I parked in my usual spot behind the shop and let myself in through the back door. The familiar ritual of opening soothed something anxious in my chest—alarm disabled, lights flooding the space with warmth, the scones I'd prepared last night waiting like small promises in the refrigerator. I slid them into the preheated oven and set the timer, then moved through the shop with the muscle memory of ten years, arranging, straightening, preparing for whatever the day would bring.

Genevieve arrived at 6:30, her backpack slung over one shoulder and her hair still wet from the shower. She was a good girl—reliable, quick to learn, never complained about early mornings or difficult customers. The kind of employee you thanked the universe for sending and tried very hard not to lose to better opportunities.

"Big day?" she asked, tying on her apron with practiced efficiency.

"Potentially," I said, sliding the first tray of scones into the oven. "I'll be gone most of the day. Deidre might stop by around lunchtime to check on things, but you should be fine."

"Is this about the murders?" She asked it casually, the way someone might ask about the weather, as if murder investigation had become just another part of my business model. Which, given recent events, wasn't entirely inaccurate.

"Yes."

"Cool. I mean—not cool that people got murdered. Obviously that's terrible. But cool that you're, like, solving it." She pulled out her phone to check the day's schedule. "The Silent Book Club has the back room reserved at two o'clock. I've got everything ready for them."

The Silent Book Club was a group of locals that picked their own books each month and came to the shop to read in silence and sip tea. It was an unusual group, but I couldn't say too much considering I'd been recruited as an honorary member of the Silver Sleuths. I still had several chapters to read of our latest true crime novel, and our next meeting was Thursday.

"Perfect," I said. "Thank you."

Dash arrived at 8:30, looking less like a small-town sheriff and more like someone who'd stepped out of a film noir—dark slacks, white dress shirt with the sleeves rolled to his elbows, his badge clipped to his belt rather than prominently displayed.

"Ready?" he asked, accepting the travel mug of coffee I handed him.

"As I'll ever be."

The drive to Sea Pines took forty minutes, cutting across the bridge that connected Grimm Island to the mainland and then following Highway 17 through a landscape that shifted from salt marsh to pine forest and back again. Dash drove with one hand on the wheel, the other holding his coffee, his eyes scanning the road with automatic alertness.

I'd brought Pickering's journal—or rather, copies of the relevant pages—along with our notes on Elder Crenshaw. The file sat in my lap like a sleeping cat that might wake up and scratch at any moment.

"What do we know about his health?" I asked, flipping through the pages again even though I'd memorized them by now.

"Administrator said he's mobile with a walker, mentally sharp most days. No dementia, no major cognitive decline. Just old." Dash glanced at me. "You nervous?"

"Shouldn't I be?"

"Probably. But you hide it well." He smiled slightly.

I found myself singing softly, the words slipping out before I could stop them. *They asked me how I knew, my true love was true... I of course replied, something here inside, cannot be denied...* The old standard felt right somehow—about smoke getting in your eyes, about being blinded by love or trust or whatever made people overlook the obvious until it was too late.

Dash glanced at me but said nothing, letting the song finish before he spoke.

"Crenshaw's not going to want to talk about any of this," he said, his expression growing serious. "He's had a long time to build his version of events, to justify whatever he did or didn't do. We're going to have to push him, and he's not going to like it."

"Then we push," I said quietly. "Ruby Bailey deserves someone asking the hard questions."

Sea Pines Retirement Community announced itself with a sign so aggressively cheerful it bordered on parody—carved wood with painted flowers and a motto that read *Where Every Day is Golden*. The grounds were immaculate in that way that required a full-time land-scaping crew and significant financial investment. Azaleas lined the curved driveway, their blooms a riot of pink and white. The main building was low and sprawling, designed to look like a grand planta-tion house but achieving something closer to a very expensive hotel that catered exclusively to people waiting to die.

The reception area smelled like flowers trying to disguise antisep-tic, with an underlying note of cafeteria food and despair that no amount of potpourri could fully mask. The receptionist—a woman in her fifties with hair the color of a new penny and a smile that suggested she'd perfected the art of professional sympathy—looked up from her computer as we entered.

"Good morning! How can I help you?"

Dash pulled out his badge. "Sheriff Beckett from Grimm Island. This is Mrs. McCoy. We're here to speak with Matthias Crenshaw. I called yesterday."

The smile faltered slightly. "Oh yes, of course. Mr. Crenshaw is expecting you. He's in the solarium—he likes to take his morning tea there. Second floor, take the elevator to your right, then follow the signs."

The elevator was the slow, gentle kind designed for people who couldn't handle sudden movements, with handrails on three sides and a mirror positioned so residents could check their appearance before emerging. I caught my reflection and was satisfied to see that I looked calm, professional, entirely unthreatening. The kind of woman who might be visiting her own grandfather rather than interrogating a potential murder conspirator.

The solarium occupied the entire east end of the second floor, its walls made almost entirely of glass that let in the morning sun with generous enthusiasm. Plants crowded every available surface—ferns and orchids and something with leaves the size of dinner plates. White wicker furniture was arranged in conversational groupings, and scattered throughout were residents in various states of activity. Some read newspapers. Others stared into space with the patient expression of people who'd run out of things to anticipate. One woman worked on a jigsaw puzzle with the concentrated focus of someone defusing a bomb.

Elder Matthias Crenshaw sat in a wingback chair near the windows, a walker positioned within easy reach. He was smaller than I'd expected—diminished by age in that way that makes former authority figures look almost harmless. His white hair was neatly combed, his cardigan buttoned against the air-conditioning that hummed through the vents. But his eyes were sharp when they fixed on us, intelligent and wary, and I revised my assessment of harmless immediately.

"Sheriff Beckett," he said, his voice carrying the cultured accent of old Charleston families. "And you must be Mrs. McCoy. I've heard about you. The tea shop woman who fancies herself a detective." It wasn't quite an insult, but it wasn't quite friendly either.

"Mr. Crenshaw," Dash said, settling into the chair across from him with careful courtesy. "Thank you for agreeing to speak with us."

"Did I have a choice?" Crenshaw's mouth twitched. "When the sheriff calls requesting an interview about a cold case, one doesn't exactly feel comfortable declining. Though I can't imagine what you think I can tell you that hasn't already been said."

I took the remaining chair, arranging my skirt with deliberate care, letting the silence stretch just long enough to become uncomfortable. It was a technique I'd learned from years of running a tea shop— sometimes you learned more from what people said to fill silence than from any direct question.

Crenshaw's fingers drummed against the arm of his chair.

"Ruby Bailey," Dash said. "You knew her."

"Everyone knew Ruby Bailey." Crenshaw's expression gave away nothing. "She cleaned houses for half the island, including mine. Twice a week, Tuesdays and Fridays. Always on time, always thorough. My wife was very pleased with her work."

"And her relationship with Reverend Pickering?"

Something flickered across Crenshaw's face—too quick to read, gone before I could identify it. "I was aware of it. Hard not to be, the way they carried on. Ruby had no shame, and George—" He paused. "George forgot that being a man of God required actual godliness, not just the appearance of it."

"You confronted her," I said. It wasn't a question.

Crenshaw's gaze shifted to me, assessing. "And what makes you think that?"

"There was a witness."

The silence that followed had weight to it, pressing down on the cheerful solarium with its bright plants and false optimism. Somewhere in the building, someone was playing piano—badly, with the halting uncertainty of someone relearning forgotten skills.

"I did speak with her," Crenshaw said finally. "In my capacity as a church elder. It was my responsibility to address matters of moral impropriety within our congregation. Ruby was conducting an affair with our pastor—an affair that was becoming increasingly public and scandalous. It reflected poorly on the church, on George's ministry, on all of us."

"What did you say to her?"

"I told her that her behavior was sinful and that she needed to end the relationship. I told her that she was jeopardizing George's marriage, his position, the respect of the entire community. I told her that if she had any decency, she would leave the island and give George the opportunity to repair his life and his relationship with God."

"And what did she say?" Dash asked.

Crenshaw's jaw tightened. "She laughed at me. Said I was a hypocrite and a fool. Said that I had no idea what George was really like, what any of them were really like. She told me to mind my own business unless I wanted everyone to know what she knew."

The air in the solarium suddenly felt thicker, harder to breathe. "What did she know?"

"I assumed she was bluffing," Crenshaw said, but his voice had gone careful, measured. "Ruby was clever—cleverer than most people gave her credit for. She cleaned houses, which meant she was in people's homes when they thought they were alone. She heard things, saw things. And she wasn't above using that information when it suited her purposes."

"Was she blackmailing you?" I asked.

"No." The word came quick and sharp. "She never asked me for money, never made any specific threats. It was all innuendo and suggestion. Letting me know she had ammunition without ever quite loading the gun."

"But you were afraid of what she might know," Dash said.

Crenshaw was quiet for a long moment, his fingers resuming their rhythmic tapping. "I was concerned. There were…irregularities in the church finances that year. Nothing illegal, you understand. Just complicated. The building fund, the community center project—there were cost overruns, unexpected expenses. George and I were working to resolve the accounting, but it looked messy on paper. If Ruby had told people that money was missing, it could have caused problems."

"How much money?" I asked.

"I don't recall the exact figures."

"Try," Dash suggested, his voice pleasant but with steel underneath.

"Nearly two hundred thousand dollars." Crenshaw's expression had gone carefully blank. "The community center was supposed to cost one hundred and fifty thousand. We'd raised two hundred thousand in donations. But the contractor—he'd estimated incorrectly, and the actual costs were significantly higher. We had to cancel the project and reallocate the funds to other church expenses."

"That's a very tidy explanation," I observed.

"It's the truth."

"Is it?" Dash leaned forward slightly. "Because from where I'm sitting, it sounds like exactly the kind of story someone tells when a significant amount of money has gone missing and they need to account for it. Two hundred thousand dollars raised for a specific project that never gets built, and the money just...redistributes itself into vague church expenses?"

"The church board reviewed and approved all expenditures," Crenshaw said stiffly.

"A church board that you controlled," I said. "That you and George Pickering controlled together."

"There were six of us," he said, though his face had gone red, the color rising from his collar like a thermometer measuring anger. "George, myself, Roger Hammond, Gene Forsythe, Douglas Sutton, and Craig Baker. All honorable men."

"Except for George, who was cheating on his wife," I said. "Surely you wouldn't consider him honorable."

His lips pinched in a thin line and his breathing grew shallow. "You know nothing," he spat.

"It just seems to me," I said as if I were making casual conversation. "That if George wasn't so honorable, then maybe you could overlook other dishonorable behavior from the members of the board."

"You're making accusations based on speculation and the word of a woman who's been dead for forty years." His voice elevated so that several heads turned our direction. "Ruby Bailey was a liar and a manipulator. She had an affair with a married pastor, disrupted an entire congregation, and got herself killed because she couldn't keep her mouth shut about things that were none of her business."

The words hung in the air like smoke, revealing more than Crenshaw probably intended.

"Got herself killed," Dash repeated softly. "Interesting choice of words."

Crenshaw seemed to realize his mistake. "A figure of speech. Obviously someone killed her—killed both of them."

"And did you tell George to stop his sinful ways and end the affair, or did you place the blame solely on Ruby's shoulders?"

"I told him to stop," he said. "But Ruby knew she was a temptress and reveled in it. Unfortunately, men are easily swayed by certain types of women and she could have put an end to things. Ruby's behavior invited danger. She was reckless, provocative. She pushed people."

"People like you?"

"I never touched her." The denial came fast. "I had nothing to do with what happened at Turtle Point. I was home with my wife that evening. We had dinner, watched television, went to bed. My wife gave a statement to the police—you can check the records."

"We have," Dash said. "Your wife confirmed you were home. But wives have been known to lie for their husbands."

"Martha would never—" He stopped himself, jaw working. "My wife was a godly woman. She wouldn't have lied, not even for me."

"What about Stephanie? Would she have lied for you?"

"Stephanie married my son two years after the murders," Crenshaw said, each word measured and deliberate. "So, no. She wouldn't have. The marriage didn't last, I'm afraid. Stephanie had...ambitions that didn't align with island life. She wanted more than my son could provide." There was bitterness in his voice now, the kind that comes from watching a family alliance crumble. "Why are you asking about her?"

"A witness saw a blond woman in a nurse's uniform at Turtle Point the night of the murders," Dash said, leaning forward slightly. "Saw her with Reverend Pickering around nine o'clock."

The color drained from Crenshaw's face, then flooded back twice as red. His hands gripped the arms of his chair until the leather creaked under the pressure. "That's impossible. Stephanie was at work that night. She worked the evening shift at the hospital. She couldn't possibly have been at Turtle Point."

"You're very certain of her whereabouts," I said, watching his face carefully. "For something that happened so long ago."

Crenshaw's face had gone from red to purple. "This interview is over. I've answered your questions, told you everything I know, which is nothing. I was home with my wife the night of the murders. Stephanie was at work. Neither of us had anything to do with what happened to Ruby Bailey and George Pickering. If you want to harass me further, you can speak to my attorney."

He reached for his walker with shaking hands, pulling himself to standing with visible effort. For a moment, I saw him as he must have been forty years ago—tall, commanding, the kind of man who was used to being obeyed. The kind of man who would have viewed Ruby Bailey's defiance as intolerable.

"One more question," I said as he prepared to leave. "Did George Pickering keep a journal? Personal records beyond the church ledgers?"

Crenshaw's walker scraped against the floor as he froze mid-step. "A journal?"

"We have it," Dash said quietly. "Every confession he heard, every secret people told him, every piece of information he collected. All written down in his own hand."

The silence that followed was profound. Crenshaw's knuckles went white against the walker's handles.

"That's—" He swallowed hard. "George wouldn't have done that. It would have violated every tenet of pastoral confidentiality."

"And yet he did," I said. "Pages and pages of other people's secrets. Financial improprieties. Affairs. Things people thought they'd confessed in confidence."

"Where did you get this journal?" His voice had gone thin, reedy.

"Does it matter?" Dash asked. "The question is whether your name appears in it, Mr. Crenshaw. Whether George documented your conversations about the church finances. Whether he wrote down what really happened to that two hundred thousand dollars."

Crenshaw's face had gone gray. He shuffled toward the elevator without another word, his walker clicking against the tile with the rhythm of a clock counting down.

"He's lying," I said.

"About which part?"

"All of it. Some of it. Enough of it." I gathered my things, suddenly desperate to be out of this place with its false cheerfulness and underlying despair. "He was afraid of what Ruby knew. The money disappeared from the church building fund and never got properly accounted for. His son's girlfriend was a blond nurse who later became his daughter-in-law—very convenient timing for a marriage that cemented her loyalty to the family."

"But we can't prove any of it," Dash said as we walked back to the elevator. "His wife alibied him. The church board approved all the financial decisions. Everything's clean on paper.

"Or she's lying to protect him," he added. "Though verifying hospital records from 1985 is going to be nearly impossible. Most places didn't keep paper records that long, and nothing was digitized back then."

"So we take Crenshaw's word for it, or we don't," I said. "And given everything else he's lied about or conveniently forgotten, I'm not inclined to believe him."

"Neither am I," Dash said. "Which means Stephanie Chester stays on our list until we can prove otherwise."

The elevator doors opened with a soft chime, and we stepped inside.

"Magnolia Gardens is twenty minutes from here," Dash said, checking his watch. "Elsie Crawford. Let's pray she's having a lucid day, and see if she can give us something more solid than Crenshaw's carefully rehearsed denials."

The drive to Magnolia Gardens took us deeper into the low country, past plantation houses and marshland, through the landscape that had witnessed centuries of secrets. I sang quietly, not quite realizing I was doing it until Dash glanced over with that slight smile.

"*In my sweet little Alice blue gown, when I first wandered down into town...*"

"That's an old one," he observed.

"My grandmother used to sing it. She said it was her mother's favorite—something about innocence and naïvety and the way we dress ourselves up to face the world." I looked out the window at the passing scenery. "Ruby Bailey put on her best dress to meet George Pickering that night. Made herself beautiful for what she thought would be an evening with her lover, planning their future together. She had no idea she was dressing for her own funeral."

"We're going to find out who killed her," Dash said. It wasn't a promise—it was a statement of fact.

Magnolia Gardens Assisted Living was smaller than Sea Pines, more intimate, with the feeling of a well-maintained home rather than an institution. The main building was actual antebellum architecture —not a replica but the real thing, carefully preserved and adapted for modern use. Magnolia trees lined the circular drive, their white blooms perfuming the air with sweetness.

The receptionist here was younger, friendlier, less practiced at professional sympathy. "You're here to see Miss Elsie? Oh, she'll be so pleased. She doesn't get many visitors anymore. Most of her contemporaries have passed, you understand. She's in the memory-care wing —take the path through the garden, it's the cottage at the back. The blue door."

The garden was spectacular—roses and jasmine and something purple I couldn't identify, all of it tended with obvious care. A stone path wound through the plantings, past a fountain where water trickled over moss-covered rocks. Birds sang in the trees, and somewhere in the distance, I could hear wind chimes.

The memory-care cottage was painted pale blue with white trim, cheerful and bright despite its purpose. Through the windows, I could see a common room where residents sat in chairs arranged in a circle, some engaged in conversation, others staring at nothing with the patient confusion of people whose minds had left them behind.

A nurse met us at the door—a woman in her thirties with kind eyes and competence. "You must be Sheriff Beckett and Mrs. McCoy. I'm Nurse Anna. Miss Elsie's having one of her good days today—very lucid, very chatty. Just keep in mind that she can tire quickly, and if she starts to get agitated, we'll need to end the visit."

"Understood," Dash said.

"She's in her room. Third door on the left. I'll be right here if you need anything."

Elsie Crawford's room was small but bright, with large windows overlooking the garden and walls covered in photographs—black-and-white images from decades past, color prints from more recent years, all documenting a life fully lived. She sat in a rocking chair by the window, a knitted blanket across her lap despite the warmth, her white hair caught back in a bun that had probably been tidy this morning but had since begun to escape in wisps around her face.

She looked up as we entered, and her eyes—pale blue and surprisingly sharp—fixed on us with immediate interest.

"Well," she said, her voice thin but clear. "The sheriff and his lady detective. Anna told me you'd be coming. Said you wanted to ask about that night. After all these years, someone finally wants to hear what I saw."

I pulled a chair close while Dash positioned himself where he could see both Elsie and the door—cop instincts never fully turning off. "Miss Crawford, I'm Mabel McCoy, and this is Sheriff Beckett. We're investigating the murders of Ruby Bailey and George Pickering."

"Forty years ago this September," Elsie said, nodding. "I remember it like it happened yesterday. Some things you can't forget, no matter how much time passes or how much your mind tries to let go of other things. I've forgotten what I had for breakfast this morning—I had breakfast, didn't I, Anna said I did—but I remember that night like it's painted on the inside of my eyelids."

"You were walking your dog," Dash prompted gently.

"Chester. Golden retriever, lived to be fifteen years old. He needed his evening constitutional—that's what my mother used to call it, a constitutional—and I couldn't sleep anyway. Never could sleep well, even when I was young. The doctor gave me pills, but they made me feel fuzzy, like my head was full of cotton. So I walked instead. Chester and I, we'd go out after dark when it was cool and quiet, walk for an hour or more sometimes."

She rocked slowly, her gnarled hands gripping the arms of the chair. "That night we walked out to Turtle Point. It was September, still warm but with that edge that tells you summer's ending. The moon was nearly full—not quite, but close enough that you could see everything clear as day almost. Chester loved the beach, liked to chase the waves and dig in the sand."

"What time was this?" I asked.

"Nine o'clock, maybe a bit after. I remember because the church bells had just finished ringing and I thought it was later than I'd intended. Chester was sniffing around near the tree line—you know how dogs are, have to investigate every smell—when I saw them."

"Them?" Dash leaned forward slightly.

"The reverend and a woman. They were standing near his car— that Buick he drove, parked back in the trees like he didn't want anyone to see it. They were arguing. Not yelling, you understand. The kind of arguing where people are trying to stay quiet but the emotion comes through anyway. Sharp voices, lots of gestures."

"Could you hear what they were saying?"

Elsie shook her head. "I was too far away, and Chester was making noise. But I could see them clearly in the moonlight. The reverend was upset—I could tell by his posture, the way he kept running his hands through his hair. And the woman, she was angry. Pointing at him, stepping close then backing away."

"The woman," I said carefully. "Can you describe her?"

"Blond hair, worn down around her shoulders. Tall—taller than me, and I was five foot five back then. She wore white—looked like a nurse's uniform, the kind they wore back then with the white dress and white stockings."

"Did you see her face?"

"Not well enough to identify her. She had her back to me mostly, and like I said, I was keeping my distance. Chester wanted to go investigate—he was a friendly dog, wanted to say hello to everyone—but I held him back. Something about the whole scene felt wrong. Private. Like I was seeing something I shouldn't be seeing."

"How long did you watch them?" Dash asked.

"Maybe five minutes. Then the woman turned and walked off toward the road—I assume she had a car parked somewhere nearby, didn't want it seen next to his. The reverend stayed by his car, just standing there looking upset. Chester and I continued our walk down the beach in the other direction. I figured whatever they'd been arguing about was their business, none of mine."

"Did you see Ruby Bailey arrive?"

"No. I'd already walked away by then. But everyone knew she and the reverend had their arrangement. I assumed she'd be coming to meet him—she lived close enough to walk to Turtle Point from her house."

She was quiet for a moment, rocking, her eyes focused on something beyond the window. "When I heard the next morning that they'd been found dead, both of them shot...I knew I'd seen something important. I went to the police station, asked to speak to whoever was handling the investigation. They brought me into a little room, gave me terrible coffee, and this deputy—young man, very earnest—he took my statement. Wrote down everything I said, had me sign it. He seemed to think it was important."

"But Sheriff Milton didn't," I said.

Elsie's mouth tightened. "Sheriff Milton was a horse's behind. He came to my house three days later. Sat in my living room drinking tea my sister made and told me very politely that I'd been mistaken. Said I couldn't have seen what I thought I saw because they had evidence that Reverend Pickering was alone until Ruby Bailey arrived later. Said I was confused, probably saw someone else entirely. When I insisted I knew what I'd seen, he got less polite. Started asking questions about my mental health, about the sleeping pills my doctor had prescribed, about whether I'd been drinking that night."

Her hands had begun to shake slightly. "He made me feel crazy. Like I couldn't trust my own eyes, my own memory. My sister—she was worried about me, said maybe the sheriff was right, maybe I had gotten confused. After a while, I started to wonder myself. But then sometimes I'd be falling asleep and I'd see it again—that woman in white, arguing with the reverend in the moonlight. And I'd know I hadn't imagined it."

"Miss Crawford," Dash said gently, "Is there anything else you remember? Any detail that might help us identify the woman?"

Elsie was quiet for so long I thought she might have drifted off or forgotten the question. Then she spoke, her voice barely above a whisper.

"No. I wish I'd stayed longer. Maybe if I had, if I'd been a witness they couldn't dismiss…" She looked at me with sudden intensity. "You believe me, don't you? I'm not crazy. I saw what I saw."

"I believe you," I said, reaching out to take her hand. Her fingers were cold and fragile, bird bones wrapped in papery skin. "Everything you've told us makes sense. You saw something real, something important, and Sheriff Milton buried it because he was corrupt."

Elsie's expression shifted then, her eyes losing their sharp focus as she looked at me. Really looked at me. Her head tilted slightly, and a smile spread across her face—sweet and confused and heartbreaking.

"Helen?" she said softly, her voice taking on a younger quality. "Helen, is that you? I thought you weren't coming until Sunday. Did you bring the buttermilk pie? You know how Daddy loves your buttermilk pie."

My throat tightened. I glanced at Dash, who had gone very still.

"Miss Crawford," I said gently, but she wasn't listening.

"Your dress is lovely, Helen. Is it new?" Her fingers plucked at my sleeve, examining the fabric with childlike wonder. "Mama would have loved to see you in it. She always said you had the best taste of all of us." Her eyes filled with tears. "I miss Mama. Do you miss her too?"

Nurse Anna appeared in the doorway, her expression sympathetic but unsurprised. "She does this sometimes," she said quietly. "Helen was her older sister. Passed away in 1973."

Elsie was still holding my hand, stroking it gently, her face peaceful now as if the confusion brought its own kind of comfort. "Stay for supper, Helen. Please stay. I don't like eating alone."

"I think that's enough for today," Anna said softly. "She's had a good spell, but she's tired now. This is how it goes—clarity comes and goes like the tide."

We stood slowly, and I squeezed Elsie's hand before letting go. She looked up at me with those pale blue eyes, and for just a moment, I saw recognition flicker there—saw her remember who I really was and what we'd been discussing. Her expression grew troubled, almost frightened.

"The woman in white," she whispered. "She came back. I know she did."

Then the moment passed, and she was looking past me again, searching for her sister who'd been gone for fifty years.

My phone buzzed with a text from Dottie: *Ready when you are. Hank and I are at the shop waiting.*

"I need to get back," I said. "Dottie and Hank are waiting on me so we can go talk to Thomas Wheeler."

Dash nodded, though I could see the tension in his jaw—the part of him that didn't like sending me off without him. But we'd already decided this approach made more sense.

I found myself singing softly, the words slipping out before I could stop them. *"Pennies in a stream, falling leaves of sycamore, moonlight in Vermont…"*

My grandmother used to say that music was just longing set to melody—longing for what we had, what we've lost, what we hope might come. The old standards understood that better than most. They dressed heartbreak in pretty melodies and called it romance.

The familiar sight of Grimm Island's bridge emerging from the mainland felt like coming home, though whether that was comfort or trap I couldn't quite decide. Below us, the marshland stretched out in shades of gold and green, eternal and unchanging, holding its own secrets in the mud and water.

Dash pulled up in front of The Perfect Steep, where Dottie and Hank waited on the bench outside, looking like two people dressed for entirely different occasions. Dottie wore bright green culottes and a patterned shirt that made my eyes cross, her cat-eye glasses perched on her nose. Hank had on his cargo shorts and that fishing vest with its seventeen pockets, each presumably containing something essential for interrogating ex-deputies.

"Be careful," Dash said as I gathered my things. "Frank Holloway left the force for a reason. If he knows something that Milton wanted buried, talking about it might make him nervous."

"We'll be fine," I assured him. "Three harmless-looking people asking questions about old times."

"You're about as harmless as a cottonmouth in tall grass," he said, but there was warmth in his voice. "Call me when you're done?"

"Promise."

He caught my hand briefly, his thumb tracing that familiar circle on my palm. Then I was out of the vehicle and walking toward Dottie and Hank, feeling his eyes on me until I reached them.

"You ready?" Dottie asked, her expression suggesting she'd noticed that little moment and would be asking questions about it later.

"Absolutely."

The afternoon had turned sultry, the kind of low-country heat that made the air feel thick enough to drink. As we pulled away from The Perfect Steep, I caught a glimpse of Chowder in the window, still wearing his blazer and bow tie, watching us leave with the solemn expression of a journalist whose story was just getting interesting.

CHAPTER
NINE

Hank Hardeman's 1987 Buick LeSabre—powder blue and pristine despite its age—hummed along Highway 17 with the steady confidence of a car that had been maintained with religious devotion. The interior smelled faintly of Armor All and the peppermints Hank kept in a crystal dish mounted to the dashboard, a detail so quintessentially him that I'd smiled when I first noticed it.

"My daughter thinks I've lost my mind," Dottie announced from the passenger seat, adjusting her cat-eye glasses as she gazed out at the passing landscape of pine trees and marsh grass. "Veronica called last night—at 11 p.m., mind you, knowing full well I go to bed at 10—to lecture me about 'age-appropriate behavior.'"

"What does that even mean?" I asked from the back seat, where I'd spread out my notes on Frank Holloway across my lap.

"It means she found out about Hank and me, and she's scandalized."

My head snapped up from my notes. So I'd been right about them. The casual touches, the way they gravitated toward each other—it hadn't been my imagination. Something warm bloomed in my chest at the confirmation, though whether it was happiness for them or envy for what they'd found, I couldn't quite say.

Dottie's voice dripped with sarcasm as she continued. "Apparently, seventy-eight-year-old women aren't supposed to have romantic relationships. We're supposed to sit quietly in our houses doing needlepoint and waiting for death like proper old ladies."

Hank chuckled from behind the wheel, his hands positioned at ten and two. "She actually said that?"

"Not in so many words. But she kept saying things like 'Mother, at your age' and 'what would people think' and 'have you no sense of propriety?'" Dottie pulled out a compact mirror, checking her lipstick with the critical eye of someone who refused to let age dictate her presentation. Today's shade was crimson—bold, unapologetic, perfectly Dottie. "I told her that I had plenty of propriety, I just chose not to let it dictate my personal life."

"I'm guessing that didn't help," I said.

"Made it worse, actually. She started crying, said I was being reckless and irresponsible, then hung up on me." Dottie snapped her compact shut with satisfying finality. "The next day she called my son Gerald to stage an intervention. Gerald—bless him—told her to mind her own business and that I deserved to be happy."

"At least one of them has sense," Hank observed.

"Gerald's always been the practical one. Takes after me. Veronica takes after her father—all emotion and propriety and worrying about what strangers think." Dottie twisted in her seat to look at me fully, and the afternoon light caught the purple frames of her glasses, making them gleam. "The real issue is that she's jealous. Forty-five years old, divorced, working eighty-hour weeks at a job that's eating her alive, and her mother is having more fun than she is. That's what's really bothering her."

The landscape rolled past us—spartina grass waving in the breeze, egrets picking their way through shallow water, the occasional house on stilts rising from the marsh like a ship anchored in green seas. The low country had a way of making even difficult conversations feel softer somehow, as if the land itself absorbed the sharp edges of human drama and gentled them into something more bearable.

"My kids aren't thrilled either," Hank admitted, taking the exit toward Beaufort. "My daughter Patricia keeps making pointed comments about 'moving too fast' and 'being disrespectful.'"

"That's complicated," I said carefully, knowing from the island gossip network that Eleanor had raised Hank's children after their mother died young. "What does your son think?" I asked.

"Michael doesn't care one way or the other. He's got his own life in Charleston—three kids, demanding job as a marine biologist, no time to worry about his old man's love life. He called last week and said as long as I was happy, that's what mattered." Hank's voice held fondness despite the complicated emotions. "But Patricia keeps saying Eleanor deserves more respect than this, that I should wait longer before moving on. She actually suggested I wait until the five-year mark, as if grief operates on some kind of official timeline."

"Five years," Dottie scoffed. "What's magical about five years? Does grief expire like milk?"

"According to Patricia, yes." Hank took a turn a bit wide and earned an annoyed honk from a truck. He waved dismissively. "Eleanor knew what she was doing though. She told me six months before she died that I wasn't allowed to mope around after she was gone. Said she'd haunt me if I turned into one of those widowers who let themselves go to seed."

I remembered Eleanor—sharp-tongued, elegant, the kind of woman who'd order Earl Grey and then tell you exactly what you'd done wrong with the steeping. She'd been a regular at The Perfect Steep, always sitting by the window with her crossword puzzle, making acerbic comments about the tourists who thought iced tea was the same as proper tea.

"She came into my shop every Thursday," I said. "Always complained that I made the tea too hot, then drank three cups."

"That was Eleanor," Hank said. "Complained about everything but kept coming back for more. Drove me crazy for forty-two years, and I loved every minute of it."

I found myself smiling despite the heaviness of our mission. There was something deeply comforting about watching two people who'd lived full lives—who'd buried spouses and raised children and survived decades of joy and grief—find each other in the messy middle of it all. It made the future feel less frightening somehow, as if happiness wasn't just for the young and uncomplicated.

"Speaking of romantic entanglements," Dottie said, turning in her seat with predatory interest, "are we going to discuss Sheriff Beckett, or are you going to keep pretending that little goodbye wasn't dripping with sexual tension?"

Heat flooded my face. "We're investigating a murder."

"We're always investigating something. Doesn't mean you have to die a nun." Dottie's eyes, magnified behind her cat-eye glasses, were entirely too knowing. "The man looks at you like you're water and he's been wandering the desert for forty days. It's actually painful to watch—all that want with nowhere to go."

"Leave her alone," Hank said, though his eyes crinkled with amusement in the rearview mirror. "Not everyone moves at your speed, Dottie."

"My speed got results. You're here, aren't you?"

"Because you told me my beef bourguignon was adequate and then invited yourself over the following Tuesday to see if I could do better with coq au vin."

"It worked, didn't it?"

I pressed my fingers against my mouth, trying not to laugh. They were terrible together in the best possible way—sharp edges that somehow fit.

"Dash is…" I started, then stopped, unsure how to finish.

"Waiting," Dottie supplied. "Very patiently, I might add. But patience runs out, honey. Even for sheriffs with sad eyes who look like they stepped out of a film noir."

"I haven't noticed—"

"Liar." Dottie turned back around, studying me in the visor mirror. "You've known him five weeks now. Long enough to know if you can see yourself spending your life with him. Either you can or you can't. Sitting in the middle just wastes everyone's time."

The question landed with unexpected weight. Could I see myself spending my life with Dash Beckett? The thought should have terrified me—it had only been five weeks, barely enough time to know someone's coffee order, let alone their soul. But the problem wasn't whether I could imagine it. The problem was that I could imagine it too easily, and that scared me more than not being able to imagine it at all.

"He keeps things close," I said finally. "His past, why he really left undercover work, what he's running from—because he's definitely running from something. I can see it in the way he watches doors, the way he goes quiet sometimes like he's somewhere else entirely. And I don't know if he'll ever trust me enough to let me in."

"So you're worried he's got secrets," Dottie said.

"Everyone has secrets. But his feel...bigger. More dangerous. The kind that might matter."

"Then ask him," Hank said simply. "Straight out. No dancing around it. You want to know who he is beneath the badge, you ask him to tell you."

The landscape had begun to shift as we approached Beaufort—marsh giving way to neighborhoods, then to the historic downtown with its antebellum architecture and tree-lined streets. Live oaks created tunnels of shade that dropped the temperature ten degrees, their branches arching over brick sidewalks and wrought-iron balconies. Beaufort had the unhurried elegance of old money that didn't need to announce itself, gardens tended by the same families for generations, history preserved in every careful detail.

Bay Street was busier than expected for a Tuesday afternoon—tourists browsing shop windows, locals running errands, the steady flow of people that kept small downtown districts alive.

"There's the hardware store," Hank said, slowing as we approached a brick storefront with cheerful red lettering. "But good Lord, look at this parking situation. There's not a spot anywhere."

He was right—every space along Bay Street was occupied, cars parked bumper-to-bumper along the entire block.

"Drop us off in front," Dottie suggested, already gathering her purse. "You can find parking and meet us inside. No sense in all of us circling like vultures."

"You sure?" Hank asked, but he was already pulling up to the curb.

"We'll be fine," I assured him, tucking Frank Holloway's folder—the one containing all our questions—into my handbag. "Two harmless ladies asking questions about old times. What could possibly go wrong?"

"That's what people say right before things go spectacularly wrong," Hank muttered, but he was unlocking the doors.

Dottie leaned over and kissed his cheek—quick, casual, the kind of gesture that spoke of intimacy and comfort rather than passion. "We'll be careful. Find a good spot for the Buick. You know how you get when someone parks too close to your doors."

"That's because people don't understand the concept of personal space," Hank said, but there was affection in his mock indignation.

We climbed out onto the brick sidewalk, and I watched Hank's powder-blue Buick disappear around the corner, still searching for that elusive perfect parking space. The afternoon had turned warm—not quite oppressive, but enough to make me grateful for the shade of the storefront awning.

"Ready?" Dottie asked, squaring her shoulders like a general preparing for battle.

"Yep," I said. "Cool as a cucumber. That's me."

The bell above the door chimed as we entered—one of those old-fashioned shopkeeper's bells that announced customers with cheerful authority. The interior of Holloway's Hardware smelled like sawdust and motor oil, metal and paint thinner, WD-40 and possibility. All the scents of creation and repair mixed into something oddly comforting, like stepping into a place where broken things could still be fixed if you had the right tools and knew how to use them.

The store itself was a labyrinth of narrow aisles crowded with merchandise organized according to some system that probably made perfect sense to the owner but looked like controlled chaos to everyone else. Screws in tiny drawers labeled with perfect handwriting, electrical supplies hanging from ceiling hooks like mechanical stalactites, plumbing fixtures arranged by size and function on pegboard walls. Everything had its place, and that place had been carefully considered and maintained with the dedication of someone who genuinely cared about helping people find exactly what they needed.

Behind the counter stood a man who looked like he'd walked out of Mayberry and decided the 1960s suited him just fine. He was slight —maybe five foot eight and a hundred and fifty pounds after a big meal—with sandy hair going gray at the temples and a face so earnest it made you want to confess your sins just so he could forgive them. He wore wire-rimmed glasses that kept sliding down his nose, a flannel shirt despite the late spring heat, and jeans that had been washed so many times they'd faded to the color of forget.

When he smiled at us, his whole face transformed into something boyish and open, the kind of smile that made you trust him with your grandmother's antique lamp or your deepest secrets.

"Afternoon, ladies," he said, his voice carrying a soft low-country drawl that wrapped around the words like honey. "Can I help you find something? We've got a special on deck stain this week if you're look-ing, and the window screens just came in—had to order them special from a supplier in Columbia, but they're good quality. Last you ten years if you treat them right."

"Frank Holloway?" I asked, approaching the counter with the careful steps of someone approaching a skittish animal.

"That's me." His smile faltered slightly, becoming cautious in the way people got when strangers knew their names. "Do I know you folks?"

"No, but we know someone who spoke very highly of you. Thomas Wheeler's brother, Marcus." I offered my hand across the counter. "I'm Mabel McCoy, and this is Dr. Dottie Simmons. We were hoping you might have a few minutes to talk about your time as a deputy on Grimm Island."

The transformation was immediate and complete. Frank's open expression shuttered like someone had thrown a switch, his body going rigid as a corpse on an autopsy table. He took a step back from the counter, his hand moving instinctively toward something beneath it—probably a phone, possibly something more dangerous. His face had gone pale, and behind his wire-rimmed glasses, his eyes held something that looked like fear seasoned with resignation.

"I don't talk about that," he said flatly, his voice stripped of all its honey warmth. "Not to anyone. Not ever. And anyone who knew Tommy Wheeler should know why."

"We're investigating the Pickering–Bailey murders," Dottie said gently, her medical examiner voice coming out—calm, professional, impossible to ignore. "Reopening the case officially. We believe Sheriff Milton buried evidence, and we're trying to find out what really happened that night in September 1985."

"Milton's in prison," Frank said, and there was satisfaction in his voice, dark and bitter as burnt coffee. "Federal prison, where he belongs. But that doesn't change what he did, what he covered up. Some things stay buried even after the person who buried them gets locked away."

"But Ruby Bailey and George Pickering deserve justice," I said, pulling out the folder we'd brought. "And Thomas Wheeler died thinking he'd failed them. Marcus said Tommy never got over that case, that it haunted him until the day his heart gave out. He was fifty-two years old, Frank. That's too young to die from carrying guilt that wasn't even his to carry."

Something flickered across Frank's face at Thomas's name—grief, guilt, anger, a complicated tangle of emotions that suggested Marcus had been right about his brother's obsession with the unsolved murders. His hand trembled slightly as he removed his glasses, cleaning them on his flannel shirt with slow, deliberate movements that looked like a delaying tactic while he decided what to say.

"Tommy was a good man," Frank said finally, his voice rough as sandpaper on raw wood. "The best partner I ever had in my three years on the force. We were young together, both of us thinking we'd make a difference, believing that doing things right actually mattered. Tommy never lost that belief, even when Milton tried to beat it out of him. Even when it became clear that honesty was a liability on Grimm Island, not an asset."

He replaced his glasses, and his eyes behind them held decades of resentment compressed into something hard and sharp. "But Grimm Island didn't want honest cops back then. It wanted cops who understood how things worked, who knew which families were untouchable and which crimes weren't worth solving. Who knew when to look the other way and keep their mouths shut about what they'd seen."

"Is that why you left?" Dottie asked.

"I left because I couldn't do it anymore." Frank's voice had gone quiet, almost apologetic, as if he were confessing a failure rather than standing up for what was right. "Milton kept asking me to do things—lose paperwork, forget what I'd seen, tell witnesses their statements weren't needed. Small things at first, then bigger ones. And I kept telling myself it was just how things worked, that I was too new to understand. But I understood."

He looked down at his hands, as if surprised to find them gripping the counter so tightly. He relaxed his fingers, stepped back.

"Tell us about the Pickering–Bailey case," I said quietly. "What did you and Tommy find that Milton didn't want found?"

Frank looked at us for a long moment, his earnest face struggling with something—fear, maybe, or the weight of secrets kept too long. Behind his wire-rimmed glasses, his eyes held the kind of wariness that came from experience rather than nature, as if life had taught him that some conversations were dangerous even decades after the fact.

The bell above the door chimed. I thought it would be Hank, but a customer entered—a woman with a canvas shopping bag, heading toward the paint section with the purposeful stride of someone who knew exactly what she needed.

"Jimmy," Frank called out, his voice carrying through the store with practiced ease, "Can you handle the front for a bit? I need to take care of something in the office."

"Sure thing, Mr. Holloway," came a young man's voice from somewhere among the aisles.

Frank gestured toward the back of the store with a slight inclination of his head, the movement almost furtive. "Come on. We can talk privately back here."

The office was small but meticulously organized in the way that suggested a man who'd learned to control what he could when so much had been beyond his control. A desk covered in receipts and invoices arranged in neat stacks, each pile squared at the corners with mathematical precision. A filing cabinet with drawers labeled by year and category in that same careful handwriting we'd seen on the screw bins out front. An old coffee maker that looked like it had survived several decades and countless pots, its carafe stained dark as river water.

Frank pulled out two folding chairs for us—the metal kind that had probably been purchased during some long-ago church surplus sale—and settled himself behind his desk with movements that were careful, measured, as if his body hurt in ways he'd learned to accommodate.

He was quiet for a moment, his hands resting on the worn wood of the desk, and I could see him gathering himself, preparing to revisit something he'd spent decades trying to forget.

"Tommy made me promise," he said finally, his voice soft. "Before I quit, he made me promise that if anything happened to him, I'd make sure someone eventually knew the truth. Someone who'd actually do something with it instead of letting it get buried again."

He took a breath, and when he spoke again, his voice had changed —gone flat and careful, the tone of someone reciting a report they'd memorized so thoroughly it had become part of their DNA.

"The call came in around 6:30 Monday morning," he began. "September 16, 1985. Samuel Morrison out jogging at Turtle Point at an hour when decent people were still in bed. Found two bodies near the tree line, called it in from the pay phone at the marina. Tommy and I were on duty that morning—we'd pulled the overnight shift and were about ready to clock out when the call came through. We got there maybe twenty, twenty-five minutes later."

He paused, his eyes going distant, focused on something we couldn't see—some scene preserved in memory like an insect in amber, perfect and terrible and impossible to forget.

"I was still a rookie in all the ways that counted when I got that call," he continued, his voice dropping lower. "Grimm Island wasn't exactly a hotbed of crime back then. Traffic stops, noise complaints, the occasional drunk and disorderly. Tommy and I had responded to one fatal car accident in all that time—teenager wrapped his truck around a tree on River Road. But that was clean compared to what was waiting at Turtle Point."

He removed his glasses, cleaning them with the edge of his flannel shirt—a delaying tactic, giving himself time to find the words.

"They were arranged," he said finally, his voice taking on the hollow quality of someone revisiting a nightmare that never quite faded, no matter how many years passed or how many miles separated him from Grimm Island. "Someone had taken the time after killing them to pose them in that embrace. But the scene—the actual scene before it got sanitized for the reports—told a different story entirely."

He leaned back in his chair, and the springs creaked like old bones settling. His eyes went distant, focused on something we couldn't see, some terrible tableau preserved in memory with the clarity of a photograph that wouldn't yellow or fade no matter how desperately you wished it would.

"Pickering died first. Single shot to the back of the head, execution style. He was on his knees when it happened, about ten feet from his car." Frank's hands moved unconsciously, positioning invisible bodies in invisible sand. "The killer must have had a gun on both of them. Forced him down. Made Ruby watch. Then pulled the trigger."

The afternoon sun slanting through the office window seemed too bright suddenly, too cheerful for what we were discussing. Outside, I could hear Jimmy helping the customer with paint colors—something about eggshell versus cream—and the normalcy of it felt obscene.

"Ruby ran," Frank continued, and his voice had gone softer, almost reverent, as if he were honoring her final moments of defiance. "Made it maybe twenty feet toward the tree line before the killer caught her. The sand showed everything—where she'd been dragged back, where she'd fought. And God, she fought hard. The beating came first. We found blood on the sand where her face had hit, where ribs had cracked under someone's fists or feet. Defensive wounds on her hands and arms where she'd tried to protect herself from blows that kept coming."

Dottie had gone very still beside me, her medical examiner brain already cataloguing the violence, understanding exactly what Frank was describing in ways I hoped I never would.

"Three gunshots to the chest," Frank said. "But here's the thing that stayed with me, that still keeps me up some nights when I can't stop thinking about it—even after the first two bullets hit, she was still trying to crawl away. The drag marks in the sand showed her fingers clawing at the ground, trying to pull herself toward the trees, toward anywhere that wasn't there. And then the killer pushed her onto her back and shot her a third time point-blank."

The silence that followed felt heavy as wet sand, pressing down on us with the weight of Ruby Bailey's last terrified moments.

"Then someone moved them both," Frank continued, his jaw working as if he were chewing on words too bitter to swallow. "Dragged Pickering's body from near his car, dragged Ruby's from where she'd fallen by the tree line, positioned them in that embrace like they were lovers sleeping peacefully. Made something beautiful out of something brutal. That's what Tommy couldn't get past—the deliberateness of it. The care someone took to arrange them just so, to create this tableau that told a story completely opposite from what had actually happened.

"Their clothes were neatly folded and placed on the back seat of Pickering's car—his shirt on bottom, then his pants, then her dress, then her undergarments on top. Stacked like laundry fresh from the dryer. That's not what happens when people are interrupted during sex. Clothes get tossed, scattered, left where they fall in the urgency of the moment. Someone took the time after they were dead to collect every piece of clothing, fold it carefully, stack it neatly. Making everything orderly except for the bodies themselves, except for the blood soaking into the sand, except for Ruby's mutilated face."

The office felt smaller suddenly, the air thicker, as if the past was pressing in on the present, demanding space it had been denied for too long.

"The tongue," Dottie said quietly, and something in her voice told Frank she knew exactly what he was about to say, had seen it herself on the autopsy table all those years ago.

Frank nodded slowly. "Tommy thought it was symbolic—silencing her even in death. Making sure everyone knew this wasn't just about murder. This was about punishment for speaking, for knowing, for saying something someone couldn't allow to be said."

"What about the footprints?" I asked, pulling us back to evidence, to things that might still matter decades later.

"Small ones. Women's shoes, maybe a size six or seven. They go back and forth, like she was pacing, and then toward Pickering's vehicle before eventually heading toward the road." Frank's hands clenched into fists on his desk. "Tommy thought whoever left those prints had come after the murders, not during. The prints were on top of the disturbed sand, on top of the drag marks. Someone came to see what had been done, or maybe to make sure it was done right. But Milton shut down any investigation into them. Said we didn't have the budget for that kind of forensic work, that footprints in sand weren't reliable evidence anyway. By the next morning, someone had been out there with a rake, smoothed over the entire area. Every print gone. Every piece of evidence that might have pointed somewhere uncomfortable just…erased."

"And Milton's official story?" I asked.

Frank's jaw tightened. "Milton didn't have a story—not one that made sense anyway. He let three different people confess over the next week. Three completely different versions of what happened, all of them knowing details that hadn't been made public. Tommy thought Milton was feeding them information, coaching them through confessions so he could appear to be solving the case while actually making sure it stayed buried. All three recanted within days, claimed coercion. By then the evidence trail was so muddied that nobody knew what was real anymore. Which was exactly what Milton wanted. Just like any high-profile case with Milton, if there was money to be made on his end, then he found a way."

"But you didn't believe the discrepancies," Dottie said.

"Tommy didn't." Frank's voice carried shame and admiration in equal measure. "I went along with it—I went along with it because I had a mortgage and a wife and twin baby daughters. But Tommy kept digging even after Milton told him to stop. He documented everything—took photographs before Milton could confiscate them, made copies of evidence, tracked down witnesses and recorded their statements properly."

"And Milton buried all of it," I said.

"Everything that mattered. Tommy made copies of everything—three sets, because he wasn't stupid and he'd learned by then that evidence had a way of disappearing when it pointed in directions Milton didn't want to go. Photographs from the crime scene, witness statements, financial records someone at the church slipped him showing discrepancies in the building fund."

"Where are those copies now?" Dottie asked.

"Safe. Not here—I'm not fool enough to keep something like that where it could be found. But I've got them." Frank's jaw tightened. "I can mail them to you. Everything Tommy documented, everything he couldn't get anyone to listen to."

"What did Tommy think happened?" I asked. "Who did he think killed them?"

"Tommy didn't have answers, just questions that kept multiplying. Every time he found something, it led somewhere Milton wouldn't let him follow. Elder Crenshaw's name kept coming up—he'd been seen arguing with Ruby Bailey in the Piggly Wiggly parking lot about a week before she died. Public enough that people noticed, remembered. Tommy wanted to question him formally, but Milton shut it down. Said we couldn't harass respected members of the community without solid evidence."

Michael had mentioned seeing Crenshaw argue with his mother at their house, but a public confrontation at the Piggly Wiggly? That suggested the tension between them had been escalating, becoming less careful about who witnessed it.

"So Milton protected Crenshaw," Dottie said.

"Milton protected whoever had enough money or power to make

the investigation disappear." Frank's voice had gone flat. "A week after Tommy tried to push forward with Crenshaw, his house was broken into. Nothing stolen—TV, stereo, his wife's jewelry all still there. But his home office was ransacked. Every file, every note he'd made about the case, gone. He'd been wise to make copies and send a set to me."

The afternoon sun slanting through the window seemed too bright suddenly for what we were discussing.

"That's when I knew this wasn't just Milton being corrupt," Frank continued. "Someone was actively cleaning up, making sure no evidence survived."

"Is that when you quit?" I asked.

"Two months later. Told my wife I couldn't do it anymore, couldn't be part of a system that cared more about protecting criminals than finding justice." He stood, moving to the window. "Tommy stayed. Kept hoping someone would eventually listen. But it ate him alive— the guilt, the frustration. He died young, and I know that case is part of what killed him."

Frank turned back to face us.

"Milton's in prison now. Some of the people who had power back then are dead or too old to matter. Maybe the truth can finally come out." He paused. "But I need you to promise something—you don't mention my name. As far as anyone knows, you found this through your own investigation. I've built a good life here. I'd like to keep it that way."

"We promise," Dottie said.

"I'll mail you everything tomorrow—Tommy's notes, photographs, copies of financial records. Everything he documented that Milton buried." His jaw tightened. "Once it's in your hands, I'm done. I've carried this long enough."

We thanked him and made our way back through the store, past Jimmy still helping customers with paint selections. Outside, the afternoon heat wrapped around us like wet wool, making the air thick enough to taste.

"Where's Hank?" Dottie asked immediately, her head swiveling to scan Bay Street. "He should have come inside by now. It's been at least twenty minutes."

I pulled out my phone and called him. It rang once, twice, three times, then went to voicemail.

"He's not answering," I said.

"Maybe he couldn't find parking close enough and decided to wait in the car?" Dottie suggested, but her voice held doubt. "You know how he is about walking too far in this heat with his back."

We started toward the municipal lot where he'd been headed, our pace quickening with each step. The Tuesday afternoon crowd seemed to part around us as if sensing our urgency—tourists window-shopping, families with strollers, people moving with the leisurely pace of those who had nowhere important to be.

I tried calling again. Straight to voicemail this time, as if the phone had been turned off or died.

"Something's wrong," Dottie said, and there was an edge to her voice I'd never heard before—fear, raw and unfiltered.

We were nearly running now, dodging pedestrians and ignoring the annoyed looks from people we brushed past. The parking lot appeared ahead, cars glinting in the sun like rows of metal soldiers standing at attention.

"There," Dottie said, pointing with a trembling hand. "That's his car."

The powder-blue Buick sat at the far end of the lot, positioned perfectly between white lines in a spot that offered good visibility and easy exit—exactly the kind of spot Hank would choose after careful deliberation. But something about its stillness made my breath catch in my throat, made every instinct I had scream that something was terribly, horribly wrong.

We ran the last fifty feet, our footsteps echoing against the pavement. As we got closer, I could see through the driver's side window, and the world seemed to tilt sideways.

Hank was slumped over the steering wheel, his body twisted at an angle that no conscious person would maintain. His arms hung limp at his sides like broken puppet strings. His fishing vest with its seventeen carefully organized pockets was rumpled, pulled askew. And his head was bent forward at an angle that made my stomach drop to my feet.

"Oh God," Dottie breathed beside me, and then louder, desperate, "Hank. HANK!"

She lunged for the door handle, wrenching it open with strength born of desperation. The door swung wide and Hank's arm fell limply to the side, dangling in the space between the car and the pavement.

"Hank!" Dottie's hands went to his neck, searching for a pulse, as she'd done with hundreds of other patients. But those were other people's bodies, strangers whose deaths she could catalog clinically. Not this. Not him.

I leaned in, trying to see if his chest was moving, if there was any sign of breathing. His skin had a grayish pallor that made my stomach clench with fear.

"Is he—" I couldn't finish the question.

Dottie's fingers pressed against his throat, searching, her face a mask of concentration that couldn't quite hide the terror underneath. The seconds stretched like hours.

"Call 911," she said, her voice barely above a whisper. "Now, Mabel. Call them now."

THE PARAMEDICS MOVED WITH PRACTICED EFFICIENCY that somehow made everything feel both more and less real—hands checking pulse points, voices calling out vitals in medical shorthand, the snap of a gurney being deployed from the ambulance that had arrived with sirens that still echoed in my ears like tinnitus.

I stood frozen three feet from the Buick's open door, my phone still clutched in my hand though I couldn't remember who I'd called or what I'd said. The afternoon sun painted everything in shades too bright, too cheerful for what was happening—Hank's limp form being transferred from driver's seat to backboard with movements that looked choreographed, rehearsed, the kind of thing you did so often it became muscle memory instead of emergency.

"Ma'am, we need you to step back." The paramedic—young, efficient, kind eyed—was already working on Hank, checking his airway, his pupils, the wound at the back of his head that had bled through his thinning hair and soaked into his collar.

Dottie hadn't moved. She stood at the driver's side door with both hands pressed to her mouth, and I'd never seen her look like this—shaken, terrified, stripped of every ounce of the clinical detachment she wore like armor. Her cat-eye glasses sat crooked on her face, and mascara had started tracking down her cheeks in dark rivulets she didn't seem to notice or care about.

"Dottie," I said, touching her arm. "Dottie, they need space."

She flinched like I'd struck her, then seemed to come back to herself. "I'm a doctor. Retired medical examiner. I need to know his condition."

The paramedic glanced up, recognition flickering across his face. "Dr. Simmons? I heard you speak at a conference in Charleston about ten years ago. Forensic pathology and decomposition patterns." He returned his attention to Hank, fingers on his neck checking pulse. "Pulse is steady at seventy-two. Responsive to pain stimuli but not conscious. Significant trauma to the occipital region—looks like blunt force, probably something heavy. We're taking him to Charleston Medical Center—closest trauma facility with neurosurgery on call."

"I'm coming with him." Dottie's voice brooked no argument.

"Are you family?"

"I'm whatever I need to be to stay with him." The medical professional was emerging from beneath the terrified woman. "And I know what questions you need to ask that he can't answer right now. When did the attack occur, any history of anticoagulant use, allergies to medication, pre-existing conditions that might complicate treatment. I can give you all of that."

The paramedic made a decision. "Get in."

The doors closed with mechanical finality, and then they were pulling away, lights flashing but sirens mercifully silent now that the emergency had been stabilized into something manageable.

"Mabel." A hand on my shoulder, gentle but insistent. "Mrs. McCoy, breathe."

I turned to find Frank Holloway standing beside me, his earnest face creased with concern and something that looked like guilt had someone taken a chisel to it and carved the emotion into permanent lines. He must have heard the sirens, must have come out to see what chaos had erupted in the parking lot on an otherwise ordinary Tuesday afternoon.

"The man in the blue Buick. He's your friend? Is he—"

"Alive." The word came out thin, reedy, like it had traveled a long distance to reach my mouth. "They're taking him to Charleston Medical Center. Someone hit him." My voice sounded like it was coming from somewhere outside myself. "While we were inside talking to you, someone attacked him in broad daylight in a public parking lot."

Frank's face went through a series of transformations—pale to flushed, shock to anger, all of it settling finally into something that looked like shame wearing an overcoat of fury. "This is my fault. I should have known—should have warned you that asking questions about this case after all these years might—" He stopped, unable or unwilling to finish the sentence.

Might get someone hurt. Might get someone killed. Might wake something that had been sleeping peacefully in the dark for four decades and preferred to stay there, undisturbed, anonymous, safe.

A Beaufort police officer was approaching the Buick now—young, professional, already pulling latex gloves from his belt. His partner stood near the rear bumper, photographing the broken taillight with the methodical attention of someone documenting evidence that might matter or might mean nothing, but procedure demanded it be recorded either way.

"You need to get to the hospital," Frank said, and the decisiveness in his voice surprised me. This was the man who'd quit law enforcement rather than be complicit in Roy Milton's corruption, who'd spent forty years running a hardware store in quiet anonymity. But underneath that mild exterior lived someone who'd once believed in justice enough to walk away from a career when justice became impossible.

"I can't." I gestured at the Buick, at the police who were now dusting the door handle for fingerprints, their movements careful and practiced. "That's our only vehicle, and I can't exactly drive it away while they're processing it. I'll have to call someone to—"

"I'll drive you." Not an offer. A statement of fact. "It's forty-five minutes to Charleston. And I can swing by my house on the way— grab Tommy's files. You'll need them sooner rather than later, and waiting on the mail seems like giving whoever did this time to regroup."

"Frank, you don't have to—"

"Yes, I do." His jaw set with unexpected stubbornness, transforming his earnest face into something harder, more determined. "Tommy died thinking this case would never be solved. Your friend is in the hospital because someone wants to keep it that way. I've kept quiet for forty years, and I'm done with quiet. The least I can do now is drive you to Charleston."

An officer approached us, notepad in hand, his young face carrying that particular earnest concern of someone new enough to the job that every incident still felt like a personal failing rather than just another Tuesday afternoon going wrong.

"Officer Turk," Frank said, the greeting carrying the easy recognition of small-town familiarity—the way everyone knew everyone else's business without needing formal introductions, the way a hardware store owner and a cop would have crossed paths a hundred times at the grocery store or the gas station or anywhere else people went about the business of living.

"How's it going, Frank?" he asked.

"Going okay. How's your mom doing? She any better?"

"Still sore, but she's going to be all right. Can't say the same about her car. Guy plowed right into the back of her. On his cell phone and never looked up."

"That's a shame," Frank said, shaking his head in disgust. "Coulda killed someone. I'm glad she's okay. This is Mabel McCoy. She's friends with the man who was hurt."

Turk turned to me, pen hovering over his notepad. "Ma'am, do you know what happened here? Did you see anything?"

"No. I was inside the hardware store with my friend Dottie." The words came out steadier than I felt. "When we came back to the parking lot, we found Hank unconscious in his vehicle."

Turk made a note in handwriting too small to read from where I stood. "And Dottie is—"

"With the victim in the ambulance," Frank supplied. "On the way to Charleston Medical Center. I offered to take Mrs. McCoy there now so she can be with her people."

"I'm sorry about your friend," Turk said. "Crime in this area is rare. And if someone had seen something they'd come forward. Probably just a transient looking for money. We'll follow up with your friend at the hospital. See if he remembers anything."

Frank led me toward his truck that was parked behind the hardware store. It was an older Ford F-150, forest green, with the kind of respectful wear that came from years of actual use rather than neglect. The interior smelled like sawdust, coffee gone cold in the cup holder, and something else I couldn't quite identify but found oddly comforting—maybe pine tar, maybe just the accumulated scent of someone who worked with his hands and didn't apologize for it.

He drove with the careful attention of someone who'd learned that rushing led to accidents and accidents led to consequences. Checked his mirrors, used his turn signals even when no other cars were visible, kept both hands at ten and two on the steering wheel like he'd been taught in driver's education and never quite let go of the lesson.

We rode in silence for several miles, the landscape shifting from Beaufort's historic district to marsh and pine forest, the late afternoon sun painting everything in shades that made me think of amber and honey and all the sweet things that could turn bitter if left too long in the heat.

My phone buzzed. Dash.

Where are you? Dottie called from the ambulance. Said someone attacked Hank.

I typed back with trembling fingers—*Frank Holloway is driving me to Charleston Medical. Hank was hit in the head in the parking lot while we were interviewing Frank. Police are examining the Buick.*

The response came so quickly he must have started typing before I finished. *I'm leaving now. Don't go anywhere alone. Stay in public spaces with witnesses.*

I stared at that last sentence—*don't go anywhere alone*—while sitting in a truck with a man I'd met less than an hour ago. A man who'd quit the sheriff's department under circumstances that could mean principled stand or guilty conscience. A man who knew we were asking questions about a murder someone had just violently tried to stop us from investigating.

Frank Holloway, who was driving me to Charleston. Who knew exactly where I'd be for the next forty-five minutes. Who could take any exit, any turn, drive anywhere he wanted while I sat in his passenger seat with my phone and my assumptions about his good intentions.

My fingers hovered over the keyboard, and I realized I was holding my breath.

Frank is getting Tommy Wheeler's evidence files. Bringing them directly to the hospital.

A longer pause this time, and I imagined Dash processing that information, recalculating timelines and priorities and probably the wisdom of letting me get into a vehicle with someone connected to a case where people were being attacked in parking lots.

Good. That's good. I'll be there in 45 minutes. Call me if anything feels wrong.

If anything feels wrong. As if wrong would announce itself politely, give me time to dial and explain before something terrible happened.

"Your sheriff," Frank observed, and something in his tone suggested he'd been aware of the texting even while keeping his eyes on the road. "He worries."

"He should worry." The words came out before I could stop them, sharper than I'd intended.

Frank's hands tightened fractionally on the steering wheel, then relaxed. "You're wondering if you made a mistake. Getting in a truck with a stranger. A stranger who used to be a cop, who quit under suspicious circumstances, who's connected to a case where someone just got their skull cracked for asking questions."

The fact that he'd said it out loud somehow made it both better and worse. "The thought crossed my mind."

"Smart." He took the turn onto Highway 21 with careful precision. "For what it's worth, I understand the concern. And I'm not offended by it. Caution keeps people alive." He paused. "My house is just up here. Five minutes. You can stay in the truck if you want—I'll leave the keys so you can drive away if you get nervous."

The offer surprised me with its matter-of-factness, its acknowledgment that my suspicion was reasonable rather than insulting. "You'd leave me your keys?"

"Rather that than have you sitting here terrified while I'm rummaging through closets for files." A ghost of a smile. "Besides, if I were planning something nefarious, I probably wouldn't announce my address and offer you the means to escape."

"Unless that's exactly what you'd do to seem trustworthy."

"Fair point." He pulled onto a gravel road, the truck crunching over stones. "Be back in a few minutes."

He disappeared inside, and I sat in his truck watching pine trees sway in the breeze, their branches moving like hands conducting music only they could hear. The afternoon was starting its slow decline toward evening, shadows lengthening across Frank's small yard, and I found myself thinking about all the places secrets could hide in plain sight.

A man running a hardware store in Beaufort. A blond nurse working in pediatrics. An elderly church elder in assisted living, his sins tucked away behind careful denials and the respectability that came from old family names and enough money to make people look the other way.

Forty years was long enough for everyone to believe they were safe. Long enough to build respectable lives on foundations of buried bodies and burned evidence. Long enough that the past should have stayed past, should have remained a story people told at dinner parties when the conversation turned to Grimm Island's scandals—*remember when that preacher was killed with his mistress? No one ever figured out who did it.*

Frank emerged from his house carrying a manila envelope so thick it had been reinforced with packing tape, the kind of precaution you took when you knew something was valuable enough to protect but fragile enough to fall apart under its own weight. The way he held it—carefully, reverently, like it was either a holy relic or a live grenade—told me everything I needed to know about what was inside.

He climbed back into the truck and set the envelope on the seat between us. It sat there like a third passenger, silent but present, heavy with more than just paper and ink.

"Everything Tommy documented," Frank said, starting the engine. "Crime-scene photos Milton claimed were lost. Witness statements that never made it into official reports. Financial records from the church. His personal notes about why he thought the investigation was being deliberately sabotaged." He pulled back onto the highway, heading toward Charleston. "Three copies originally. The one that got stolen from his house when someone broke in. One he mailed to a lawyer in Columbia. I figured the lawyer must have died because nothing came of that. And this one, that he gave me for safekeeping."

"Did you ever look through it?"

"Once. Right after Tommy died."

The landscape rolled past—marsh grass turning golden in the declining light, the occasional house on stilts rising from the wetlands like something from a fairy tale about people who'd learned to live with floods.

Charleston emerged on the horizon like a promise or a threat depending on your perspective—church steeples and bridge spans, the city spreading along the harbor with centuries of practice at being beautiful. We crossed the Ashley River as the sun dropped lower, painting the water in shades that made me think of fire and blood and all the things that looked lovely from a distance but burned when you got too close.

Charleston Medical Center announced itself with the visual grammar of hospitals everywhere—multiple buildings connected by covered walkways, parking garages stacked like concrete layer cakes, the emergency entrance marked with letters that glowed red even in daylight, demanding attention, promising help, suggesting that whatever brought you here was serious enough to require fluorescent lighting and people in scrubs.

Frank pulled up to the main entrance. "Go. I'll park and find you inside."

"You don't have to stay—"

"I'm staying." He said it quietly, almost apologetically. "At least until your sheriff arrives. Someone attacked your friend in broad daylight, and I—" He paused, seeming to search for the right words. "I'd feel better knowing you weren't alone until he gets here."

The automatic doors slid open with a pneumatic hiss that sounded like the hospital breathing out, and I stepped into air-conditioning aggressive enough to raise goose bumps on my arms despite the humid warmth I'd left behind. The lobby smelled like every hospital lobby I'd ever encountered—antiseptic trying to mask fear, coffee fighting a losing battle with institutional cleaning solution, wilting flowers in vases near the information desk where someone had left them as offering or apology or both.

The volunteer at the desk was elderly, kind faced, wearing a pink jacket that marked her as someone whose job was helping people find their way through the labyrinth. Her name tag read *Dorothy—20 Years of Service*, and she looked up at me with practiced sympathy that suggested she'd directed many worried people toward many trauma bays.

"I'm looking for Henry Hardeman," I said, surprised my voice came out steadier than I felt. "Brought in by ambulance not long ago."

She typed with two-finger precision, squinting at her computer screen through glasses that had slipped down her nose. "Emergency department, treatment bay four. Are you family?"

"Yes." I'd apologize to God for the lie later, but right now I needed to get to Hank.

"Through those doors, follow the blue line on the floor. Take a left at the nursing station. Bay four will be on your right." She printed out a visitor badge with my name in letters large enough to read from across a room.

The blue line on the floor led me through corridors that all looked identical—beige walls, motivational posters about hand-washing, the distant sound of monitors beeping in rhythms that meant something to people who spoke that particular language. I followed the line like Dorothy in Oz, except this yellow brick road led to trauma bays instead of emerald cities, and there was no wizard waiting at the end.

Dottie stood outside bay four with her arms wrapped around herself like she was physically holding her ribs together. She'd lost her cat-eye glasses somewhere—probably in the ambulance—and without them she looked diminished, older, as if the glasses had been holding up not just her vision but some essential part of her carefully constructed armor.

"Mabel." She straightened when she saw me, trying to pull herself together. "They won't let me in while they're doing the CT scan. Said I'm making everyone nervous hovering around."

I pulled her into a hug, felt her shake against me. "What did they say about his condition?"

"Someone hit him hard enough to crack his skull. They're checking to see if there's bleeding in his brain." Her voice wavered. "At his age, that's the real worry. Even a small bleed can turn into something serious."

"But he's alive."

"He's alive." She said it like a prayer.

The door to bay four opened and a doctor emerged—Asian, forties, wearing scrubs printed with cartoon dinosaurs. His name tag read *Dr. James Chen, Emergency Medicine*.

"Dr. Simmons," he said. "Your friend is stable. The CT showed a small subdural hematoma, but it's not expanding. We're monitoring closely, but I'm cautiously optimistic it won't require surgical intervention."

"Prognosis?" Dottie asked, her voice steady.

"Guarded but good. Responsive to stimuli, pupils equal and reactive. We're keeping him sedated for the next twelve to twenty-four hours to prevent agitation." He paused. "At his age, recovery will be slower. There may be lingering effects—headaches, confusion, memory issues related to the incident. But barring complications, I expect full recovery."

The tension in Dottie's shoulders released fractionally. "Can I see him?"

"Briefly. He's not conscious, but you can sit with him." Dr. Chen's expression softened. "Head wounds bleed extensively. The paramedics cleaned him up, but he looks worse than he is."

"I've seen worse," Dottie said, but her hand found mine and squeezed hard before she disappeared into the bay.

I watched through the small window as she approached the bed where Hank lay surrounded by monitors and IV lines. She stood there for a long moment just looking at him, then bent and pressed her lips to his forehead with such tenderness it made my throat tight.

"There's a waiting area on the second floor," Dr. Chen said. "Quieter. Dr. Simmons has your number—she'll call if there's any change."

Frank found me in the waiting area ten minutes later, still carrying the manila envelope. He looked uncomfortable in the way people did when they ventured into hospitals for reasons other than their own medical care.

"Any news?" he asked.

"Stable. Small brain bleed but not expanding." I gestured to the chair across from me. "They're keeping him sedated."

Frank settled into the chair, the envelope balanced on his lap. He held it carefully, like it might catch fire if he wasn't vigilant. "I should probably leave this with you and go. Let you handle things."

"Thank you," I said. "For everything. For driving me here, for trusting us with Tommy's evidence."

"Thank Tommy." He set the envelope on the table between us. "He's the one who documented the truth when everyone else was looking away." He stood, hesitated. "Be careful. People who've kept secrets this long won't give them up easily."

After he left, I sat alone in the waiting area with the envelope on the table. I didn't open it. Somehow spreading crime-scene photographs across a hospital coffee table felt wrong—disrespectful to Ruby Bailey and George Pickering, disrespectful to Hank lying sedated in a trauma bay because someone wanted these secrets to stay buried.

My phone buzzed. Walt.

Bea and I are en route. Deidre is closing the library early. ETA 40 minutes.

I sent back: *Hank is stable. Dottie is with him.*

Good. We're bringing food. Hospital cafeteria is inedible.

Footsteps echoed in the hallway—rapid, purposeful. Dash appeared in the doorway, and his eyes found mine immediately, catalogued that I was whole and unharmed, and some of the tension in his shoulders released.

He crossed the room and pulled me into his arms—brief, fierce, more telling than words. "You're okay."

"I'm fine. Hank's stable." I pulled back enough to gesture at the envelope. "And Frank brought Tommy Wheeler's evidence. Everything Milton buried."

Dash settled into the chair beside me, his hand finding mine. "We'll go through it. But not here."

"Agreed."

We sat in silence for a moment, his thumb tracing circles on my palm—a gesture that had become familiar over the past weeks, grounding.

The door opened and Dottie appeared, looking steadier now that she'd seen Hank breathing. "He looks terrible. Like someone tried to cave in his skull, which I suppose someone did. But his vitals are stable and Dr. Chen seems competent."

She settled into a chair, finally noticing the envelope on the table. "Is that—"

"Tommy Wheeler's files," Dash confirmed.

"We should—" Dottie started, then stopped. "No. Not here. This deserves better than a hospital waiting room."

"After we talk to Stephanie Donaldson," Dash said.

He pulled out his phone, made a call. We could hear his half of the conversation—Sheriff Beckett, badge number, requesting staff information for an active investigation. Professional, clipped, the voice of someone who expected cooperation and usually got it.

He hung up a minute later. "Stephanie Donaldson works in the pediatric ward here. Three days a week including Tuesdays. She's scheduled until 7 tonight—still has another hour on her shift." He looked at his watch. "If we're going to talk to her, we do it now before she leaves for the day."

The revelation settled over us. We were in the same building as the woman who might have killed Ruby Bailey and George Pickering.

"I'm coming with you," I said, picking up Frank Holloway's file.

Dash nodded. "Let's go."

The elevator to the third floor moved with the grinding reluctance of machinery that had seen better decades and resented being reminded of them. A small sign near the buttons announced that scheduled maintenance was planned for next month, which—based on the groaning sounds the elevator made—seemed optimistic bordering on delusional.

The pediatric ward announced itself before we'd even stepped off the elevator. Cheerful in the aggressive way that only spaces designed for sick children could be—primary colors splashed across walls, cartoon animals wearing stethoscopes and displaying improbable joy about medical procedures. A giraffe near the nurse's station was demonstrating proper hand-washing technique with a grin that suggested it had never actually encountered germs in its life.

The corridor stretched ahead of us, lined with more murals— elephants juggling medicine bottles, lions taking temperatures, a rhinoceros that appeared to be explaining the food pyramid to a group of zebras. The absurdity of it pressed against the seriousness of why we were here, making everything feel slightly tilted, off-balance.

Office 312 sat at the end of the hallway, its door partially open. Through the gap I could see a woman at a desk—blond hair that had gone silver at the temples in that expensive way that required either excellent genes or an excellent colorist, wearing scrubs printed with teddy bears holding balloons. She was bent over paperwork, pen moving in quick, efficient strokes that suggested decades of practice at documentation.

Dash knocked—not aggressive, just firm enough to announce intent.

"Yes?" She looked up with the harried impatience of someone trying to finish paperwork before shift change, her pen still poised over whatever form she'd been completing. "Can I help you with something? I've only got about twenty minutes before I need to be out on the floor."

"Stephanie Donaldson?" Dash kept his voice neutral, professional.

"That's me." She set down her pen with a slight edge of annoyance—not rude exactly, just the briskness of someone whose time was limited and who dealt with interruptions constantly. "Is this about one of my patients? Because if it's a CPS issue, you'll need to coordinate with—"

"I'm Sheriff Dashiell Beckett from Grimm Island. This is Mabel McCoy. We're following up on an old case, and we were hoping you might be able to answer a few questions."

The shift was subtle but immediate. Her shoulders went from busy-nurse posture to something more guarded. "An old case." The words came out careful, measured. "I'm not sure how I could help with anything from Grimm Island. I haven't lived there in years."

"But you did live there in 1985," I said, watching her face.

Her hand, which had been resting on the desk, curled slowly into a fist. "Sure. I'd just finished nursing school and was living with my parents to save money. That was all a long time ago."

"Tell me about Ruby Bailey," Dash said, as if he were simply mentioning the weather. "And George Pickering."

The pen she'd set down rolled off the desk and clattered to the floor with a sound that seemed far too loud. Neither of us moved to pick it up. Stephanie's face had gone the color of hospital walls—that particular shade of beige that wasn't quite white but wasn't quite anything else, just the absence of healthy color.

"I—" She swallowed, her throat working visibly. "That was a terrible thing. Everyone on the island was shocked."

"You knew them," I said. Not a question.

"Everyone knew about them." She'd found her footing slightly, though her knuckles were white where she gripped the edge of her desk. "The affair was the scandal of the year. You couldn't go to the grocery store without hearing about it."

"But you knew them personally," Dash clarified. "You were a nurse at Charleston Medical in 1985. You were dating Matthias Crenshaw Jr., whose father was Elder Crenshaw—on the church board with Reverend Pickering. You got a front row seat to the scandal."

"It's not like they tried to hide it." Each word was coming out more clipped now, more defensive. "Matt's father was very involved in the church. The whole situation with Reverend Pickering was embarrassing for the family. But I didn't know either of them on a personal level."

"Where were you the night of September 15, 1985?" Dash asked.

"At work." Too quick, too practiced. "I worked the evening shift at Charleston Medical. 7 to 3 a.m."

"Can you prove that?"

Her jaw tightened. "It was forty years ago. I don't exactly keep my timesheets from 1985. But yes, I was at work. I remember because everyone was talking the next day about what had happened."

"A witness reported seeing a blond woman in a nurse's uniform at Turtle Point that night," I said, keeping my voice gentle. "Around 9 p.m. The woman was arguing with Reverend Pickering near his car."

Stephanie's face did something complicated—a series of micro-expressions that cycled through too quickly to identify individually but left an overall impression of panic poorly suppressed. "Then your witness is mistaken. Or saw someone else. There are lots of blond nurses."

"In 1985, you drove a white sedan," Dash continued. "A Honda Accord, according to DMV records."

"So did half the nurses at the hospital. White was a popular color." But she'd stood now, her chair rolling backward and hitting the wall with a thud. "Look, I don't know what you think you're investigating here, but I had nothing to do with what happened to those people. I was at work. I didn't even find out about it until the next day when it was all over the news."

"What do you remember about that day?" I asked. "When you found out?"

"I remember thinking it was horrible. That Ruby Bailey had a young son who'd just lost his mother. That Reverend Pickering's wife and children must have been devastated." She crossed her arms over her chest, a defensive posture that made her look smaller. "I remember Matt's father being upset because it reflected badly on the church, and Matt saying we should stay out of it, that it was none of our business."

"Elder Crenshaw was very concerned about the scandal," Dash observed. "About what it would do to the church's reputation. To his son's future."

"Everyone was concerned. It was a mess." Stephanie had started to pace now, small movements behind her desk like a caged animal testing the boundaries of its enclosure. "But being concerned about a scandal isn't a crime."

"No," Dash agreed. "But murder is."

She stopped pacing. "I didn't murder anyone."

"We didn't say you did," I pointed out gently. "We're just trying to understand what happened that night. Two people died, Ms. Donaldson. Two people whose deaths were never properly investigated because the sheriff at the time was corrupt. Surely you can understand why we need to ask these questions."

"I understand that you're harassing me at my workplace based on some witness who maybe saw someone who maybe looked like me forty years ago." Her voice had gained strength now, indignation replacing fear. "I understand that you're implying things without evidence. And I understand that I don't have to stand here and listen to it."

"You're right," Dash said evenly. "You don't. But we're going to keep investigating. We're going to keep asking questions. And eventually we're going to figure out what really happened that night. So if there's anything you want to tell us now—anything that might help us understand—this would be a good time. Because even if you didn't kill them, but have information that could help us with this case and don't share it, I won't hesitate to charge you with obstruction. There's no statute of limitations on a murder investigation."

Stephanie moved to her desk, pulled open a drawer, and extracted a business card. "This is my attorney. If you have any further questions, you can direct them to her. I'm not saying another word without legal counsel present."

She held out the card and Dash took it, reading the name with no visible reaction. Then he pulled out his own card and set it on her desk.

"When you're ready to tell us the truth," he said quietly, "Call me. Ruby Bailey deserves justice. Don't you think so?"

"I think Ruby Bailey made her own choices and those choices had consequences," Stephanie said, and there was something bitter in her voice now, something that had been fermenting for decades. "I think she knew exactly what she was doing when she started that affair. And I think trying to dig up the past forty years later doesn't change anything except to hurt people who've moved on with their lives."

"Have you moved on?" I asked, surprising myself. "Because you seem pretty upset for someone who's moved on."

Her eyes met mine then, and for just a moment I saw past the defensive nurse in teddy bear scrubs to something rawer underneath. Anger, maybe. Or grief. Or guilt that had been wearing the mask of righteousness for so long it had forgotten which was which.

"I think you should leave now," she said quietly.

We left her standing behind her desk, arms still crossed, looking smaller and older than when we'd arrived. The cheerful animals in the corridor seemed to mock us as we walked back to the elevator—all those impossible smiles, all that aggressive joy painted over the reality of sick children and dying patients and secrets that wouldn't stay buried no matter how deep you dug the grave.

The elevator doors closed behind us, and I found myself humming without quite meaning to—a few bars of "Gloomy Sunday."

"Death is not dream, for in death I'm caressin' you..."

The words seemed appropriate given how thoroughly Stephanie had tried to bury the past and how determined we were to dig it back up.

"She fits the description," I said finally. "Blond nurse, white sedan, connected to the church through Crenshaw. But we can't prove she was actually there."

"Not yet," Dash said. "But she's hiding something."

"We need to go through Pickering's journal again," I said, the idea taking shape as I spoke. "More carefully this time. Look for entries that might connect to Stephanie even if her name isn't mentioned directly."

Dash's expression sharpened. "That's a good idea. We need to look at it from the angle of who might *not* be mentioned. It's rare that people sin alone."

I watched the floor numbers descend. "Pickering documented everything people told him. If Stephanie was involved in something worth hiding—an affair, the embezzlement, anything—there might be an entry."

Dash nodded, his brow narrowed in thought. "We were looking for Ruby and George and Elder Crenshaw in that journal. We weren't looking for Stephanie because we didn't know she was connected yet."

The elevator deposited us back on the second floor, and before the doors had fully opened, Bea's voice carried across the waiting area.

"Well? Did she crack like an egg or clam up like a—well, like a clam?"

She was perched on the edge of her chair, her silk caftan pooled around her like she was holding court, phone in one hand and what appeared to be a half-eaten sandwich in the other.

Walt sat across from her with his notebook open, pen poised, looking every inch the judge waiting for testimony. Deidre had commandeered an entire row of seats and spread what looked like several decades worth of church bulletins across them in some organizational system only she understood.

"Told us to talk to her lawyer," Dash said, settling into a chair with weariness.

"Well, fiddlesticks and molasses." Walt made a note with more force than necessary. "Though I can't say I'm surprised. Anyone with half a brain lawyers up these days, guilty or innocent."

"Where's Dottie?" I asked, suddenly noticing her absence.

"Back with Hank," Deidre said. "She won't leave his side. Said she'd stay there even if he's unconscious, just in case he wakes up confused and needs a familiar face."

"I'm just glad they're not sneaking around anymore," Bea said, staring down at her nails. "Secret affairs are fun for a time, but it's never long before someone catches you copping a feel in a storeroom."

"Hmm," I said, wondering how long Bea had known about Hank and Dottie. She'd made a living uncovering people's secrets.

"So what did Stephanie say before she lawyered up?" Deidre asked.

"That she was at work that night," I said. "That she knew about the affair because everyone did. That she didn't know Ruby or George well, just knew of them through Matt's father being on the church board."

"But she fits the description," Dash added. "Blond nurse, worked at Charleston Medical, drove a white sedan. Everything matches what Elsie Crawford told us about the woman at Turtle Point."

"Matching a description isn't proof," Walt said, ever the pragmatist. "Not after forty years."

"No," I agreed. "But she was scared. Not just annoyed at being questioned—actually frightened. She denied being at Turtle Point, claimed she was at work, but she couldn't meet our eyes when she said it."

"So what's next?" Bea asked, setting down her sandwich.

"We need to go through Pickering's journal again," Dash said. "Look deeper at the entries and the sins committed."

"And Michael Bailey," I added. "We're going to his house to look through the box of his mother's belongings. He said his grandparents gave it to him after the funeral but he's never opened it. Could be letters, photographs, personal items—anything that might tell us what Ruby knew or who she was afraid of."

"It's getting late," Deidre observed, glancing at her watch. "Will he see you?"

I pulled out my phone and dialed Michael Bailey's number. He answered on the third ring.

"Mr. Bailey, it's Mabel McCoy. I know it's late, but we'd like to take you up on your offer—to look through that box of your mother's things. Would tonight work?"

A pause. "You found something?"

"We're following some new leads. And we think there might be something in your mother's belongings that could help—letters, maybe, or notes. Anything that might tell us what she knew."

"Come now," Michael said. "I'll be waiting."

Michael Bailey lived on the north end of Grimm Island, in one of the newer developments that had sprung up in the nineties when the bridge made commuting to Charleston feasible. Not the old-money estates on the water, but respectable—the kind of neighborhood where doctors and lawyers and successful business owners built comfortable lives. His house was a two-story Colonial with black shutters and a wide front porch, set back from the street with mature landscaping that suggested he'd been here awhile.

The front yard had been converted into a vegetable garden—tomatoes already staked despite it being only May, beans climbing up trellises, herbs growing in neat rows that suggested someone who found comfort in making things grow.

He answered the door in jeans and a button-down shirt, barefoot, looking more human than he had at the funeral home in his professional armor. His hair was slightly mussed, and he held a coffee mug that suggested he'd been settling in for a quiet evening before we'd called.

"Come in," he said, stepping aside. His living room was comfortable in an impersonal way—furniture chosen for durability rather than beauty, bookshelves lined with volumes about grief counseling and bereavement, everything neat and organized and slightly sterile. The home of someone who dealt with death professionally and didn't want it bleeding into his personal space.

"I have to admit," Michael said as we settled into chairs that were comfortable without being memorable, "when you called I hoped it meant good news. Progress."

"We've found some things," Dash said carefully. "Evidence that was buried by Sheriff Milton. We're following new leads that suggest your mother's murder might have been connected to problems with the church finances."

Michael's face went very still. "What kind of problems?"

"Money that went missing," I said carefully. "Your mother was cleaning houses for church board members. She might have overheard something, seen documents, figured out something she wasn't supposed to know."

"And someone killed her for it." Michael's voice had gone flat. "Not because of the affair, but because she knew too much."

"We don't know that for certain yet," Dash said. "But we're trying to piece it together. That's why we need to look through her belongings— see if she left any clues about what she knew or who she was afraid of."

"The box is in the attic. I've never opened it. Never wanted to." Michael stood abruptly. "I was ten when they gave it to me. Too young to know what to do with it. Then I just…kept putting it off. I've lived with the memory of her all this time, thinking that would be enough."

He disappeared up a narrow staircase, and we sat in his living room listening to footsteps overhead, the creak of floorboards, the sound of boxes being moved. The house itself felt watchful, as if it had absorbed decades of other people's grief through Michael's professional presence and learned to hold sorrow without judgment.

When he returned, he was carrying a cardboard box that had been reinforced with packing tape, the kind of precaution you took when something was too precious to risk falling apart. He set it on the coffee table with the careful reverence of someone handling relics.

"My grandparents said these were things Mama would want me to have someday," Michael said quietly. "Her Bible. Some photographs. Letters. I don't know what else."

Dash had pulled on latex gloves, and he cut through the packing tape with a pocketknife that looked like it had seen decades of use.

The box opened with a sigh, releasing the scent of lavender sachets and old paper, time preserved in cardboard.

Photographs came out first—Ruby Bailey young and beautiful, holding a baby who must have been Michael. Ruby in her choir robe looking solemn and proud. Ruby with other women, all dressed in their Sunday clothes, smiling for the camera.

"She was so young," Michael said, his voice rough. "Thirty-two. I forget that sometimes. She's been dead longer than she was alive."

Letters came next, tied with ribbon that had faded from what might once have been pink to the color of old bone. Dash untied the first bundle, unfolded the top letter with the care of someone handling evidence that might crumble.

My dearest Ruby,

I know we shouldn't be doing this. I know what we have is wrong in the eyes of God and the church and everyone who matters. But when I'm with you I can breathe. You make me remember who I wanted to be before I became what everyone expected.

George Pickering's handwriting—neat, careful, the script of someone who'd been taught penmanship in an era when it mattered. The words of a man caught between duty and desire, guilt and longing.

"Love letters," Michael said flatly. "From Reverend Pickering."

"Several dozen of them," Dash confirmed, setting the bundle aside carefully. "We'll need to go through these more thoroughly. May we take the box with us? We'll document everything and return it when we're done."

Michael nodded. "Take it. Take whatever you need. I don't want them back. I thought I was through being angry with her. Seeing all this makes me realize I'm not."

Dash continued working through the box methodically. More bundles of letters, all tied with that faded ribbon. A journal with a worn leather cover. Photographs of Ruby at different ages—some with baby Michael, others with people I didn't recognize. Everything carefully preserved, as if Ruby had been preparing for the day when someone might need to understand her life.

And then, tucked inside a Bible with a cover that had been handled so often the leather felt like cloth, Dash pulled out a bankbook.

Charleston Savings and Loan. Ruby Bailey's name in neat script across the front.

He opened it carefully, and I watched his expression shift as he scanned the entries. He turned it so I could see.

Monthly deposits going back three years. But these weren't the small amounts you'd expect from a housekeeper picking up extra jobs. Fifty dollars here, a hundred there, and then—starting in early 1985— several deposits of five hundred dollars. The final balance, dated September 10, 1985: $15,247.

"That's a lot of money," Michael said quietly, looking over our shoulders. "How did she—" He stopped, understanding dawning on his face. "The church funds."

"We don't know that," I said quickly, though the numbers were damning. A housekeeper in 1985 would have made maybe two hundred dollars a week if she was lucky. These deposits were far beyond what cleaning houses would earn.

"She was stealing from the church," Michael said, his voice hollow. "With Reverend Pickering. That's what this was about. Not just an affair—they were embezzling together and someone found out."

"Or someone was giving her money," Dash said carefully, still studying the bankbook. "Pickering could have been supporting her, helping her save up to leave. That doesn't necessarily mean she was involved in any theft."

But even as he said it, I could see the doubt in his expression. Large deposits, multiple times over several months—that was more than help. That was serious money.

At the bottom of the box, wrapped in tissue paper that had yellowed with age, was a photograph. I unfolded the tissue carefully.

A large group photo, maybe twenty people standing together outdoors with what looked like picnic tables in the background. The kind of photograph churches took at summer events—everyone arranged in rows, some sitting, some standing, all smiling at the camera. The colors had that faded, and several faces were slightly blurred from movement.

I turned it over. On the back, in neat handwriting—*First Methodist Church Picnic, July 4, 1985.*

"Church picnic," I said, studying the faces more carefully. Ruby Bailey stood near the back, her smile careful and composed. George Pickering was front and center, his arm around a woman who must have been his wife. And scattered throughout the group were other faces I didn't recognize.

"Who are you looking for?" Michael asked.

"Stephanie Chester," I said. "The woman we interviewed tonight. She claimed she barely knew your mother or Reverend Pickering, but if she was at church events…"

I scanned the faces more carefully—so many people, some in focus, some not. Then I spotted her. Third row, slightly to the left. A young blond woman standing between an older man and a younger man who looked enough like him to be his son.

"There," I said, pointing. "That's her. And I think that's Elder Matthias Crenshaw beside her, and his son on the other side."

"So she was at church events with them," Michael said quietly. "Along with everyone else in the congregation."

We carefully packed everything into the box—the letters still tied in their bundles, the bankbook, the church picnic photograph, the journal. Everything that might hold answers to what had happened that September night. Michael walked us to the door, watching as Dash carried the box to the car.

"I don't know what to hope for anymore," Michael said quietly. "That my mother was innocent and died for nothing? Or that she was guilty and got what thieves deserve?" He looked out at his vegetable garden, the tomatoes he'd staked so carefully. "Either way, she's still dead."

"Either way, she deserves the truth," I said.

He nodded slowly. "Call me when you know something. Good or bad, I want to know."

The drive back to my house took only ten minutes through streets that had gone quiet for the night. Porch lights glowed from the houses we passed, and somewhere in the distance I could hear the foghorn from the harbor. Ruby Bailey hadn't been the simple victim of a jealous crime of passion. She'd been tangled up in something—embezzlement or the appearance of it, money that looked stolen whether it was or wasn't, involved in complications that had gotten her killed.

"I'm coming in," Dash said. "Just for a few minutes. Need to make sure everything's secure."

I didn't argue. The day had been long enough, violent enough, complicated enough that having him check the windows and doors and alarm system felt less like overprotection and more like sensible precaution.

Inside, Chowder greeted us with the offended dignity of a dog who'd been left home during what was clearly an eventful day. Genevieve had dropped him off hours ago when she closed the shop, and she'd changed him into very dapper striped pajamas, but they were rumpled in a way that suggested he'd been napping.

"I know," I told him, scooping him up. "It was a long day for everyone."

He woofed softly and then padded to his doggy door and let himself into the backyard. Dash moved through the house with professional thoroughness—checking window locks, testing the alarm system, making sure nothing looked disturbed. Finally satisfied, he returned to the kitchen where I was making tea I didn't really want but needed something to do with my hands.

"Someone attacked Hank this afternoon," he said quietly. "In broad daylight in a public parking lot. It could have been plain bad luck. A random attacker. But it could also be because we're asking questions that are making someone very nervous."

"I know."

"I'm going to drive to Beaufort first thing in the morning and talk to the investigating officers. Maybe we can get some camera footage from a gas station or one of the businesses. It's a long shot, but I've had greater miracles happen in cases like this."

"This has been a long week," I said. "We've got a lot of information to go through. We've asked a lot of questions, and we don't have a lot of answers."

"And tomorrow we're going to keep asking them. Going to go through Tommy Wheeler's evidence, read through Ruby's letters, push harder on people who've kept secrets for decades." He leaned against the counter. "That makes you a target."

"Then I'm a target." I poured water over tea leaves, watched them unfurl in the heat. "Ruby Bailey was thirty-two years old when someone killed her. Beat her badly enough to break bones, then shot her three times. She deserves better than me backing down because I'm scared."

"I'm not asking you to back down." He crossed the kitchen, and his hands found my shoulders. "I'm asking you to be careful. To not take unnecessary risks. To remember that whoever did this is still out there, still has everything to lose if the truth comes out."

"I'll be careful," I said, turning to face him.

"Promise me."

"I promise."

We stood there in my kitchen, close enough that I could see the worry in his eyes, the way the day had worn on him too. Hank in the hospital. Stephanie's evasions. Michael Bailey's grief turning to anger as he learned his mother might have been a thief.

"I should go," Dash said finally, though his hands were still on my shoulders.

"Yes," I said, though I was reluctant to move out of his grasp.

He sighed and kissed me on the forehead. "Tomorrow."

"Tomorrow," I agreed.

Then he was gone, and I watched as his taillights disappeared down Harbor Street.

Inside, I locked the door, set the alarm, and carried my untouched tea upstairs with Chowder waddling behind me.

"It's just the thought of you…the very thought of you, my love."

I hadn't sung that song since Patrick died. There was something in it—some quality of longing made beautiful, of absence made into art —that pressed against my chest until I couldn't breathe. The kind of romantic ache that felt dangerous, like opening a door to a room you'd locked for good reason.

But tonight it had slipped out unbidden, humming itself into existence while I thought about locks being checked and alarms being set and the particular way Dash had looked at me in my kitchen. Not with Patrick's easy certainty—we'd known each other since childhood, had moved from friends to lovers with the inevitability of water finding its level. This was different. Careful. Deliberate. Two people choosing each other rather than simply recognizing what had always been there.

The song wound through my thoughts as sleep finally came, and for once the yearning in it didn't make me weep. It just made me wonder what tomorrow might bring.

CHAPTER
ELEVEN

Wednesday morning arrived wrapped in fog so thick the harbor disappeared entirely, leaving only the mournful call of the foghorn and the scent of salt marsh that crept through every crack and crevice of The Perfect Steep. I stood behind my counter, staring at a teapot I'd apparently been holding for the better part of five minutes without pouring a single cup, while Carly watched me with the expression of someone witnessing a slow-motion catastrophe.

"You're doing that thing again," she said.

"What thing?"

"That thing where you're physically present but your brain is somewhere else entirely. I'm going to assume you're solving murders in your head. 'Cause you're definitely not making tea." She gently extracted the pot from my grip. "Mrs. Hartwell has been waiting for her English Breakfast for ten minutes. She's started tapping her nails on the table. You know what that means."

I did know. Mrs. Hartwell's nail-tapping was the auditory equivalent of a countdown timer on a bomb.

The door swung open, and Walt appeared with a clipboard in one hand and a determined expression that hinted he was about to reorganize my entire life whether I liked it or not. Behind him came Bea in an emerald caftan that looked like it had been woven from peacock feathers and audacity, struggling slightly with a folding table. Deidre brought up the rear, her ever-present tote bag on one shoulder and what appeared to be a tactical planning board tucked under her arm.

"We're commandeering your back room," Walt announced, not bothering with preamble.

"I can see that," I said, watching as they maneuvered the table through the doorway with the kind of coordinated effort that suggested they'd planned this operation down to the last detail. "Good morning to you too."

"No time for pleasantries." Walt was already disappearing into the back room, the sound of furniture being rearranged with precision echoing through the doorway. "We've got a situation that requires immediate tactical response."

"A situation," I repeated.

"You," Bea said, pointing at me with one finger heavy with turquoise rings. "You're running yourself into the ground trying to run this shop and solve a murder. Both are full-time jobs. It's not sustainable, and frankly, watching you try is exhausting for the rest of us."

"I'm fine—"

"We're staging an intervention," Bea declared. "A hostile takeover, if you will. The Silver Sleuths are taking over tea shop operations. You're going full-time on the investigation."

I opened my mouth to protest, but Carly was already untying my apron. "They're right. You can't keep doing both. And honestly? I'd rather work with them than watch you set another batch of scones on fire."

"That was one time—"

"Yes, but it still smells like someone set a Christmas tree on fire."

I pursed my lips together, trying not to be insulted. I never burned things in the kitchen, and I wasn't a fan of what this slipup was doing to my reputation. Grace covered a lot of sins, but apparently not burning the scones.

"It was cinnamon scones," I said for lack of anything better in my defense. "And there are worse things than the smell of Christmas trees."

Carly muttered something under her breath and went to wait on a customer at the register.

The bell over the door chimed, and Dash walked in wearing his uniform and an expression that suggested he hadn't slept much better than I had. His gaze found mine immediately, something passing between us that felt too weighted for a Wednesday morning in a tea shop—concern, determination, and something else I wasn't ready to name.

"Tell me you have coffee," he said.

"This is a tea shop."

"Tell me you have something with enough caffeine to jump-start a corpse."

"I have a French press in the back for emergencies." I gestured toward the back room, where Walt's organizational sounds had reached a crescendo. "Though fair warning, it's become Silver Sleuth headquarters."

"Excellent." He headed toward the back, then paused, turning back with his hand on the doorframe. "You're not going to fight them on this, are you? The takeover?"

"So you're in on it too?" I asked, brow arched in question.

He just grinned. "You're a stubborn woman, Mabel McCoy. I don't know why I look forward to these moments."

Twenty minutes later, I stood in my own back room feeling like a stranger at my own party. The space had been transformed into something that looked like a cross between a war room and a particularly organized craft fair. The murder board now occupied the entire back wall, photographs and documents arranged with the kind of precision that suggested Walt had used a level and possibly a protractor. Tommy Wheeler's files spread across the folding table in neat stacks, each labeled with color-coded tabs. Even the lighting had been adjusted—a clip-on lamp now illuminated the center of the workspace with the intensity of an interrogation room.

Chowder had claimed the one armchair as his command post, wearing the yellow hoodie I'd dressed him in this morning—a casual choice that suggested he wasn't particularly invested in today's investigation. He watched the proceedings with half-lidded eyes.

"Dottie called from the hospital," Bea announced, consulting her phone. "Hank's children arrived about an hour ago. They'll stay with him through lunch, which gives Dottie time to work with us this morning."

"How is he?" I asked.

Walt's expression tightened in a way that said more than words. "Awake. Alert. Can't remember a blasted thing about Tuesday afternoon. The neurologist says the trauma wiped out everything from when he dropped you at the hardware store to when he woke up in the hospital. It's just gone."

"Convenient," Dash muttered, pouring himself coffee from the French press with the concentration of someone performing surgery. "For whoever hit him while he was looking for parking."

"Medically sound, though," Deidre added, pulling out her reading glasses. "Head trauma affects memory consolidation. It's not unusual for patients to lose hours or even days around the time of injury. Sometimes it comes back, sometimes it doesn't."

"We need to go through everything systematically," Walt said, tapping the murder board with a pointer he'd produced from somewhere. "No more reactive investigation. We're getting strategic."

Dash leaned against the wall, coffee cup in hand, that intense focus I was beginning to recognize settling over his features. "Agreed. The attack on Hank could be coincidence, but nothing was stolen from him. The car wasn't taken. If it's connected to the case, and I think it is, then someone's escalating. Which means we need to be smarter about how we move forward."

He pulled out his phone, scrolling through messages. "I heard back from the Beaufort investigators this morning. They pulled footage from every business with cameras in the area around the municipal parking lot where we found Hank."

"And?" Walt leaned forward, his coffee forgotten.

"Not much." Dash's frustration bled through each word. "The parking lot itself doesn't have cameras—budget cuts from two years ago. The restaurants along Bay Street have security, but their cameras face their own entrances and registers, not the street or parking areas. Best they got was footage from the bank on the corner—shows Hank's Buick driving past toward the lot around 2:47 p.m. yesterday, but the angle doesn't capture the lot itself."

"How convenient," Bea said, her voice sharp as glass. "The one afternoon someone gets beaten half to death in broad daylight, there's no footage of the actual attack."

"There's more," Dash continued, his jaw tight. "A clothing boutique two blocks over had a camera that captures part of the sidewalk. Around 3:10 p.m.—which fits our timeline for when the attack likely occurred—they picked up someone walking quickly away from the direction of the parking lot. Dark clothing, average height, but the angle's wrong and the image quality is poor. Can't make out features or even determine gender with certainty."

"So we've got nothing," Deidre said flatly.

"We've got timing," Dash replied. "Hank dropped you off at the hardware store around 2:45. You were inside with Frank for roughly twenty-five minutes. That gives us a window between 2:50 and 3:10 when someone attacked him in broad daylight in a public parking lot on a Tuesday afternoon."

"It was crowded too," I said, remembering the packed streets, the tourists, the families strolling Bay Street. "That's why he had to drop us off in the first place—there wasn't any street parking available."

"Which means someone either got very lucky," Walt said slowly, "or they knew exactly when and where to find him. Knew he'd be alone in that parking lot while you two were busy talking to Frank."

The implication hung in the air like smoke. Someone had been watching. Waiting.

"The Beaufort PD is treating it as assault with intent," Dash said.

"They're canvassing businesses, interviewing anyone who might have been in or near the lot during that time frame. But so far, no witnesses have come forward. The lunch crowd had thinned out by then, and most people were either inside shops or along the waterfront where the weather was nicer."

"Whoever did this picked their moment carefully," Deidre observed, her voice quiet but firm. "Knew when to strike, where the cameras weren't, how to make sure they couldn't be identified."

"And made absolutely certain Hank couldn't identify them," I added, thinking of his blank expression in the hospital, the way he kept repeating "the dates don't match" without remembering what dates or why it mattered. "The memory was stolen from him as efficiently as if someone had reached into his skull and plucked it out."

Walt's pointer tapped against his clipboard with sharp, staccato beats. "Then we operate under the assumption that whoever attacked Hank is connected to this case. And that means we're dealing with someone who's willing to hurt people to keep their secrets buried."

"Which means we need to be systematic," I said, moving to stand beside the board. The faces from the church picnic photograph stared back at me—dozens of people frozen in time on a July afternoon that was supposed to be about celebration, not murder. "Let's go through what we know for certain."

"Excellent idea," Walt said. "The facts don't lie. Victims—Reverend George Pickering and Ruby Bailey. Both killed September 15, 1985, at Turtle Point. Both shot. .38 caliber weapon never recovered."

"Both having an affair that was public knowledge by summer of '85," Deidre added, consulting her notes. "Though the affair itself started at least a year earlier, possibly longer, from witness accounts."

"So by the time that church photograph was taken at the July 4 picnic, the knowledge of their affair was well known," I said, shaking my head. "And everyone looks so happy in the photograph."

"The longer you live in life," Walt said, "the more you'll find that people don't like to upset the apple cart. Doing the right thing takes work. And there are a lot of people who think they want to do the right thing, but they don't want to put in the work. Work takes a toll on you, and your family."

Bea grunted and said, "Don't forget the missing money from the church. Money that disappeared between 1984 and early 1985, though the actual timeline of when it was taken is unclear."

"The church board closed the investigation after the murders," Deidre said, flipping through her notes. "Blamed the victims, moved on within weeks."

And here's where it gets interesting," Bea added, pulling out a folder with her characteristic flair. "I've been digging into what happened to the finance committee members after 1985. Elder Crenshaw bought waterfront property in 1986—cash purchase. He sold it a few years ago and made an easy million in profit. I found old permits Roger Hammond took out to renovate and restore his historic family home. He turned it into a bed-and-breakfast twenty years ago. And Gene Forsythe opened a sporting goods store on the mainland. All significant expenditures, all within two years of the murders."

"People come into money," Walt said, though his tone suggested he didn't believe his own words.

"Not in those amounts, not all at once, not all from the same church finance committee," Bea countered. "When multiple people from the same small group suddenly have cash to spend? That's not coincidence. That's embezzlement."

Walt nodded. "They all seemed to invest it wisely. They made profit from those investments."

"Easy to do when you're spending someone else's money," Dash said.

"Which brings us to motive." I studied the list of persons of interest, feeling that familiar itch between my shoulder blades that meant I was missing something obvious. "We've been operating under the assumption that this was a crime of passion—jealous spouse, outraged congregation member, someone who couldn't handle the scandal of the affair."

"But?" Walt prompted.

"But what if the affair was just convenient?" The idea had been forming slowly, pieces clicking together like a puzzle I'd been solving in my peripheral vision. "What if someone stole that money, and when suspicion started to fall on them, the affair provided perfect cover? Kill the lovers, frame them for the theft, let everyone believe it was about sin and shame when it was really about the money."

The bell chimed again, followed by a voice I recognized as Mr. Blackwood asking about the daily special. Carly's response involved the word "delightful" used three times in one sentence. The domestic normalcy of the tea shop felt surreal against the backdrop of what we were discussing—murder, theft, decades of lies.

"Let's talk about Tommy Wheeler," Dash said, pulling out a file folder thick with photocopied documents. "Retired cop, served under Milton, but according to everything I've found, he was one of the good ones. Kept trying to investigate things Milton buried."

"Including this case," I said. "His notes show he kept investigating even after Milton closed it, even when everyone else had moved on."

"He was building something," Walt added, spreading out pages covered in Tommy's handwriting. "Look at the dates on these notes—they span over a decade. 1986, 1989, 1993, picking up intensity in '96, '97, '98. He was chipping away at it whenever he could, interviewing people, digging through financial records. And here—" he pointed to a notation in Tommy's day planner, "—a meeting scheduled with FH for September 23, 1998. Three days later, Tommy's dead."

"Frank Holloway," I said. "Unless there's another FH involved in this case we don't know about."

Deidre pulled out a butterscotch candy, unwrapping it with deliberate slowness. "At this point, I don't believe in coincidences anymore. Tommy dies right before sharing what he found? That's not bad luck, that's murder."

"Can't prove it, though," Dash said. "I pulled the death certificate. Natural causes, signed off by the coroner at the time. No autopsy was done."

"Who was the coroner in 1998?" I asked.

"Dr. Vernon Keats," Dottie's voice came from the doorway, where she'd appeared like a perfectly timed stage entrance, still wearing her coat and carrying a travel mug. "He died in 2003. Liver failure. The man drank like Prohibition was coming back." She shrugged off her coat, revealing her signature cat-eye glasses and a mint-green cardigan. "He had a small practice here on the island for a while."

"I remember him," Deidre said. "Never went to him myself. He was a pill pusher."

Bea snorted. "Among other things."

"He was rarely sober," Dottie continued. "But for the island he was easy enough for the council to post as coroner. All he'd need to do is sign death certificates. Any death that showed obviously signs of foul play they'd send to me in Charleston."

"Right," Walt said finally. "So it's not out of the realm of possibility that Wheeler died not of his own volition. But we'll put a pin in that for another day. We can't solve all the world's problems."

"But we can solve this one," I said, pulling the manila folder closer. Tommy Wheeler's file—the one Frank had given us at the hospital. The edges were soft with age, corners bent from being handled over the decades. Someone—probably Tommy himself—had written *Pickering–Bailey* across the tab in blue ink that had faded to almost gray.

Inside were witness statements, crime-scene photos, autopsy reports we'd already seen, and notes in Tommy's cramped handwriting. But tucked into the back pocket of the folder was a smaller envelope, sealed and yellowed with time.

"What's that?" Deidre asked as I worked my finger under the flap. The old glue gave way with a sound like tearing silk.

Inside were deposit slips. Five of them, from Grimm Island Community Bank, dated between January and June of 1985. Each one showed a deposit to the "New Hope Recreation Center Building Fund" account. The amounts varied—$2,500, $3,200, $4,100, $5,000, $2,800.

"Look at the signature line," Walt said, leaning in close enough that I could smell the coffee on his breath.

Each slip was signed *G. Pickering* in the same neat script we'd seen in the journal. But something about the signatures looked off. Too perfect. Too uniform.

"These don't match his handwriting in the notebook," I said, comparing them to an open page of Pickering's journal that lay nearby. The journal entries had natural variation—some letters slanted more than others, the pressure varied with his mood. These signatures were identical, like they'd been traced.

"Forgeries," Dash said quietly.

Bea picked up one of the slips, holding it up to the light from the window. "The paper stock is right for the time period. The bank stamp is authentic—see how it's slightly off-center?"

"That was their style back then," Deidre said, adjusting her reading glasses to examine the slip more closely. "I remember because I helped with the church bookkeeping for several years in the eighties. Every deposit slip had that same off-center stamp. The teller—Mrs. Kowalski—had terrible aim with that thing, but she'd been at the bank since the fifties and nobody had the heart to correct her."

"So someone made these deposits using forged signatures," Dottie said. "Someone was stealing from the recreation center fund and making it look like Reverend Pickering was responsible."

"There's a note," I said, unfolding a piece of paper that had been tucked behind the deposit slips. Tommy's handwriting again, this time more hurried, the letters cramped together like he'd been writing fast.

Found these in evidence box marked Financial Records. Not part of official file. Sheriff Milton told me to lose them. Said case was closed and this would only muddy waters. But these don't match Pickering's known handwriting samples. Someone framed him. Need to verify signatures before I go to Milton again.

The note was dated October 3, 1985—just over two weeks after the murders.

"Tommy knew," Walt said, his voice rough. "He knew someone had framed Pickering."

"The question is," Dash said, "did Milton bury it because he was part of it, or because someone with more power told him to?"

I stared at the deposit slips, at those too-perfect signatures, and felt something cold settle in my stomach. Someone had been embezzling from the church building fund, using Reverend Pickering's name to cover their tracks. And when Pickering started asking questions about the missing records, when he threatened to go to the bank for copies, they'd killed him to keep him quiet.

"We need a handwriting expert," I said. "Someone who can prove these signatures are forged."

"And we need to go through Pickering's notebook again," Dash said. "See if he documented anything about discovering the embezzlement, about who might have had access to forge his signature."

"Financial records, building fund meetings—anything that connects to this," Walt added, already making notes with his characteristic precision.

"Or maybe whoever was stealing reported the records as missing themselves," Bea said quietly. "To cover their tracks when Pickering started asking questions."

I moved to the table where we'd spread out the church picnic photograph, the one from just two months before the murders. The original print from Michael Bailey's box had been faded and small, but Walt had worked some kind of technological magic after he'd scanned it into his laptop.

"My grandson showed me this trick," Walt said with obvious pride. "You scan the photograph, then use this program to sharpen the pixels and increase the resolution. Makes everything clearer. Brings out details you couldn't see in the small print." Walt adjusted his reading glasses as he studied the enlarged version.

"All right," he said, pulling out a notepad with the precision of someone about to catalog evidence. "Let's identify everyone we can. Between all of us, we should know most of these faces."

Bea leaned forward, her reading glasses catching the light. "Lord, look how young everyone was. That's Martha Hendricks in the front row—see the woman with the enormous hat? She always wore those things to outdoor events. Died of ovarian cancer, bless her. Her daughter married that awful man from Columbia who ran off with his receptionist."

"Betty Walters," Deidre said, pointing to a plump woman holding a paper plate piled high with food. "She made the best deviled eggs on the island. Brought them to every church function for thirty years. Her son is the one who opened that tackle shop on the pier."

"Roger Hammond." Walt indicated a man in the middle row with salt-and-pepper hair. "Died in a single-car accident on Highway 17. His widow Linda sold their house within six months and moved to Hilton Head. Never came back, not even for funerals of friends."

"He was on the finance committee," I said.

I studied Roger Hammond's face—pleasant enough, smiling at the camera, one hand resting on the shoulder of the woman beside him.

"That's Gene Forsythe next to him," Bea added, tapping a heavyset man with a thick mustache who stood with his arms crossed. "His grandson runs the sporting goods store now, but I heard he's looking to sell to developers for a bunch of condos."

"Who's that?" I pointed to a thin man with wire-rimmed glasses standing at the edge of the group, slightly apart from the others as if he'd been caught trying to leave the frame.

"Craig Baker," Walt said. "Accountant. We play dominoes together at the senior hall on Friday mornings. I was going to try and corner him there and see what he remembers about that time. He's sharp as a tack. And I'll know if he's lying to me. We play poker on Monday nights, and he's a terrible liar."

Deidre had moved on to another section of the photograph. "Oh, there's Patsy Jenkins and her husband James. Patsy made the best peach cobbler. James died of a heart attack about twenty years ago, and Patsy moved to Florida to be near her daughter."

"Stay focused, Dee," Walt said. "We don't need a society column report."

"I am focused," she protested. "I'm providing context. These are real people, not just names on a list."

She was right, of course. Even in the midst of a murder investigation, these were neighbors, fellow church members, people who'd brought deviled eggs and peach cobbler to picnics. People who'd raised children and paid mortgages and lived entire lives on this island.

"There," I said, pointing to a young man in the back row with dark hair and an earnest expression. "Who's that? He looks kind of familiar."

Dottie leaned closer. "That's Douglas Sutton. He would've been—what, early twenties in this picture? He came to Grimm Island right out of seminary in New York. Had no family or anybody down here. Deidre, didn't your Aunt Phyllis put him up for a time, until he got his feet under him?"

"She did," Deidre said, nodding. "He stayed in the guesthouse for the first year or so. Helped her around the house with handyman type things. He met Anne Winslow a couple of years after he moved here and married her. They never had any children of their own as I recall."

I studied Douglas Sutton's young face in the photograph—earnest, smiling, standing beside his mentor George Pickering with what looked like genuine admiration. Had he known about the embezzlement at that time?

"And there's Stephanie Chester," Deidre said, her finger hovering over a blond woman in the second row. She wore white—a sundress that seemed to glow in the July sunlight—and stood close to a dark-haired young man whose hand rested at the small of her back. "That would be Matthias Crenshaw Jr. Never liked him."

"He was a bit of a weasel," Bea said. "Reminded me of Eddie Haskell. I was friendly with his mother, Martha. At least for a little while. People in my profession usually don't keep friends long."

"That happens when you sleep with people's husbands," Dottie said, rolling her eyes. "You've never been a victim, Bea. Stop laying it on so thick."

Bea shooed her hand toward Dottie and said, "Hush up, this is my story." Then she cleared her throat. "Anyway, Greta used to say Stephanie was the best thing that ever happened to Matt," Bea said. "Settled him down, gave him purpose. Before Stephanie, he was directionless—dropped out of college, couldn't hold a job. He was an entitled brat, so I don't think work was something he wanted. But after they married, he ended up finishing college and went to medical school. I think Stephanie wasn't too excited to work while he was going to school. There were rumors neither of them were faithful. I guess it was at least partially true because she ended up marrying a surgeon barely a month after the ink on her divorce papers was dry."

"Still doesn't explain why she might have been meeting Pickering the night of the murders," I said.

The photograph was coming alive as they identified face after face—neighbors, acquaintances, people whose lives had intersected at a church picnic on a summer day. Some had stayed on the island, their stories continuing in ways both ordinary and extraordinary. Others had left, carried away by time or tragedy or simply the pull of somewhere else.

"Wait," I said, leaning closer to a figure partially obscured by shadow in the back row. The angle of the sun, the position of the trees—something had created a pocket of shade that made his features harder to see. But the build was familiar. The way he stood, slightly apart from the group. "Who's that?"

Dottie squinted, then sucked in a breath. "Well, well, well... That's interesting."

"What?" Dash moved closer, following her gaze.

"That," she said, "is Frank Holloway."

The room went very still.

I studied the figure more carefully now. Younger by decades, maybe mid-twenties, wearing plaid shorts and a polo shirt, and standing next to a pretty young woman with dark hair. They were each holding a baby about a year old. His face was partially in shadow from the oak trees overhead, but the bone structure was unmistakable once you knew to look for it.

"Frank Holloway," I said quietly.

The name landed like a stone in still water. Frank Holloway, at the church picnic. Part of the congregation. Part of the community. And he'd never mentioned it.

"He positioned himself as an outsider," I said. "Someone who knew Tommy professionally, who quit the force and moved to Beaufort. Not someone who was there, who knew these people, who sat in those pews every Sunday."

"Why lie about that?" Deidre asked.

Walt's expression had gone hard. "Because Frank Holloway knows more than he's told us. And that makes him either a witness we need to push harder, or something much worse.

I pulled Pickering's notebook closer—the composition book with the faded marbled cover that Reverend Sutton had given us. We'd read through it before, but now I was looking for different things. Not just obvious connections to Ruby or the affair, but names, patterns, anything that might point to other people involved in whatever had gotten Pickering and Ruby killed.

The pages were filled with Pickering's observations about his congregation—some entries straightforward, others cryptic, all of them revealing the private struggles of people who'd trusted him with their secrets.

I flipped through slowly, reading more carefully this time.

"'June 1984—Mary Jane G. confessed that her daughter has been seeing a married man. Prayed with her about guiding her daughter back to righteousness.' Who's Mary Jane G.?" I asked. "Anyone have an idea?"

"Never heard of her," Bea said. "She must not have been in my circle."

"Oh, that's easy," Deidre said. "Mary Jane Goodall. But I don't remember her having a daughter. I think she had two boys."

"Didn't she remarry after her husband left her?" Dottie asked. "That was a scandal. She had those two boys barely a year apart and then he took off to parts unknown. Never came back to see his kids as far as I know."

"She did get remarried," Deidre said. "Not even a year after she was abandoned. I was glad for her. But I don't remember who she married. He wasn't an islander, and they moved off to the city. But she stayed connected to the church. As far as I know, the new husband never went with her."

"We've got to find a reason she'd meet with Pickering the night he was killed," I said. "Maybe he confronted her about her affair with a married man on her mother's behalf."

"I can look and see if there's any connection between Mary Jane

Goodall and Stephanie Crenshaw," Dash said. "That shouldn't be hard to find. Who else do we need to look for?"

I kept reading, looking for more. "March 1985—'Doogie brought deposit slips for recreation center fund. Numbers look good on paper. Board pleased with progress.'"

"Who's Doogie?" Dottie asked, reading over my shoulder.

"No idea," I said. "Never heard anyone called that around here."

"No," Dottie said, her glasses slipping down her nose. "I haven't either."

"Keep reading," Dash said. "See if there are more entries about this Doogie person or the recreation center fund."

I kept flipping pages and skimming over Reverend Pickering's words. "Jordy Kerr had a gambling problem and lost his house payment at the racetrack. Asked for financial help from the church so his wife doesn't kill him. Amos Bledsoe lost his job and he and his wife Carla were struggling to put food on the table. They asked for groceries to tide them over until he can find work. Drew Watson's wife found his stash of *Playboy* magazines and made him sleep on the couch."

"I always knew he was a perv," Bea said. "It was in the eyes. He had shifty eyes."

"Well, he's dead now, isn't he," Dottie said. "So it hardly matters."

"Here we go," I said. "April 1985—'Doogie said deposit records are missing. The board wants to move forward with breaking ground. Will have to go down to the bank and get copies.'"

I kept reading, but there were no more entries about Doogie or the recreation center fund. The later entries focused on other pastoral matters and concern about the gossip about him and Ruby.

"August 30, 1985—'I'm going to have to make a decision soon. The children are grown, so I don't have to worry about them. But what do I do? My vows are with June and my heart is with Ruby. I'm starting to question everything. I can leave the church. I can leave my wife. But I don't know if I can leave Ruby.

"'I know June knows. I can tell by the way she looks at me. That's my fault. Ruby and I haven't been as careful as we should have been.

Elder Crenshaw continues to scold me like a child, but he can't remove me from my position. Not with what I know. But I do know things can't stay the same. I know there are whispers through the congregation, and many of the families Ruby cleaned for have quietly let her go. She can't afford to stay here any longer. She needs a fresh start. We both do.'"

The back room had gone very quiet except for the sound of Carly handling customers in the front and Chowder's rhythmic snoring from his armchair.

"We're missing something," Walt said, studying the murder board with his arms crossed. "We know about the embezzlement, we know about the affair. But we still don't know who actually pulled the trigger."

"Jane Sutherland might know," I said. "Bea, did you ever get anywhere with her after she hung up on you?"

Bea shook her head, frustration evident in the tight line of her mouth. "I've tried three more times. She won't answer my calls anymore. I even sent her an email—very carefully worded, very professional—explaining that we're officially reopening the case and that her testimony could help bring justice for two murder victims. Nothing. Complete silence."

"Then we move forward without her," Dash said. "At least for now."

Dash stood, moving to the murder board with the restless energy of someone who needed to move to think. "All right. Let's organize what we know. We've got too many threads—we need to see how they connect."

He pulled down a blank section of the board and started writing, his handwriting surprisingly neat for someone who seemed to do everything with intensity.

VICTIMS:

- Reverend George Pickering—shot execution style
- Ruby Bailey—shot three times, tongue removed
  postmortem

- Both positioned to look like lovers

MOTIVE—MONEY:

- $200,000+ missing from church building fund
- Forged deposit slips with Pickering's signature
- Multiple finance committee members made large purchases 1986–1987
- Pickering's notebook: "he can't remove me from my position. Not with what I know"

MOTIVE—COVER-UP:

- Affair was public knowledge—scandal but not murder-worthy
- Embezzlement would ruin reputations, families, careers
- Frame the dead lovers as thieves—who would question it?

"The affair was the perfect cover," I said, watching the pattern emerge. "Everyone expected a crime of passion. A jealous spouse, an outraged congregation. But the real motive was money."

"And Pickering figured it out," Deidre added. "That's what got him killed. He knew someone was stealing from the church, forging his signature.

"So now we know Frank lied to us." Dash's voice had gone hard, that lawman edge replacing the warmth I'd grown accustomed to. "He positioned himself as an outsider who knew Tommy professionally. But he was in that church photograph—part of the congregation, sitting in those pews every Sunday. He knew these people personally, and he never said a word about it."

"Why lie?" Deidre asked, though her tone suggested she already knew the answer.

"Because he's protecting someone," Walt said, his pointer tapping against the board with sharp, staccato beats. "Or protecting himself."

"We need to confront him," Dash said. "Today. Before he has time to prepare another story or warning reaches him that we've found him in that photograph."

"What about Crenshaw?" Bea asked, her rings clicking against her coffee cup. "Pickering wrote that Crenshaw couldn't remove him from his position because of what he knew. That's blackmail material. That's motive."

"And Stephanie," I added, remembering the way she'd shut down at the hospital, that carefully controlled fear in her eyes. "We need to know if she's Mary Jane Goodall's daughter. That birth record search—how long will it take?"

Dash was already pulling out his phone. "An hour, maybe two. I can access the database from my laptop in the car."

"Then that's priority one," Walt said, ever the tactician. "Run the search on the way to Beaufort. We need to know if there's a family connection before we question anyone else."

"I'm coming with you," I said to Dash, and held up a hand before he could protest. "I was there the first time we interviewed him. I'll know if his story changes, if he contradicts what he told us before. And you shouldn't be going alone—not after what happened to Hank."

Something flickered in Dash's expression—concern warring with the knowledge that I was right. "Fine. But we do this my way. Official interview, recorded, by the book."

"Wouldn't dream of interfering," I said, echoing Bea's earlier promise with a smile that probably looked more confident than I felt.

The truth was, my hands had started trembling the moment we'd identified Frank in that photograph. He'd sat across from us in his meticulously organized office, his earnest face radiating honesty as he told us about Tommy's crusade for justice, about Milton's corruption, about how he'd quit because he couldn't stomach what was happening. And all of it—every word—had been built on a foundation of lies.

Walt stood, already gathering his tactical-planning materials. "Dottie, you approach Stephanie at the hospital. Bea, keep trying Jane Sutherland—if we can get her to confirm anything about what she saw, it strengthens our case. Deidre, you're on research. I want everything you can find about Mary Jane Goodall—marriage records, employment history, anything that might connect her to Stephanie Donaldson."

"What about Elder Crenshaw?" Dottie asked.

"Tomorrow," Dash said, checking his watch. The late morning light slanting through the window caught the worry lines around his eyes, making him look older suddenly, or maybe just tired. "Once we know what Frank has to say and whether Stephanie is connected to Mary Jane. We approach Crenshaw with all our evidence lined up, not half-formed theories that he can dismiss."

It made sense. It was smart, strategic, the kind of methodical police work that solved cases. But every instinct I had screamed that we were running out of time, that whoever had put Hank in the hospital was watching us get closer, planning their next move while we planned ours.

"Everyone else goes home after we leave," Dash continued, his voice carrying that note of command that suggested arguing would be futile. "Lock your doors. Don't answer questions from anyone about the investigation. And text me when you're home safe."

"Very authoritarian," Bea observed, but there was approval in her voice rather than criticism.

"Very practical," Deidre said quietly. "Hank's in the hospital with a cracked skull. We'd be fools to ignore the danger."

The Silver Sleuths dispersed with less theatrical flair than usual, the weight of what we'd discovered settling over all of us like morning fog—heavy, obscuring, impossible to ignore. Even Bea's exit was subdued, her usual dramatic sweep reduced to a quick squeeze of my shoulder and a whispered, "Be careful."

After they'd gone, the back room felt strangely empty despite being full of evidence and murder boards and the lingering scent of coffee gone cold in forgotten cups. Dash stood at the board, studying the church photograph with an intensity that made the muscles in his jaw jump.

"He never mentioned being part of the congregation," I said, the realization still stinging. Dottie and I had sat across from Frank in that small office while he told us about Tommy's investigation, about

Milton's corruption, about how hard it had been to be an honest cop on Grimm Island. And not once had he said, *"I knew these people. I sat in those pews every Sunday. I was there."*

"It's a significant omission," Dash said, his tone more analytical than angry. "He positioned himself as an outside observer when he was actually part of the community. That changes the nature of his testimony."

"Do you think he knows who killed them?" I asked.

Dash was quiet for a moment, considering. "Maybe. Or maybe he knows something that would point us in the right direction, and he's been sitting on it for forty years." He glanced at me. "Either way, we need to ask him directly. See how he responds when confronted with the photograph."

"We should go," I said, because standing here speculating wouldn't get us answers, and the drive to Beaufort was long enough that we needed to leave soon if we wanted to catch Frank before his store closed. "Let me tell Carly she's closing up tonight."

Dash caught my wrist as I moved past him. "If Frank gets hostile, you let me handle it. Agreed?"

"Agreed," I said. "Though I doubt he's going to attack us in broad daylight in his own hardware store."

"Probably not. But people do surprising things when they're cornered." He released my wrist. "Let's go talk to Mr. Holloway about his church attendance."

Twenty minutes later, we were on Highway 17 heading toward Beaufort, the midday sun painting the marsh grasses in shades of gold and amber. Dash drove with one hand on the wheel, the other typing commands on the mobile data terminal.

"Got it," he said finally. "Stephanie Michelle Chester, born January 12, 1963, in Charleston. Mother listed as Ruth Arceneaux Chester. Father listed as Raymond Chester."

"So not connected to Mary Jane Goodall," I said, disappointed.

"Keep digging," he said, turning the laptop toward me. "Do a search on her father and see what comes up."

I clicked on Raymond Chester's name and watched the screen fill with information. "Born August 1930. Died April 2013. Married to Ruth Arceneaux in May of 1957 until her death in 1973... Well, well, well," I said, my attention perking up. "Married Mary Jane Goodall in 1974."

"That's why you always keep digging," he said, grinning. "Good work."

My heart started beating faster. "So Stephanie Chester is Mary Jane's stepdaughter."

"Looks like it."

"So when Pickering counseled Mary Jane about her daughter's affair with a married man in 1984, he was talking about Stephanie." The pieces clicked together with the satisfying finality of a lock turning. "Stephanie was having an affair, her mother went to Pickering for guidance, and then Pickering ended up dead."

"Along with his own mistress," Dash added. "Which makes Stephanie either a suspect or a witness. Either way, she lied to us when she said she barely knew Pickering."

The highway stretched ahead of us, cutting through the low country like a promise or a threat—I couldn't decide which. The marshes on either side shimmered in the noon sun, their tall grasses swaying in rhythms older than memory. Every few miles, a weathered church steeple punctured the horizon, white paint peeling like old secrets coming loose.

Somewhere ahead, Frank Holloway was probably ringing up a customer's deck stain or explaining the difference between Phillips and flathead screws, thinking his careful omissions would hold for another day. Thinking we wouldn't find the photograph. Thinking the past would stay buried where he'd helped plant it.

But the past had a way of resurfacing—not dramatically, not all at once, but in small revelations that accumulated like water behind a dam. One photograph. One inconsistency. One lie by omission. And suddenly the whole structure was trembling, ready to break.

"What if he runs?" I asked. "Frank, I mean. What if we spook him and he disappears?"

"Then we know he's guilty of something," Dash replied. "And we put out a BOLO and find him. But I don't think he'll run. He's been here since 1986, built a life, a business. People who run don't put down roots like that."

"Unless the roots are the disguise," I said. "What better way to look innocent than to stay in one place, be respectable, never draw attention?"

Dash's hands remained steady on the wheel. "Then we're about to find out which Frank Holloway is real—the honest ex-cop, or the man who's been hiding a murder."

CHAPTER
TWELVE

Holloway's Hardware looked exactly the same as it had yesterday—same cheerful red letters, same brick façade that had probably been there since Eisenhower was president, same bell that announced our arrival with oblivious enthusiasm. But walking through that door felt different this time, like returning to a restaurant where you'd found a hair in your food. Everything appeared normal on the surface, but you couldn't quite forget what lay beneath.

Frank Holloway glanced up from behind the counter, and I watched recognition hit him like a physical blow. His earnest expression—the one that had seemed so genuine during our first visit—flickered and died.

"Sheriff Beckett," he said, his voice flat and unwelcoming. "Mrs. McCoy. Wasn't expecting to see you folks again so soon."

"Funny thing about photographs," Dash said, pulling out the church picnic picture and laying it on the counter between a display of cabinet hinges and a bin of assorted washers. "They have a way of telling stories people forgot to mention."

Frank's face went through several interesting color changes—pale to flushed to pale again, like watching a very anxious traffic light. His hand moved toward the photograph, then stopped, hovering above it as if touching it might burn him.

"July 4, 1985," I said, keeping my voice pleasant. "First Methodist Church. That's you in the third row, isn't it? Holding one of your daughters. Your wife, Sandra, beside you."

The silence that followed felt about as comfortable as a mammogram.

"Jimmy," Frank called toward the back of the store, his voice strained. "Can you handle the front for a bit? Need to talk to these folks in my office."

We followed him past displays of power tools and paint cans stacked like colorful towers, into the small office that smelled like old coffee and unspoken confessions.

Frank sank into his desk chair, the old wood creaking under his weight like a sigh.

"Sandra and I were members," he said, hands flat on the desk as if anchoring himself. "Joined about six months before I started working for Milton. She grew up Methodist. Wanted the girls raised in the church."

"And you didn't think to mention this when we came asking about a double homicide that happened at your church?" Dash's voice was pleasant. Too pleasant. The kind of pleasant that meant someone was about to find themselves in very deep water.

"I didn't think it mattered." Frank pulled off his glasses, cleaned them with his flannel shirt—buying time to construct his defense. "Spent decades trying to forget I was ever part of that place. Sandra and I left six months after the murders. Couldn't sit in those pews anymore, listening to whoever replaced Pickering talk about God's love while everyone pretended two people hadn't been executed and dumped on the beach."

"But you knew them," I said. "Ruby Bailey cleaned houses. Did she clean yours?"

"Once a week. Tuesdays." Frank's jaw tightened like a vise. "She was good at her job. Efficient. The girls liked her—she'd bring them little toys from the dollar store sometimes. Nothing expensive, just little things. Stickers. Cheap bracelets. Sandra used to make her lunch."

"And Pickering?"

"I knew him the way you know a pastor. Shook his hand after service. Sat through his sermons. Brought covered dishes to potlucks." Frank looked up at us with weary eyes. "But I didn't know them. Not really. Didn't know Ruby was being threatened by Crenshaw. Didn't know about the embezzlement until Tommy started investigating. Just knew what everyone else knew—they were having an affair, and someone killed them for it."

"Did you suspect who killed them?" Dash asked.

Frank was quiet for a long moment, wrestling with something internal. "Everyone suspected everyone. That's what Milton's circus accomplished—three different people confessing, all of them recanting, nobody knowing what was real anymore. But I didn't have answers then, and I don't have them now."

The room felt heavy with the weight of old secrets and older guilt.

"I'm sorry I wasn't more forthcoming," Frank said finally. "I told myself it didn't matter that I'd been there. That being a congregant didn't make me complicit. But I see how it looks—like I was hiding something. I wasn't. I was just trying to keep my distance from something that nearly destroyed my partner."

Dash gathered the photograph, slid it back into the folder with deliberate precision. "If you think of anything else, call me." He pulled out a business card, set it on Frank's desk. "Someone's already been hurt trying to stop this investigation. The next person might not be so lucky."

Frank nodded, his face ashen. "I understand."

We left him sitting in his office, surrounded by decades of paperwork and the ghosts of decisions made when he was young enough to think running away would solve anything.

Outside, the humidity hit like walking into a steam bath.

"He's telling the truth," I said, sliding into the passenger seat of Dash's SUV. "He doesn't know who killed them. He's just scared and ashamed."

"Yeah." Dash started the engine with more force than necessary. "But he confirmed what we suspected. This wasn't about passion. It was about money."

The drive back to Grimm Island felt longer than usual, the highway stretching out through marsh and pine forest that all started looking the same after a while. Dash was quiet—that focused quiet where I could practically hear his brain working through evidence, sorting and cataloging possibilities.

"I want to review Tommy's files tonight," he said finally. "See if there's anything that points more definitively at Crenshaw or the other board members."

"What about Stephanie?"

"Her too. But I want leverage first. Real evidence, not just connections." His hands tightened on the steering wheel. "Scared people don't talk unless silence becomes more dangerous than confession."

We crossed back onto Grimm Island as the afternoon light started its slow fade toward evening. The familiar sight of live oaks and antebellum houses should have felt like coming home. Instead, it felt ominous—all that carefully maintained beauty hiding something festering underneath.

That's when my phone rang. Dottie's name flashed on the screen.

"Mabel," she said without preamble. "Where are you?"

"Just crossed the bridge from Beaufort. What's wrong?" The urgency in her voice made my stomach clench.

"It's Jane Sutherland. Someone found her body an hour ago."

The bottom dropped out of my stomach. "Where?"

"The Flamingo Motel." Dottie's voice had gone clinical—that medical examiner tone she used when things got too real for normal emotions. "Mabel, she was shot. Same caliber as Pickering and Bailey."

Dash's head snapped toward me. He was already reaching for his radio.

"What room?" I asked, though part of me already knew the answer like a song you've heard before.

"Twelve," Dottie said. "Same room number where Ruby and Pickering used to meet."

Through the phone I could hear the controlled chaos of the hospital—monitors beeping, voices murmuring instructions, machines keeping people alive who wanted to die and people dying who wanted to live.

Jane Sutherland. Who'd investigated the church finances in 1985. Who'd tracked Ruby's and Pickering's movements like a bloodhound following a scent. Who'd left town the moment their bodies were found and stayed gone for decades, scared enough to abandon her entire career and disappear into someone else's life.

"We're five minutes away," I told Dottie. "I'll call you back."

I hung up and looked at Dash, whose knuckles had gone white against the steering wheel. "Why would Jane Sutherland come back to Grimm Island after all these years? Why stay at the Flamingo?"

"Maybe she was coming to meet someone—maybe even Bea. Or maybe the killer found out she was still alive and lured her back." Dash's voice was grim. "But they made a mistake this time. Fresh crime scene means fresh forensic evidence—DNA, fingerprints, security footage from a renovated motel that definitely has cameras. If ballistics confirms it's the same gun, we've connected three murders across four decades."

Something almost predatory flickered across his face. "They stayed hidden for decades by being smart. But desperation makes people careless."

Five minutes later, we pulled into the parking lot of the Flamingo Hotel, and I barely recognized the place. Gone was the seedy motel where Ruby and Pickering had conducted their affair for fifty dollars a night and the desk clerk's practiced blindness. Someone had poured serious money into transforming it—cream-colored siding that gleamed even in the fading afternoon light, sage-green shutters, tasteful brass lettering where the old neon flamingo had once flickered its invitation to sin. The parking lot held Teslas and Range Rovers instead of Ruby Bailey's Mercury Cougar with its dented bumper and impossible dreams.

Yellow crime-scene tape fluttered across room twelve's door like a funeral ribbon.

Dash's patrol vehicles crowded the small lot. Deputy Harris stood near the entrance with the hotel manager—a man in his thirties wearing the kind of carefully casual clothes that cost more than my monthly mortgage, gesticulating with the desperate energy of someone trying to contain a public relations disaster. Probably explaining how this sort of thing never happened at the new Flamingo, as if renovation could exorcise ghosts.

Harris spotted us and walked over, his young face looking older than it had this morning. Murder did that—aged you in hours instead of years.

"Sheriff. Mrs. McCoy." He nodded at me. "Victim is Jane Sutherland, sixty-four. Checked in yesterday afternoon under her own name, paid cash for two nights. Housekeeping found her around one o'clock."

My stomach twisted into a knot. Jane Sutherland. The reporter who'd investigated the church finances, who'd tracked Ruby's and Pickering's movements, who'd fled Grimm Island the moment their bodies were discovered and never looked back.

Until now.

"What do we know?" Dash asked, his sheriff's mask sliding into place.

"Single gunshot to the back of the head. Execution style." Harris flipped through his notebook with trembling fingers. "County ME is inside now. Says it's a .38 Special—same caliber as the '85 murders."

Same caliber. Room twelve. The coincidence was about as subtle as a brick through a stained-glass window.

"Time of death?"

"Between midnight and 3 a.m based on body temperature and rigor. No signs of struggle. No defensive wounds."

"Security footage?" Dash asked.

"Yeah, part of the renovation. Manager's got it queued up in the office. This way."

Harris led us past room twelve toward the small office tucked behind the lobby. The hotel manager—whose name tag read Preston—had the footage ready on a laptop, his hands fidgeting with a pen like a nervous tic.

"This is from last night," Preston said, clicking play. "1:30 a.m."

The footage was grainy black and white, but clear enough. A figure approached room twelve—medium height, dark clothing, baseball cap pulled low. The person's face never turned toward the camera, not even for a second. Deliberate avoidance.

A knock on the door. Waiting.

After a moment, the door opened. Jane appeared in the frame—just a sliver of her, backlit by the room's lamp. She stepped back. Let the person in.

My heart sank like a stone.

"She opened the door willingly," I said.

"Or whoever it was gave her a reason to trust them," Dash replied, his voice flat. "Claimed they had information about the case maybe."

Eighteen minutes later, the figure emerged. Same careful avoidance of cameras, same deliberate movements. The person disappeared toward the parking lot, and the camera lost them in the shadows between streetlights.

"Did anyone report hearing a gunshot?" Dash asked Preston. "Other guests? Staff?"

Preston shook his head. "That's the thing—we had three other rooms occupied last night, but nobody heard anything. The rooms have pretty good soundproofing from the renovation, but still..." He shrugged helplessly.

"Parking lot footage?" Dash asked.

Preston clicked through files with shaking fingers. "We've got three cameras out there, but..." He pulled up another video. "Whoever this was knew where to walk. Stayed in the blind spots like they'd studied the layout."

I watched the footage loop, that medium-height figure moving with purpose through carefully calculated routes. That could have been anyone. Elder Crenshaw was too frail to move like that. But Stephanie? She had the right build. Or it could be someone we hadn't even considered—someone who'd been watching from the shadows all along.

"I need copies of all this footage," Dash said to Preston. "And the guest registry for the past week."

"Already pulled it for Deputy Harris," Preston said, looking relieved to be helpful rather than the bearer of bad news.

"Can we see the scene?" Dash asked Harris.

"Yes, sir," Harris said, handing us latex gloves and paper booties at room twelve's door. "County ME asked that we keep contamination to a minimum while they're still processing."

Room twelve had been transformed into something you'd see in a home decorating magazine. Soft gray walls. White linens. Black-and-white photographs of the low country in simple frames. Furniture that looked expensive because it was trying very hard to look simple and understated.

But no amount of money could change what this room had been. What it had witnessed.

Jane Sutherland lay on the floor beside the bed, positioned on her side as if she'd simply lain down to rest. Silver hair cut in a sleek bob. Tailored navy slacks and a silk blouse that probably cost more than most people's weekly salary. Small pearl earrings. Wedding ring on her left hand—so she'd married after leaving Grimm Island. Built a whole new life.

The county medical examiner—a man in his forties with wire-rimmed glasses—was photographing the wound. He glanced up when we entered.

"Sheriff Beckett." He straightened. "Dr. Martinez."

"Anything else you can tell us beyond what you shared with Harris?" Dash asked.

"Used one of the hotel pillows to muffle the shot," Dr. Martinez said, gesturing to a bloodstained pillow that had been moved aside for evidence collection. "Explains why no one heard anything. Smart thinking on the killer's part."

Dash's jaw tightened like a cable under stress. "Rush the ballistics on that casing."

"Already planned on it given the circumstances."

Jane on her knees, a hotel pillow pressed to her head to silence her final moments. The past catching up after four decades of running.

Through room twelve's window, the late afternoon sun was starting to slant golden across Waterfront Street. Soon the dinner crowd would be heading out—couples dressed for the restaurants, families finishing their beach day, tourists with their shopping bags and sunburns.

Normal people having normal evenings, completely oblivious to the fact that someone had been executed twenty feet away.

Jane Sutherland had run from Grimm Island in 1985. Had built a new life somewhere safer. Had stayed silent for decades, carrying her secrets like stones in her pockets.

And someone had tracked her down anyway.

"If ballistics confirms it's the same gun," Dash said quietly, "we're dealing with someone who's been killing for forty years and thinks they're untouchable."

"We need to find that gun," I said.

He looked at me, and I saw the determination in his eyes mixed with something else—worry. Not just for the case. For me. For all of us asking questions someone clearly didn't want asked.

"We will," he said. "Time for conversations without kid gloves." He pulled out his phone. "Stephanie Donaldson and her ex-father-in-law are going to explain exactly why this secret is worth killing for."

Outside the Flamingo, the late afternoon sun was painting Harbor Street in shades of amber and rose, the kind of light that made even the most ordinary things appear touched by magic. The evening hour was approaching, and I realized I hadn't eaten since my morning scone.

"I need food," I said. "And something stronger than tea after the day we've had."

Dash glanced at his watch. "Magnolia's should be open. Good

food, quiet atmosphere. We can talk without half the island listening in."

Ten minutes later, we were walking through the restaurant's front door. "Two of us for dinner," I told the hostess at Magnolia's, a woman in her thirties whose crisp white blouse and practiced smile suggested she'd been managing the evening crowd here for years. "Somewhere quiet, if you have it."

She led us to a corner table on the screened porch where the evening light filtered through jasmine vines. The harbor spread below us, all silver water and bobbing masts, deceptively peaceful after the horror we'd left behind.

Our waitress, Riley, appeared with menus and the kind of smile that suggested she'd mastered the art of reading her customers' moods. "Y'all look like you've had a day," she said gently. "Can I start you with something to drink?"

"Moscato," I said without hesitation. "The sweetest you have. And we'll need a few minutes with the menu."

"Sweet tea for me," Dash added.

Riley nodded and disappeared, returning quickly with a glass of wine that caught the porch lights like liquid gold. The first sip was exactly what I needed—sweet and light and utterly uncomplicated, washing away the metallic taste that crime scenes always left in my mouth.

"Better?" Dash asked, watching me over his glass of tea.

"Getting there." I studied the menu, though my appetite felt fragile. "The she-crab soup, I think. Something warm."

"Grouper for me," Dash told Riley when she returned. "Blackened, if you do it that way."

"Perfect choice," Riley said. "Miss Adelaide's soup is legendary—she adds just enough sherry to make you forget your troubles without making you forget your manners."

The food arrived with admirable speed, my soup bowl releasing steam that smelled like comfort and old Charleston recipes. The first spoonful was everything Riley had promised—rich and creamy with that hint of sherry that warmed from the inside out.

"Jane Sutherland had something she needed to finish here," I said, watching a great blue heron stalk something in the shallows beyond the restaurant's dock. "Something worth risking her life for."

Dash was about to respond when a familiar voice called across the porch.

"Mabel! Sheriff Beckett!"

We looked up to find Reverend Sutton approaching, dressed in a navy shirt and tie. He moved with the careful grace of someone who'd learned to navigate social situations without causing offense, his smile warm but carrying an undercurrent of concern.

"Reverend," I said, genuinely pleased to see him. "Please, join us if you have time. We could use some perspective."

He hesitated for a moment, then pulled out the empty chair. "I don't want to intrude. I just finished dinner with the elders when I saw you sitting out here. I'm sure you've both had a day. I heard about Jane Sutherland."

"You knew her," Dash said. It wasn't a question.

Sutton's expression grew somber as he settled into the chair. "Jane wasn't a member of our congregation, but she was certainly interested in it. Bright young woman, worked for the *Gazette*. She'd manage to miss service and show up after so she could ask questions." He paused, accepting Riley's offer of coffee. "I think she wanted people to see she was asking them. It served her purpose better than her making a one-on-one appointment during the week. Jane came to me several times in the months before the murders, asking about church finances, board meetings. Said she was working on a story."

"What kind of story?" I asked, watching his reaction carefully.

"She never said specifically, but she was persistent about the building fund. Wanted to know who had access, how decisions were made about expenditures." Sutton stirred cream into his coffee with deliberate movements. "I was young, naïve. I thought she was just interested in how churches operated. It wasn't until after George and Ruby died that I realized she'd been investigating something specific."

"Did you tell her anything?" Dash asked.

"Nothing confidential. Basic information about our structure, who served on which committees. But Jane was clever—she asked the right questions to piece together a larger picture." His voice dropped. "I've always wondered if my answers contributed to what happened to George and Ruby."

The evening air had grown cooler, carrying the salt scent of low tide mixed with jasmine from the restaurant's garden. Through the screens, couples strolled along the harbor boardwalk, their voices a gentle murmur against the backdrop of lapping waves.

"George kept detailed records," I said carefully. "We've been reading through some of his pastoral notes."

Something flickered across Sutton's face. "George was meticulous about documentation. Sometimes obsessively so. He carried the weight of everyone's secrets."

"Including financial irregularities," Dash said.

Sutton was quiet for a long moment, his hands wrapped around his coffee cup. "George suspected several board members were skimming from the building fund. Elder Crenshaw in particular had access to the accounts, made unilateral decisions about expenditures." His voice dropped. "George documented what he could—dates, amounts, patterns of withdrawals that didn't match approved projects. But Elder Crenshaw was powerful, had allies on the board. George knew he needed ironclad proof before making accusations."

"Did he share his concerns with you?"

"Some. He was my mentor, but he was also protective. Said there were dangerous people on this island, that asking the wrong questions could get someone hurt." Sutton's expression grew troubled. "I was twenty-four, fresh out of seminary. George thought he was shielding me from how deep the corruption went."

"And you think that's what got him killed?" I asked.

Sutton nodded slowly. "George was getting close to exposing them. And Ruby—poor Ruby knew what George had discovered. That knowledge made her a liability too."

"And Jane Sutherland figured it out anyway," I said.

"Jane was a journalist. She knew how to follow paper trails, how to ask questions that seemed innocent but weren't." He looked between us. "Finding her at the motel…it feels like the past refusing to stay buried. Everyone knew that's where George and Ruby went. It was the worst-kept secret on Grimm Island. "

We talked for another twenty minutes, Sutton sharing memories of the church, the tensions he'd sensed but not understood, the fear that had settled over the congregation after the murders. By the time we parted ways in the parking lot, the sun had set completely, leaving Harbor Street painted in streetlight and shadow.

"Interesting man," Dash said as we climbed into his SUV.

"Very," I agreed, though something about the conversation nagged at me. "He knew more than he was saying."

"I bet most pastors know things that would make your hair curl," he said. "No one keeps secrets better than pastors and cops."

The drive back toward The Perfect Steep took us through quiet residential streets where porch lights were beginning to flicker on. Families settling in for the evening, children being called inside, the island's peaceful rhythm continuing despite the violence that had shattered it that afternoon.

"Don't forget to drop me at the tea shop," I said. "My car is still parked in the lot."

"I remember," Dash said, his voice husky with exhaustion. "Though I was hoping to walk you to your door."

My lips twitched with amusement. "You still could. If you follow me back."

"Good idea. I want to make sure you get inside okay. Not that I'm doubting Chowder's security measures. He's very thorough."

"He'll appreciate the compliment," I said. "Though he's probably rather put out with me considering how much time I've been away lately."

We were still three blocks away when we saw the smoke.

"That's coming from Harbor Street," Dash said, his foot finding the accelerator. My heart was already racing before we turned the corner and saw the fire trucks, their red-and-blue lights painting the buildings in urgent, dancing colors. The Perfect Steep stood intact, thank God, but smoke was billowing from the back of the building, dark against the evening sky.

"The back room," I breathed, understanding flooding through me like ice water. "Someone set fire to the back room."

We pulled up behind the fire trucks as Captain Dozier approached, his face grim beneath the brim of his helmet.

"Mabel," he said, relief evident in his voice. "Thank God you weren't inside. Looks like someone broke in through the rear entrance, doused the back room with accelerant, then lit it up."

"How bad?" I asked, though I was almost afraid to hear the answer.

"Could have been worse. A group of people out for a walk saw the smoke and called it in quick. We got here before it spread to the main shop." He gestured toward the building. "Back room's a total loss, though. Everything in there is gone. And it's a mess. I'm sorry."

Everything. The murder board, the evidence copies, all our carefully organized research. Days of work reduced to ash and smoke.

"You'll want to call your insurance company," Captain Dozier continued. "But you'll need to close down for a few days until the arson investigation is finished."

Dash was already on his phone, calling for a crime-scene team. I stood staring at the building that had been my sanctuary, my livelihood, now violated and partially destroyed because we'd gotten too close to something someone wanted to keep buried.

"Mabel!"

I turned to see Walt jogging toward us, his face flushed with exertion and worry. Behind him came Deidre, moving as quickly as her sensible shoes would allow.

"We came as soon as we heard on the police scanner," Walt said, breathing hard. "Are you all right?"

"I'm fine. But the back room—all the evidence."

"Is perfectly safe," he said. "I expected something like this would happen. Which is why I took everything important home with me this afternoon."

I stared at him. "Everything?"

"Tommy Wheeler's files, George Pickering's journal, all the original evidence, every copy we made, every photograph." His smile was sharp as a blade. "Forty years in intelligence taught me to always assume the enemy is watching. Only thing in there was the murder board and the photocopies I made. If someone was desperate enough to attack Hank in broad daylight, they were certainly desperate enough to destroy evidence."

Relief flooded through me so completely I had to lean against Dash's SUV to stay upright.

Walt's expression grew serious. "After this and Jane Sutherland's murder, I think we can confirm that we're not just investigating a cold case anymore. We're hunting someone who's still very much alive, very much threatened, and very much willing to kill to keep their secrets."

The fire trucks were beginning to pack up, the immediate danger over. The Perfect Steep would need repairs, would smell like smoke for weeks, but it would survive. More importantly, our investigation would survive.

"Don't you worry, dear," Deidre said. "We'll have this place cleaned up in no time. Once they let us in of course. And insurance should cover everything. I've done plenty of research into insurance companies. Let me handle it. I'll make sure you get every penny you're owed."

"Thank you," I said, my voice hoarse with emotion. The reality hadn't quite sunk in yet. And I felt helpless.

"Tomorrow," Dash said quietly, "We start pushing harder. No more gentle inquiries. Someone just showed us how desperate they are."

I looked at the smoke still rising from my violated sanctuary, at the friends who'd rallied to my side, at the man whose presence had become as essential as breathing. Tomorrow we would indeed push harder.

"I guess we should go home," I said. "Tomorrow is another day."

Walt nodded. "Scarlett O'Hara would be quite proud of you. Chin up, sailor. Things are always more beautiful when they're rebuilt from the ashes."

We walked around back to the parking lot where my powder-blue Karmann Ghia waited alone beneath a streetlight, droplets of water beading on its hood like tears from the fire department's hoses.

It was then Deidre grabbed hold of my arm and said, "Good grief. Tomorrow is Thursday. Where are we going to have book club?"

CHAPTER
THIRTEEN

Thursday morning arrived wrapped in the kind of pristine coastal light that made tragedy feel impossible, as if the universe hadn't gotten the memo about arson and murder and the general unraveling of civilized society. I'd been awake since 4, watching shadows retreat across my bedroom ceiling while Chowder snored beside me.

My house felt too quiet, too normal, as if yesterday hadn't happened—Jane Sutherland murdered in cold blood, my tea shop's back room reduced to char and memory. The insurance adjuster was scheduled to arrive at 7. The fire inspector at 8. My life parsed into appointments with people whose job was to catalog disaster with professional detachment.

"Time to face the day," I told Chowder, who opened one eye with the kind of skepticism that suggested facing the day was optional and he was choosing to opt out.

I slipped out of bed and into my silk peignoir—a pale blue number with ivory lace I'd found at one of the boutiques in town. Even now, especially now, maintaining these small elegances felt like armor against chaos. If I was going to face insurance adjusters and fire inspectors, I was going to do it properly dressed, starting from the foundation.

"Oh no, you don't get to stay in bed," I told Chowder. "We have work to do. Justice to pursue. Criminals to catch."

He yawned, displaying an impressive array of teeth and general disinterest in justice, but followed me downstairs with the resignation of someone who knew breakfast was contingent on cooperation.

I let him out into the back garden for his morning constitutional while I made coffee strong enough to wake the dead—which, given recent events, might have been useful. The morning light streaming through my kitchen windows had that peculiar quality of early summer, all golden promise and hidden threats, like honey laced with arsenic.

The melody came unbidden as I poured cream into my cup—"Black Coffee," the Peggy Lee version that was all cigarette smoke and 3 a.m. regrets. I found myself singing softly while waiting for Chowder to finish his garden inspection.

"I'm feelin' mighty lonesome, haven't slept a wink..."

The song was supposedly about lost love but really it was about any kind of loss—the kind that kept you up at night, drinking coffee that had gone cold because even bitter comfort was better than none.

Chowder scratched at the door, ready for breakfast and fashion. I filled his bowl with the chicken and rice mixture that cost more than most people's lunches, then studied the clothes in his closet.

I selected his navy blazer with brass buttons. If we were going to face insurance adjusters and fire inspectors and whatever fresh horror Thursday had planned, we were going to do it in style.

"Arms up," I instructed after he'd finished eating and performed his post-breakfast face-cleaning ritual.

He lifted his paws with practiced ease, and I slipped the blazer onto him, adjusting the brass buttons until he looked ready to command a small yacht.

"Commodore Chowder at your service," I said, patting him gently.

The drive to The Perfect Steep took six minutes with no traffic, Chowder riding shotgun in his special car seat, the morning air carrying salt and possibility through my cracked window. Harbor Street was still mostly quiet at this hour—only Beaumont's Bakery showed signs of life, Clarence already at work behind the lit windows, preparing the pastries that made locals flock to his counter. The other shops remained dark, their owners still at home drinking coffee and preparing to face another day of tourist season on Grimm Island.

The Perfect Steep stood dark, crime-scene tape across the back entrance like a yellow accusation.

The fire inspector was already there—a woman in her fifties with competent hands and eyes that had seen too many deliberately set fires. She introduced herself as Captain Morse and led me around back to survey the damage by the harsh light of morning.

The back room where we'd held our murder investigation meetings, where Walt had created his tactical timeline and Dottie had spread her medical knowledge like tarot cards revealing death's secrets —all of it was gone. Charred beams reached up like blackened fingers, accusing the sky of witnessing and doing nothing.

"Definitely arson," Inspector Morse said, making notes on her tablet with quick, efficient strokes. "Someone jimmied the back door lock—crude but effective, probably a crowbar. Once inside, they doused everything with accelerant. Based on the pour patterns and smell, I'd say regular gasoline, about two gallons' worth. They wanted this room specifically destroyed—didn't even try to spread it to the main shop. The fire break between your back room and main shop is what saved the rest of the building. Too bad there aren't cameras in the back parking lot."

"Pretty bold to break in here when anyone could've seen them," I said.

"Yeah," Morse said. "Though it was dark outside and this area of town dies down pretty quickly in the evenings because most of the shops close by 6. He probably would've been in a car. Pulled into the back lot, parked in the shadows, and then broke in. Was probably in and out in ten minutes or less. Tell your sheriff to check the local gas stations, see if anyone stopped and filled up a gas canister."

I nodded, thinking that was a good idea.

"How long before I can reopen?"

"Health department has to clear you after cleanup. Week minimum, probably two. The main shop has smoke damage—it'll need professional cleaning, every surface sanitized. Can't serve food or beverages until then."

My heart sank. Two weeks without The Perfect Steep. Two weeks of Mrs. Pinkerton without her morning English Breakfast. Two weeks of routine shattered, income stopped, life disrupted because someone wanted our investigation silenced.

Genevieve arrived as the insurance adjuster was documenting damage. She looked stricken, standing on the sidewalk clutching her purse like a life preserver.

"I'm so sorry," I told her before she could speak. "I'll pay you for the full two weeks, of course. This isn't your fault."

"It's not about the money," she said, though the relief in her eyes suggested it was at least partially about the money. "Will you be okay? The shop—can it be fixed?"

"Everything can be fixed with enough time and money," I said. "We'll come back better than before."

She hugged me then, quick and fierce, and then left, probably to go look for another job. I stood watching the inspector and adjuster circle my wounded shop like vultures with clipboards.

"Mabel!"

I turned to find Walt's pristine sedan pulling up to the curb, all four windows down despite the morning humidity. Walt sat ramrod straight behind the wheel, his veterans cap positioned with mathematical precision. Deidre occupied the passenger seat, clutching what appeared to be a cardboard box of files. In the back, Bea's burgundy silk caught the morning light while Dottie sat beside her, her purple cat-eye glasses glinting in the sun.

"Emergency Silver Sleuth meeting!" Walt called out the driver's window. "Your house, oh-nine-hundred hours!"

"It's 8:45," I pointed out.

"Then you should hurry. Punctuality is the courtesy of kings." He was already pulling away from the curb. "Follow us!"

Dottie leaned across Bea to call out, "Hank's awake and quite cranky this morning, so I left his children with him. He's wanting to come home, and everyone in the hospital knows it."

Bea waved her ringed fingers out the window. "We'll get your spare key from under the ceramic frog, dear!"

They drove off toward my house, leaving me standing on the sidewalk with Chowder, who looked up at me with an expression that suggested even he found this morning surreal.

There was nothing to do but follow them, Chowder trotting beside me with the dignity of a small diplomat navigating dangerous territories.

My dining room table was quickly becoming command central as Walt unpacked the box Deidre had been carrying. He spread Tommy Wheeler's evidence across my grandmother's mahogany table with military efficiency while the others settled into chairs around him.

"Coffee's in the kitchen," I said, gesturing toward the doorway. "I'll make a fresh pot."

"No time," Walt said, already organizing documents into piles. "We need to move fast. Whoever killed Jane and torched your shop is escalating. Panic makes people sloppy, but it also makes them dangerous."

"Speaking of dangerous," Bea said, pouring coffee with the deliberate precision of someone defusing a bomb, her rings catching the morning light like tiny prisms, "I drove past the Methodist church this morning. 6 a.m and the parking lot had more cars than a Wednesday prayer meeting usually draws."

The coffee's bitter aroma mixed with her expensive perfume—something French and aggressive—creating an oddly comforting combination of luxury and necessity.

"Early for a Thursday," Deidre observed, her reading glasses sliding down her nose as she consulted her ever-present notebook, the one where she recorded everything from grocery lists to murder suspects with equal dedication.

"Prayer meeting maybe," Walt suggested, his fingers drumming against the mahogany table. "Some churches do those before work hours. Gets the faithful started right."

"Or," Bea said, setting down her coffee cup with deliberate precision, "they're having emergency meetings about us reopening the investigation. The scandal of George and Ruby was bad enough forty years ago. Everyone accepted that George and Ruby stole that money and got killed for it—crime of passion mixed with righteous anger about theft. Nice and neat. But if we prove they were innocent of the embezzlement..."

"Then someone else was guilty," Deidre finished quietly. "Someone who's been letting a dead man take the blame for forty years."

"The families of those board members are still prominent," Walt added. "The Hammonds, the Forsythes, the Bakers—their children and grandchildren still live here, still attend that church. If it comes out their fathers knew the real thief and covered it up, took hush money to stay quiet..."

"That's the kind of truth that would tear a congregation apart," I said, understanding dawning like cold water down my spine. "People who've believed one version of history for four decades finding out it was all a lie. Maybe we're on the wrong track. Maybe it's not the same killer."

The morning light streaming through my lace curtains painted everything in watercolor washes of gold and shadow, making even our grim purpose seem somehow softer, though I knew that was just another of the low country's beautiful lies.

I filled them in on Inspector Morse's findings, watching their faces shift from curiosity to anger as I described the crowbar marks on my back door, the deliberate pouring of gasoline in patterns meant to destroy everything we'd gathered.

"Inspector Morse said we were lucky last night. That group of people out for their evening walk called it in immediately when they saw the smoke. Another ten minutes and the fire would have breached the wall between the back room and main shop. The arsonist knew what they were doing—poured gasoline specifically in the back room where we'd been working, wanted those specific materials destroyed."

"What about security cameras?" Walt asked immediately, leaning forward with the intensity of a bloodhound catching scent.

"None in the back parking lot," I said, my fingers wrapping around my coffee mug for warmth I didn't really need. "But Morse said to check island gas stations. Someone bought a couple of gallons of gas somewhere, and in a town this small, someone might remember."

The floorboards creaked—that particular spot three feet from the doorway that Patrick had always meant to fix but never gotten around to, one of those small imperfections that had become part of the house's personality—and Dash materialized in the doorframe like he'd been conjured by our collective need for authority. His uniform was crisp despite the early hour, but I could see the exhaustion written in the lines around his eyes, the slight shadow of stubble he'd not bothered to shave.

"We need to push harder on Stephanie Donaldson," Dash said. "Jane Sutherland is dead. Hank's in the hospital with a cracked skull. Your shop was torched. Someone's panicking, trying to shut this investigation down. That means we're close, and we need to push before they do something worse."

He looked at me. "Stephanie wouldn't be so worried if she was telling the truth about being at Turtle Point. We've got to confront her with what we know about her being in Pickering's journal. With bodies piling up, we can't afford to be gentle anymore. She's working today—her shift started at 9—I've already checked."

"What about us?" Walt asked, looking slightly offended at being left out of the action.

"Keep working the financial angle," Dash said. "Go through those church records again, see if there's anything we missed about the building fund. Check with your contacts about those board members who made interesting financial decisions just after the murders."

"And Elder Crenshaw?" Deidre asked.

"We'll go see him this afternoon after Stephanie," Dash said. "No advance warning. The element of surprise might shake something loose, especially if he's been sitting on information for forty years."

We caught Stephanie in the hospital cafeteria during what must have been a late morning break. She sat alone at a corner table, picking at a salad while scrolling through her phone. The cafeteria buzzed with the controlled chaos of medical staff grabbing quick meals between crises—doctors in scrubs gulping coffee, administrators in suits discussing budgets, the constant flow of people trying to fuel themselves for whatever emergency came next.

She didn't see us until we were already pulling out chairs at her table. Her fork stopped halfway to her mouth, a piece of lettuce dangling precariously.

"You can't keep bothering—"

"Your stepmother Mary Jane went to Reverend Pickering for counseling," Dash said quietly, sitting down with the casual authority of someone who belonged wherever he decided to be. "About your affair with a married man."

The lettuce fell back onto her plate. Around us, the cafeteria bustled with a mixture of those who were worried or grieving and those who were picking at food to pass the time, but our table had become an island of tense silence.

"That's not—" She stopped, looked around at the nearby tables. A group of residents sat three tables over, too exhausted to pay attention to anything but their coffee. "That was forty years ago. You don't understand."

"Then help us understand," I said, keeping my voice gentle. "Pickering called you that Friday."

Stephanie's face flushed, then went pale. She set down her fork with excessive care, like it might shatter if she moved too quickly. "I don't know what you're talking about."

"Elsie Crawford saw you," Dash said simply. "Nine o'clock. Blond woman in a white nurse's uniform, arguing with Reverend Pickering by his car."

"Who cares?" she shrugged. "Elsie Crawford has mashed potatoes for brains now."

Dash smiled, but it was the kind of smile that sent shivers down the spine. It was a look I hadn't seen before, and I held my breath as I waited for the standoff between them.

"We don't need Elsie's testimony," Dash said. "Do you think we'd be here talking about your affair if we didn't have something else? And guess what, Jane Sutherland was murdered yesterday. You're going to need to give me a very good alibi for where you were between the hours of midnight and 3 a.m Wednesday morning. Because otherwise, I can hold you for seventy-two hours in a cell while we get things sorted out. There's no statute of limitations on murder, Ms. Donaldson."

"I didn't kill anyone," she said, her face paling and panic evident in her eyes.

"Then I'd start talking," Dash said.

She looked around the cafeteria as if searching for an escape route. A doctor at the next table glanced over, and she forced a smile that looked more like a grimace. Stephanie's hands trembled as she reached for her water glass. She took a sip, then another, buying time while her world tilted on its axis.

"You don't understand what it was like," she finally said, her voice barely above a whisper. "Being twenty-two and stupid and thinking you're in love with someone who keeps promising to leave his wife. Sure I was dating Matt Crenshaw, but that was obligation. Our families were friends. He was easy. But I never loved him. And obviously we weren't meant to be. I'm still amazed I made it ten years with that sniveling wimp."

She laughed, bitter and short, and pushed the hair that had fallen over her forehead back behind her ear. "Pickering called me that Friday afternoon. Said Mary Jane had come to him, begged him to intervene. She asked him to counsel me about my iniquities." The words came out like shards of glass. "That's what he called it.

"I wore my white uniform. I was supposed to be off shift at 7, but we had an emergency come in and everyone was stuck at the hospital. I slipped out as soon as I could. No one noticed with all the chaos." Her voice had gone flat, emotionless. "Pickering was there by his car when I arrived. Standing in the moonlight looking so righteous, so disappointed. Like he had any right to judge when everyone knew about him and Ruby Bailey."

"What did you talk about?"

"He said I was destroying my family. That Mary Jane was heartbroken. That I needed to end it immediately or he'd tell everyone—the hospital board, Greg's wife, the whole island."

Her knuckles were white against the coffee cup. "I told him he was a hypocrite. Carrying on with Ruby while his wife sat home. He said it was different—he was planning to leave June, make things right with Ruby, get married."

"You argued," I said, not a question.

"I laughed at him. Told him he was deluding himself if he thought the church would let him divorce and remarry his mistress. That Ruby was smarter than him—she knew he'd never leave June and the respectability." Stephanie's eyes opened, focusing on something beyond us. "He got angry. Said I didn't understand real love, that what he and Ruby had was blessed despite the circumstances. And that the elders wouldn't have a choice in the matter if they knew what was good for them."

"Then what?" Dash's voice was gentle but insistent.

"I left. Got in my car and drove away." She met our eyes then, and I saw truth mixed with four decades of fear. "I stopped at a payphone and called into the hospital. The nurse who answered was one of my good friends and I told her I forgot to clock out. She clocked out for me at just after 9:30. She didn't know she'd given me an alibi.

"I was the last person to see Reverend Pickering alive. When I heard the next morning—both of them dead, shot at Turtle Point—I knew how it would look if I said anything."

"So you said nothing," Dash said.

"I said nothing. Ended the affair with Greg. Married Matt two years later—someone safe from a good family." Her laugh was hollow. "Matt never knew about any of it. Still doesn't. I built my whole life on that silence."

"Did you see anyone else?" I asked. "Another car?"

She thought, her forehead creasing. "There was a dark sedan parked down the beach. But I was so angry, so focused on leaving, I didn't really look."

"Make? Model?"

"Dark. Four doors. That's all I remember." She straightened, pulling herself together like armor. "I've told you everything. I left George Pickering alive and arguing with God about his hypocrisy. Someone else killed him and Ruby. Someone else cut out her tongue."

The detail made me shiver. She'd said it so matter-of-factly, but the violence of it—silencing Ruby even in death—spoke of rage beyond simple murder.

"Go back to your rounds," Dash said finally. "But stay available. We may have more questions."

Stephanie took her food tray and walked away, dumping the half-eaten salad in the trash. She didn't look back.

Dash and I sat for a moment in the buzzing cafeteria, processing what we'd learned.

"Someone with a dark sedan," I said quietly. "That's not much to go on."

"No," he agreed, standing. "But it's more than we had. Let's go see what Elder Crenshaw has to say about his financial windfall in 1986."

We made our way out of the hospital, passing through the automatic doors into the humid morning air that hit like walking into a wet blanket.

The drive to Sea Pines felt longer in the morning light. I found myself humming something I couldn't quite place—an old hymn maybe, something about truth and revelation, about secrets laid bare in unforgiving light.

Through the window, the low country rolled past in shades of green and gold, beautiful and treacherous as everything in the South, hiding its dangers beneath a surface of aggressive hospitality.

Elder Crenshaw was in the garden when we arrived at Sea Pines, sitting in his wheelchair beneath a massive live oak that filtered the late morning sun into lace patterns across his lap. A blanket covered his legs despite the warmth—the thin blood of age always feeling winter even in summer's grip. A nurse hovered nearby, watering potted geraniums with the careful attention of someone being paid to look busy.

"Fifteen minutes," she said quietly. "He tires easily."

But when Crenshaw looked up at us, his eyes were sharp as broken glass, nothing tired about them.

"Come to accuse me of more crimes, Sheriff?" His voice carried that particular brand of Southern hostility wrapped in politeness, sweet tea with arsenic.

"Come to ask about money," Dash said, settling onto the bench across from him while I remained standing, watching the play of emotions across the old man's face. "And about someone called Doogie."

The name hit him like a physical blow. His fingers tightened on the blanket, knuckles going white as old bone.

"Where did you hear that name?"

"Pickering's journal," I said. "Multiple entries about Doogie bringing deposit slips, Doogie handling the building fund paperwork."

Crenshaw's laugh was dry as Spanish moss. "Doogie. Lord help us, I haven't heard that name in decades."

The old man studied us for a long moment, and I could see him weighing forty years of silence against whatever conscience he had left. The garden around us hummed with late morning life—bees in the azaleas, a mockingbird running through its stolen repertoire, the distant sound of a lawn mower—all of it feeling too alive for the conversation we were having about decades-old death.

"Who was doing it?" I asked.

"I had my suspicions, but no proof. George said he'd handle it quietly. Give the thief a chance to confess, make restitution." His voice turned bitter. "George always believed in redemption."

"But that's not what happened."

"No." The word came out heavy, final. "George confronted the thief that Friday. September 13. I know because the person came to me that evening, panicked. Said George was going to ruin everything."

"What did you do?"

"I told him to confess. Take his punishment. That stealing from God was worse than stealing from Caesar." He looked up at us, eyes red rimmed. "Then he reminded me that George wasn't the only one in sin. He knew about…some things I was dealing with. Things to do with my personal finances. I got in a bit of trouble with illegal betting. The mafia. I went to George for help, and I knew this trading of sins we were confessing to one another would bind me in ways that could never be untangled.

"But it wasn't only George who knew about your sins," Dash said.

"No, it wasn't."

Dash leaned forward. "And two days later, George and Ruby were dead."

"Yes."

"And the money that appeared in your account afterward?" Dash pressed. "The other board members got similar amounts. Roger Hammond, Gene Forsythe, Craig Baker."

Crenshaw's face crumpled like old parchment. "Blood money. All of it. After George and Ruby died, we were told it was from an anonymous donor who wanted to help the church move forward. It was enough to cover the debts I owed. And enough to start my wife and me on a new path. A safe path. If I hadn't taken the money I'd probably be as dead as George."

"Who gave you the money?" I asked.

The mockingbird above us switched songs, launching into something that sounded foreboding.

"I'm old," he finally said. "I know my days on this earth are numbered. I'm at peace with it. I've long since cleared my conscience. And the truth is, I saw no other way out. I would have still made the same choice if I were given it today. It makes me guilty of many things, but not of murder. George was guilty too. And he paid the price."

"No one deserves to pay with their life," Dash said.

Crenshaw shrugged. "Or maybe God was tired of George disgracing the pulpit and took vengeance into his own hands."

"Who killed him?" Dash asked. "Who paid off your debts?"

Crenshaw's gaze grew distant and his voice soft. "He killed that woman. The reporter. She knew everything. And would have blown the case wide open if he hadn't gotten to her. Must have scared her. Or had something on her too. Because next thing we know she'd packed up and left town. But she came back. And now she's dead. He's very clever. He'll kill me too. Even in a place like this. But like I said, I've made peace with death."

"Give me a name," Dash said again, his voice leaving no room for argument or more rabbit trails.

Crenshaw smiled, displaying obscenely white dentures. "A name by any other name…"

CHAPTER
FOURTEEN

The afternoon sun slanted through my lace curtains like an accusation, painting golden stripes across the murder board where Reverend Douglas Sutton's name had been written. My dining room, which had hosted years of gentle tea conversations and genteel gossip, now thrummed with the electric energy of six people who'd just discovered they'd been played for fools by a man of God.

"Reverend Sutton," Dash said. "Doogie was a nickname given to him at seminary, according to Crenshaw. Apparently he was something of a boy genius."

"Boy sociopath is more like it," Deidre said.

Walt's pointer, which had directed us through so many theories, now tapped against the timeline with sharp, agitated beats. "That sanctimonious fraud has been conducting our investigation like an orchestra, pointing us toward everyone but himself."

"To be fair," I said. "Everyone in this case has been guilty of something. No wonder it was so easy for Reverend Sutton to throw suspicion at Reverend Pickering."

"We should stop calling them reverends," Dottie said. "I can think of a lot better names for the whole lot of them. Especially after what happened to Hank. And that poor Jane Sutherland. Did we ever find out why she was here?"

Bea cleared her throat and moved to the side bar. "She was here because of me. I'd finally gotten her to agree to meet with me." Bea smoothed down a nonexistent wrinkle in her caftan. "I wish I hadn't stopped smoking. Now would be an excellent time for a cigarette."

"You could vape," Walt said.

"I don't know," Bea said. "There's something about smoking an actual cigarette. It lends itself to a certain panache. There's an elegance to it."

"You mean it looks cool," Deidre said, rolling her eyes. "It also shortens your wind."

"Which is why I no longer smoke," Bea said shortly. "Who wants a sidecar?"

"I'll take one," Dottie said. "Hank's kids are driving me crazy. Nervous Nellies if I've ever met them. It must be the generation. We were certainly made of stronger stuff."

"Yeah, cigarettes and sidecars," Walt said. "Bea, will you please get on with your story about Jane."

"Oh, right," she said, waving a hand dismissively. "Anyway, I can be rather convincing. And I told her that forty years had passed and all the original suspects were either too old or too dead for it to matter much. I even told her I'd come to her in Atlanta to hear what she'd uncovered during her investigation. I'm afraid I laid it on rather thick." She sighed and squeezed a lemon into the shaker. "I mentioned justice and doing the right thing. And look where that got her. With a bullet in her brain."

"It's not your fault, Bea," Dash said. "A man like Douglas Sutton has been playing chess for the last forty years. Don't think he didn't know exactly where she was all this time. He could have killed her at any moment."

"Unfortunately I have to live with the fact it was the moment I brought her here," she said. "And I feel guilty because I was supposed to meet with her in that very room. He killed her before I was able to meet with her, and what I felt was relief."

Deidre went over and put a hand on Bea's shoulder. "That's a perfectly normal reaction, to be grateful you're alive when the outcome could be so different. But don't take the blame for something that lies completely at the feet of a madman."

Bea nodded and looked down, trying to compose herself. I'd never seen Bea so emotional. She wasn't the type to wear her heart on her sleeve. But in this moment, she looked every bit her age—and there was a frailty about her I'd never noticed before.

"He'll pay for his crimes," Walt said, nodding his head sharply

I stood at the head of the table, still in the silk dress I'd worn to Sea Pines, though it now felt wrinkled with revelations. The fabric whispered against my skin as I moved closer to study the board, trying to see what we'd missed all along.

"How did Sutton know everyone's Achilles' heel?" Dottie asked. "He was so young."

"His office shared a heating vent with Pickering's," Dash explained. "Every private conversation, every confession—Sutton heard it all. Not through divine providence but through architectural coincidence and criminal intent."

The room smelled of Earl Grey and betrayal, with undertones of Bea's Chanel No. 5. Chowder sat at my feet in his book club attire—a hunter-green smoking jacket with a black velvet lapel—watching the proceedings with the patient dignity of a dog who'd seen enough human foolishness to no longer be surprised by it.

Dottie adjusted her purple cat-eye glasses, the late afternoon light catching the rhinestones and throwing tiny rainbows across the murder board. "Ruby cleaned both offices. She would have noticed discrepancies, found evidence. Not to speak ill of the dead, but she was an opportunist. She was looking for a way out. A way to support herself and her son. There's no proof she was as enamored with Pickering as he was with her, but he was her ticket out of town. Poor woman signed her own death warrant with a mop and bucket."

"Not to change the subject," Deidre announced, checking her watch. "But it's quarter to six. Book club is supposed to start in fifteen minutes, and I know Walt will start having heart palpitations if his schedule is disrupted." She paused, looking around the room at our makeshift war council. "Though given the circumstances, perhaps we should postpone book club?"

"Postpone nothing," Bea declared, shaking the tumbler aggressively before pouring it into her sugar-rimmed glass. "I figured out the killer within three chapters. That book was a real snoozefest. I motion we skip the book discussion entirely and focus on the real mystery."

"I second that," Dottie said immediately. "Hurry up with that sidecar, Bea. I'm dry as dust."

"All in favor?" Walt asked.

Five hands rose in unison, everyone except Dash, who had learned to go with the flow when it came to the eccentricities of our group.

Bea set to work with the skill of someone who'd spent decades perfecting the art of afternoon drinking.

"We need him to confess," I said, my fingers unconsciously finding the pearl necklace at my throat. "Crenshaw's testimony won't be enough. Not after forty years of everyone believing Sutton was above reproach."

Through the window, I caught Mrs. Pembroke pretending to water her already drowned petunias while obviously watching my house. Her hose had been trained on the same pot for five minutes, creating a small flood that was currently threatening her garden gnomes. And I'd noticed Patsy Hindman had been lingering across the street, pretending to let her golden retriever, Oscar, sniff around the palm trees while she surreptitiously glanced toward my front porch.

"Look at that," Walt muttered, following my gaze. "Better than security cameras, having those two as neighbors."

I moved to the murder board, studying the timeline we'd constructed. "He's controlled this narrative for forty years. Given us just enough truth to make us trust him while steering us away from himself." I found myself humming *Only a Paper Moon*—appropriate, given how we'd all been fooled by something that wasn't real.

"What pulls a man like Sutton?" Walt asked, his tactical mind already working. "Pride. Ego. The need to be the smartest person in the room."

"Exactly," Dash said. "He can't resist showing off his intelligence. It's why he gave us Pickering's journal—he wanted us to see how clever he'd been, using it to point us everywhere but at himself."

"What if I call him, tell him we've found something in the evidence—something we can't quite understand. Appeal to his expertise, his superior knowledge of the people involved."

"Make him think he's still in control," Dottie added, understanding immediately. "That we need his wisdom to interpret what we've found."

"He won't be able to resist," Bea said. "Men like him never can when you tell them they're the only one smart enough to help."

I picked up my phone. It rang three times before Sutton answered. "Mabel. This is unexpected. It's not often I get calls from members who belong to the other church in town." He laughed at his own joke and I followed suit, trying to play it nice and easy.

"Reverend, I'm so sorry to bother you, but you know we've been tasked with the Pickering-Bailey cold case and we found something strange in one of the evidence boxes that Milton locked away."

"I'd heard you lost everything in the fire at your tea shop," he said, sympathetically. "Such a tragedy. For the case and for your business. But I know you'll bounce back stronger than before. Patrick would be very proud of your tenacity."

I narrowed my eyes and felt the flush of anger creep up my neck. And then I burst his bubble.

"Oh, I know everything will be okay. The Lord always provides. And Walt was able to save all the work we'd done from the fire. You know how prepared he always is."

"Of course," Sutton said slowly, though I could hear the disappointment in his voice. "It's good you've got mentors with such wisdom."

"I was calling because there's just something we have to be missing. There's a pattern we can't quite figure out. You knew these people better than anyone—could you possibly come by—just so we could get your personal insight on everyone involved?"

"A pattern?" His voice sharpened with interest. "What kind of pattern?"

"Something about the dates and the way things line up. Thursday deposits, but that's not all. There's more, but I don't want to influence your interpretation. You might see something we're missing."

"Of course. I see this as my Christian duty and civic responsibility to try to right the wrongs George made against our community. I can be there in about fifteen minutes."

"You know where I live?" I asked.

"Of course," he said. "Everyone on the island knows your house. See you soon."

The line went dead, and I set the phone down carefully.

"Ten minutes," Dash said, calling into dispatch. "I need unmarked units posted around the neighborhood. Stay out of sight."

We arranged the evidence strategically—financial records visible but not obviously incriminating, the timeline prominent but incomplete, as if we were still trying to connect dots that wouldn't quite align.

Exactly fifteen minutes later, the doorbell rang with the punctuality of a man who believed tardiness was a sin just below embezzlement and murder.

I opened the door to find him in a black suit, his thin frame held with righteousness. He smelled of peppermint and old books, the scent of dusty absolution.

"Reverend, thank you for coming. Please come in and make yourself comfortable. We're just baffled."

He entered my home with confidence. The Silver Sleuths were arranged around the dining table, papers spread before them in artful confusion.

"You have quite the setup here," he said, looking at the intricate murder board and the stacks of papers and interviews, financial letters, and the blown-up picture of the church picnic the summer before Pickering and Ruby were murdered. "It's fortunate it was only your tea shop that was damaged. You had a lot more to lose here in your home."

"Yes, fortunate," I agreed, trying to look relieved instead of like I wanted to stab him in the eyeball with one of the long toothpicks on the bar.

"Now what about this pattern you mentioned," he said, moving to the board with the eagerness of a teacher about to correct particularly slow students.

I began carefully, gesturing to the board. "We've been trying to reconstruct that night, but there are so many gaps. Stephanie told us about her argument with Pickering at 9, but we can't figure out what happened next."

"A tragic evening," Sutton said, moving closer to study our timeline. "What specifically puzzles you?"

"Well," Dottie said, adjusting her purple cat-eye glasses, "When I did the autopsies, I placed time of death between 10 and midnight. The physical evidence confirmed they'd been intimate, but the positioning afterward—that staged embrace—that was done postmortem. Someone arranged them deliberately."

"Like they were making a statement," Walt said.

"But what puzzles me," I said, studying the timeline, "Is that Stephanie saw Pickering at 9, argued with him, and left around 9:15. That means Ruby arrived after that, or was waiting somewhere nearby."

"The killer had to have been watching," Sutton offered, moving closer to the board. "Waiting for the right moment."

"From where though?" Bea asked. "How do you watch without being seen?"

"Turtle Point has plenty of tree cover and marsh grass," Sutton said smoothly. "The killer could have been anywhere. The moonlight that night was strong enough to see by, but it also creates deep shadows."

"You remember the moonlight from that specific night?" Walt asked, and I could see him testing, probing.

Sutton didn't miss a beat. "Everyone remembers that night, Mr. Garrison. The whole island was talking about the moon—unusually bright for September. Like God himself was providing a spotlight." He paused, then added smoothly, "Or so people said at the time. You know how memories become collective on an island this small."

He was right, of course. The police reports had noted the clear night, the nearly full moon. But there was something about the way he said it—too ready, too rehearsed.

"What we can't figure out," I said, redirecting before he got suspicious, "is why they folded their clothes. Frank Holloway told us the clothes were stacked neatly on Pickering's back seat. Who does that in a moment of passion?"

"Perhaps they weren't in a rush," Sutton suggested. "If they thought they had all night…"

"Or someone else folded them," Dottie said quietly. "After."

The room went still for a moment, everyone playing their parts perfectly—confused investigators grateful for any insight their helpful pastor could provide.

"The money is what really puzzles us," Walt said, tapping a financial record with deliberate frustration. "These deposits into the church building fund—they're all over the place. Some Thursdays, some Fridays. No real pattern we can find."

I watched Sutton's shoulders relax slightly at Walt's apparent confusion.

"Church finances were always complicated," Sutton offered, his voice taking on a teaching tone. "Multiple donors, various fundraising events. George wasn't the most organized bookkeeper."

"That's what Elder Crenshaw said," I lied smoothly. "Though he was quite confused about the whole thing. Kept talking about someone named Doogie? Said it was important but couldn't remember why."

Sutton's hand stilled on the edge of the table. Just for a second. Then he forced a chuckle. "Poor Matthias. His mind really is going. Doogie could be anyone—a donor, perhaps. Or nothing at all. You know how the elderly sometimes fixate on random details."

"Probably," Bea agreed, then added with studied casualness, "Though it's funny—Pickering wrote Doogie in his journal several times. Always connected to deposit slips."

"May I?" Sutton asked, gesturing toward the journal we'd left strategically open.

"Please," I said. "We're hoping fresh eyes might see something we're missing."

He bent over the journal, and I watched his face as he read his own nickname in Pickering's handwriting. His jaw tightened almost imperceptibly.

"This could be anyone," he said finally. "A code name, perhaps. George did like his little mysteries."

"A code name," Walt repeated thoughtfully. "For someone on the inside. Someone who had access to the church accounts."

"The finance committee had six members," Deidre said, consulting her notes. "You were on it, weren't you, Reverend? As assistant pastor?"

"I handled some administrative duties, yes," Sutton said carefully. "But George oversaw all the finances himself. Very particular about it."

"Except someone was stealing," I said softly. "And Ruby figured it out. That's what got them killed, isn't it? Not the affair—the money."

Sutton straightened slowly, and for the first time, I saw calculation in his eyes as he reassessed the situation. We weren't as lost as we'd appeared.

"That's quite a leap," he said, his voice still steady but missing its earlier warmth.

"Is it?' Dash asked from his position by the window. "Union Theological Seminary in New York keeps good records. From 1976— Douglas 'Doogie' Sutton. Your alternate name in their files. Same man who became assistant pastor here in 1983."

Sutton went completely still.

"And Ruby cleaned both of your offices," I added, watching his face. "Yours and Pickering's. She emptied your trash, saw the duplicate deposit slips. That's what she meant when she told Pickering she knew where the money was going—she wasn't talking about some bank account. She meant your office."

"She could have meant anything," Sutton said.

"The timeline keeps bothering me," I said, crossing to where our evidence sprawled across the table like tea leaves waiting to be read. "Pickering's last journal entry—September 14—says they were meeting at Turtle Point to talk about leaving. Not their usual Tuesday or Thursday at the Flamingo, but Sunday night. Someone knew exactly where they'd be."

"Someone who'd been listening," Dash said quietly from his position by the window, his voice carrying that edge of certainty when pieces finally click.

"Through a heating vent, perhaps," Dottie said, adjusting her purple cat-eye glasses. "Your office shared one with Pickering's, didn't it, Reverend? You mentioned once how you could hear him practicing his sermons."

The silence stretched taut as piano wire. Sutton's eyes moved from face to face, calculating—measuring the distance to the door against six senior citizens who'd proven surprisingly adept at solving murders, weighing decades of successful deception against truth closing in from all sides.

"You made mistakes, Reverend," Dash said, emphasizing his title. "You thought you had the power because you knew things that could discredit those who might turn you in. Blackmail, if you will. You could have just sat on things and let the secret die with you. But you followed Hank and Dottie and Mabel to Beaufort. Haven't you ever heard that curiosity killed the cat? You followed Hank to that parking lot and hit him over the head. You could have killed him."

"I don't know what you're talking about," he said stiffly.

"That's the great thing about technology," Dash said. "It's really hard to get away with crimes nowadays. The toll road cameras caught your vehicle and license plate crossing the bridge into Beaufort."

Sutton shrugged. "I let people borrow my car all the time," he said. "Anyone who is in need, really. It's part of my job to tend to my flock."

"And then you really made a big mistake," Dash continued on, as if Sutton hadn't spoken at all. "You killed Jane Sutherland. Ballistics came back showing that it's the same gun that was used to kill Ruby and George. I've got warrants for your house, car, and the church office. There are cops going through your things as we speak. Wonder what we'll find? Not only is it the same weapon, but the crime-scene team found a partial fingerprint in the oils on our victim's face. Did you decide to absolve her of her sins?"

"You know," Sutton said finally, his voice different now—stripped raw, exposed as a nerve, "George always thought he was so clever. Writing everything down in that journal, collecting secrets like communion wafers. But he never realized the biggest secret was right next door, listening to every word through thin walls and shared ventilation."

"The money," Walt said. It wasn't a question.

"My money," Sutton corrected, and there was something almost relief in his voice, as if forty years of performance had finally exhausted him. "Money I'd earned through while having to cover for George and every other member of our leadership team. They truly were terrible people. I felt I was justified. George paid himself three times what I made. Three times! He had a wife and kids, and a piece on the side. He was getting his cake and eating it too. Why shouldn't I?"

"So you embezzled," I said.

"I took what was mine." His voice had risen to sermon pitch, but this was a different kind of sermon—one about resentment fermented into rage. "Every Thursday, my day off, I'd make deposits. Small amounts transferred to the building fund, then redirected. I was care-ful. Methodical. It would have worked perfectly if that woman hadn't—"

He stopped himself, but it was too late.

"If Ruby hadn't found the duplicate deposit slips in your trash," Dash finished.

Sutton's laugh was bitter as communion wine gone to vinegar. "She threatened to tell George everything unless I helped them run away. Can you imagine? That whore and her hypocrite lover, black-mailing ME?"

"So you killed them," Dottie said flatly.

"I followed them to Turtle Point." The words poured out now like a confession he'd been rehearsing for four decades. "Watched them from the trees. Waited until they were…distracted. Vulnerable. George never even saw me coming. I took them by surprise. Had them both kneel. I knew I had to make it quick. There was no need drawing it out. I'd already decided their sentence. One shot to the back of the head while he was still naked, still flushed with his sin."

"And Ruby?" I asked, though my throat felt tight.

"She ran." His eyes had gone distant, seeing that night instead of my dining room.

"Screaming about the money, about her son, about God knows what. So I shot her before she could draw attention. You never know who might be hidden nearby." He laughed, somewhat maniacally, and it brought chills to my skin.

"I shot her again. She fell to the ground, but she was still making so much noise. Even as the blood darkened the sand beneath her. Then I shot her again and there was nothing but silence. Not even the birds or the trees made a sound. I cut out her tongue, just to make sure she couldn't make any more noise."

"Then you positioned them," Walt said grimly. "Made it look like a crime of passion."

"Everyone expected it. Jealous spouse, outraged church member— the narrative wrote itself." He seemed almost proud. "I even provided the perfect evidence to guide the investigation. George's journal. Witness statements suggesting other suspects. For forty years, it worked perfectly."

"Douglas Sutton," Dash said formally, pulling out his handcuffs, "You're under arrest for the murders of George Pickering, Ruby Bailey, and Jane Sutherland, and the attempted murder of Hank Hardeman."

Sutton lunged sideways with surprising agility, making for the door. But Chowder—my brilliant, brave, fearless boy—had been waiting. He launched himself at Sutton's ankle with the precision of a heat-seeking missile, his teeth finding their mark just above the dress shoe.

Sutton went down hard, his knee cracking against the hardwood floor with a sound like judgment day. "Get him off! Get this hellhound off me!"

"Good boy, Chowder," I said calmly, though my heart was racing. "That's enough now."

Chowder released his grip but maintained his position, standing over the fallen reverend with the dignity of a small but victorious gladiator.

Dash cuffed Sutton while reading him his rights, the metal clicking with the finality of a church bell tolling for the last time. Through the window, I could see Mrs. Pembroke practically pressed against her fence, her watering can forgotten, as the cops that had been waiting for this moment descended through the front door.

"Forty years," Sutton muttered. "Forty years of being this island's moral compass, and you destroy it all for a whore and her hypocrite lover."

"No," I said, meeting his eyes steadily. "You're not judge, jury and executioner. Someone in your position should know that better than anyone."

By 7:30, the murder board bore Walt's neat inscription—*CASE CLOSED*. The sidecars had given way to champagne—Bea had hidden a bottle in my refrigerator when she'd first come in. Apparently, she'd had a feeling we were going to need it tonight.

"Dom Pérignon 1996," she announced. "Been saving it for something special. Figured catching a killer qualifies."

"Almost anything qualifies for you to take a drink, Bea," Deidre said.

"You used to be a lot more fun before you became a stick in the mud," Bea shot back.

The celebration continued, warm and wonderful. But as the evening wore on, Dash caught my arm gently, drawing me aside near the window where Mrs. Pembroke couldn't quite see us through her curtains.

"I need to head out soon," he said quietly, his thumb brushing against my wrist in that way that made my pulse skip. "Got to process Sutton properly, and the media have this all over the ten o'clock news.

Forty-year-old murder solved by the Silver Sleuths. They'll be camped outside the station."

"Of course," I said, though I felt a small pang of disappointment. "Duty calls."

"Breakfast tomorrow?" he asked, and there was something hopeful in his eyes that made my stomach perform its familiar acrobatics. "You'll have mornings off for a little while, until the tea shop opens back up."

"We can get pastries and coffee from Beaumont's and have a water-front picnic."

"Romantic," he said, mouth quirking in a half smile. "We need to talk, Mabel." His voice dropped lower, more intimate despite the cele-bration happening around us. "About us. About what this is becom-ing. I meant what I said before—I'm finding it difficult to leave you at the end of each day."

I remembered that conversation, the intensity of it, the promise of something more that we'd been dancing around since this investiga-tion began.

"Tomorrow then," I agreed. "Breakfast and…conversation."

Twenty minutes later, after Dash had left with a final look that promised tomorrow's conversation would change things between us, Bea caught my eye and nodded toward the kitchen.

She ushered me toward the mudroom, where no one could hear us. The celebration noises faded to a distant hum, like happiness happening in another room, another life.

"Sugar," she said, and her voice had lost all its theatrical flair. This was Bea stripped of performance, and somehow that made her words heavier. "We need to talk about your sheriff."

"Now?" I asked, though I knew the answer. Some conversations chose their own timing.

She reached into her purse—that magical repository that seemed to exist in more dimensions than physics should allow—and pulled out a manila envelope, thick with who knew what. The weight of it in her manicured hands felt like holding someone else's tragedy.

"I do what I do," she said simply. "I dig into people's lives. Can't help myself—it's like breathing or mixing cocktails. Compulsive. And honey, Dashiell Beckett..." She paused, choosing her words like selecting bullets. "He has secrets that would make your blood run cold."

The envelope felt heavier than paper should, like holding someone else's grief, someone else's guilt.

"I'm not saying he's bad," Bea said softly, her hand covering mine. "Good people can have terrible secrets. But sugar, you're falling in love with him—I see how you light up when he walks in, how you lean toward him like a plant toward sun. You deserve the whole truth, not just the charming sheriff who shows up at exactly the right time with exactly the right words."

"Maybe the past should stay buried," I said, surprising myself.

"Maybe," Bea agreed. "But secrets are like bodies in the marsh, honey. They always surface eventually. Better you know on your terms than have it explode when you least expect it."

She squeezed my hand once, then turned back to the celebration, leaving me alone with the envelope and the weight of decision.

Some secrets, I thought as I slipped the envelope in the kitchen drawer unopened, could wait for another day. But even as I walked back to join the others, I knew that day would come sooner than I wanted.

The envelope sat heavy in the back of my mind, counting down to a revelation I wasn't sure I was ready for. But then again, I hadn't been ready for widowhood, for murder, for falling in love again either.

Maybe being ready was overrated.

Maybe the only thing that mattered was being brave enough to open the envelope when the time came.

But not tonight. Tonight was for victory and friendship and the knowledge that Ruby Bailey and George Pickering finally had the justice they deserved.

Tomorrow, though—tomorrow might be for harder truths.

PRE-ORDER CHILLED TO THE BONE

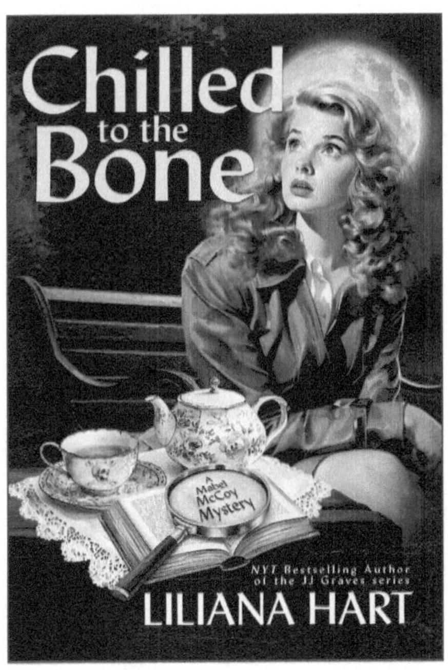

Chilled to the Bone
June 23, 2026

THE LIES WE TELL

By her calculations, Grace Meredith had exactly five and a half seconds to take out six targets before an alarm sounded. She had a round in the chamber and five in the magazine of her M40A5. Piece of cake.

She ignored the mosquitoes the size of hummingbirds searching for exposed flesh, and she disregarded the sweat that dripped steadily down her spine as she looked through the scope of her rifle. The temperature was in the mid-nineties, but the canopy of trees that blanketed the area held the heat in like an oven and slowly baked anyone who didn't have shelter with a running AC. Her body and mind were disciplined, so the discomforts barely registered.

Colombia wasn't known for its gentle climate. Or gentle anything for that matter. Gemino Vasquez was Colombia's baddest arms dealer, and lately his biggest client had been North Korea. But Vasquez had something Grace wanted very badly. Something that would bring in a big, fat paycheck from the South Korean government.

She shifted slightly, and the bark of the large tree branch she'd lain on for the last four hours ground against her stomach. But her focus was absolute. Not even the hundred-and-fifty-foot drop to the ground could distract her.

The orange sun blazed just over the tops of the trees, but it would disappear completely in another twenty minutes. By the time it was gone, she'd have the flash drive in hand and already be across the border to Venezuela.

Grace did one final check of all her equipment and took a deep, steadying breath, slowing her heartbeat so her pulse would be in time with-b each shot. She'd hit the sentry at the top of the Vasquez compound first and then take the rest in order from left to right. She pushed her feet against the tree for balance. The clock ticked in the background of her mind as she put the slightest amount of pressure on the trigger.

"One," she whispered. She didn't wait to watch him fall but moved to the next target. Five seconds until the report from her rifle reached their ears. Five seconds for five more kills.

Two...

Three...

Four...

Five...

Six...

Grace didn't stop to check the accuracy of her shots. She never missed a target. She hung her rifle on a tree branch, already missing the feel of it in her hands. Time was of the essence now, and she couldn't afford to be burdened with too much equipment—she'd have to leave it behind. The new guards would be driving up soon for the shift change, and she had to be long gone by then.

She unzipped her supply pack, pulling out a lightweight pipe no longer than her forearm. It looked completely worthless at first glance. In reality, it was a military prototype she'd borrowed from her former life. She hit the button on each end of the pipe and it expanded in length until it was almost as tall as she was, and then she hit the button in the center and waited as wings made out of a synthetic material unfurled to complete the hang glider.

"No time like the present," she said, swallowing as she perched on the edge of the tree and looked out across the jungle. She had a straight shot into the compound, but any shift in wind would have her hurtling into trees. Falling to her death wouldn't bring her the money she needed, so she had no choice but to take a leap of faith. Literally.

Fifteen minutes until all hell breaks loose.

Grace grasped the bar and jumped. The bottom dropped out of her stomach as she free-fell for just a brief moment, and then the air caught beneath the wings and she soared through the treetops like a phantom. It took all her strength and concentration to keep the glider on a straight path to the compound roof, and when her feet touched the ground her muscles were fatigued and her skin coated with perspiration.

She hit another button on the long metal tube and the glider folded itself back up until it was small enough to fit back in her pack.

The body of the first sentry she'd shot lay face down in the greenish-blue water of the swimming pool. A hazy cloud of blood ballooned from under him, and his arms and legs floated like waving ribbons.

Her eyes and ears were alert, but all that greeted her was growing darkness and silence. Even the animals and birds in the jungle knew something bad was about to go down.

Grace unhooked the harness and pulled her SIG from a thigh holster. She stood silently next to the gray door that led from the roof down a set of stairs to the main floors of the house. Two heartbeats passed before she opened the door and slipped inside. It was quiet, but that wasn't unusual at this time of the day according to her intel—six sentries on duty surrounding the compound, only two guarding Vasquez's private suite of rooms.

Vasquez's stupidity only made her job easier.

Grace walked silently down the thickly carpeted hallway as if she weren't about to steal the schematics for a new superweapon—a weapon that used state-of-the-art laser technology—and sell it to another country. But the closer she got to Vasquez, the more her spine tingled in awareness that something was wrong. That tingle had saved her life more than once, and she never ignored it. The hallway opened up into a landing just as she reached Vasquez's private rooms. Weak light filtered through the windows and cast rainbows as it pierced the glass chandelier that hung overhead.

She saw firsthand exactly why her spine was tingling.

Both sentries were slumped against each other—a dead man's embrace—one with a broken neck and the other with a hunting knife in his carotid. Efficient work considering the size of the sentries.

She pushed the bodies out of her way with her foot and eased the door open, her trigger finger at the ready on her SIG. All that mattered was the flash drive. If she didn't produce it, then she didn't get paid.

She crept into the room. The smells of new death were thick and cloying in the heat, and she could taste the fresh blood in the back of her throat with every breath she took. Dust motes danced in the air, and long shadows were cast in the fading sunlight.

Grace waited for her eyes to adjust and listened for sounds of footsteps, but all she heard was the gentle whir of the wicker fans that rotated slowly on the ceiling. She moved silently, staying close to the wall as she checked his suite.

Vasquez's bedroom was bigger than her whole apartment—the furniture oversized and ornate, the colors garishly red. He was set up for sex. The interesting kind of sex by the looks of things. Restraints and various whips and other tools lined one whole wall, and torn condom packages littered the floor. It looked like Vasquez had a busy day. Too bad his afternoon hadn't turned out so hot.

Gemino Vasquez's body lay spread-eagle on his bed. He was naked, and his eyes were open and unseeing. Two shots to the center of the forehead screamed of a professional hit. He hadn't been dead long. She couldn't stop the bitter disappointment when she saw the flash drive was gone from the chain on his right wrist.

"Hell," she whispered and moved to check the covers of his bed, just to make sure it hadn't come off in the struggle. But she knew in her heart it was long gone. Professionals didn't leave loose ends behind. And this was definitely professional. What ticked her off even more was that whoever did it managed to sneak in right under her nose. He had to have known she was watching through her scope and snuck in through the one blind spot she had at the back of the compound.

The stir of air behind her was the only warning she had before an arm locked around her throat.

"Looking for this?" a deep voice whispered in her ear. He held the flash drive in front of her face.

He pressed close against her back and squeezed his arm tighter around her throat so she had to breathe shallowly through her nose. Grace winced as he pressed his fingers against the pressure points of her wrist, and her pistol fell uselessly to the floor with a dull thunk.

Fear never had a chance to take hold. It was anger that drove Grace. Anger that had kept her alive the last couple of years. And she knew how to wield it. She threw her head back and aimed her heel at his knee simultaneously. He dodged her blows as if he'd been expecting them, but the distraction was enough for him to loosen his grip. She swept her leg and brought him to his knees, reaching down for the knife in her boot. The blade gleamed once in the fading sunlight just before it was knocked out of her hand and across the room.

He outweighed her by close to eighty pounds, and he had a good eight inches on her in height. They grappled and rolled, each one blocking the other's strikes with only seconds to spare. It was a well-choreographed dance.

A familiar dance.

The surprise of recognition took her off guard, and she looked up into laughing blue eyes framed by thick, dark lashes she'd always been jealous of. She had time to register that he'd let his hair grow—a shaggy mane of ink black that curled just over his ears and collar, and a face that was covered in a short, stubbled beard—just before her legs went out from under her. She hit the carpet with a thud. A hard body pressed her into the floor, and he held her wrists captive above her head.

"Hello, darling." His breath whispered against her skin. "You've been practicing. Who's your new sparring partner?"

"Gabe," she said. "What do you want?" She bucked beneath him, annoyed at the familiarity of his weight on her.

"I want you, of course." His lips glanced across her cheek to the corner of her mouth, and she sucked in a breath that brought her body even closer to his. After everything he'd done, he was still the only man who could make her feel less than whole when their bodies weren't fused together. She hated him for it. She hated herself for it.

"Go to hell." She struggled against him, but he shifted his weight to hold her down.

"I've been there, thanks." He cupped his hand against her cheek—gently—softly. "You still feel good against me. Stop wiggling and we'll talk. Don't you want to at least hear my offer? Especially since I did your dirty work for you."

She stilled her body and relaxed, hoping he'd get distracted long enough for her to make a move, and she spoke through gritted teeth. "I don't want anything you have to offer. Just give me the flash drive."

"I figure we have exactly four minutes to get out of this place before the new guards show up for the shift change and Armageddon begins. All I'm asking is that you come back with me and hear me out. If you decide to turn me down, then I'll give you the flash drive with no hard feelings, and you can claim your bounty."

Grace stared at him and tried to decide if he was bluffing. "You know I don't trust you."

"Yes, I believe you've told me that before," he said, his gaze hard. "But what I'm offering will pay more than double any of the jobs you've recently taken. Hear me out."

"Fine." She knew her options were limited. "What are we waiting for?"

"Our rendezvous point is on the other side of the border," he said, rolling off of her. She ignored the hand he reached out to help her up. "We've got twenty minutes to get there or we miss our ride."

Grace had no choice but to follow him out of one hell and into another.

***

The woman hadn't changed a bit in all the years he'd known her. She still kept her deep auburn hair braided tightly down her back while she was working. But he knew what it looked like spread across his pillow, and he knew what it felt like as it slithered like silk across his chest—glorious—a bright flame that was cool to the touch.

He looked at her critically, trying to decipher exactly why he was still attracted to her after the two years they'd spent apart. There wasn't just one thing about her that stood out, but the entire package. Her face was thinner now—her cheekbones more pronounced—but it was still the face of a sea goddess. Eyes the color of emeralds, slightly tilted at the corners, and full lips that haunted his dreams. She was every desire he'd ever had wrapped in one tiny package.

He let his gaze drift down her body. She was thinner all over. The lush curves he remembered were gone, replaced by a compact body of pure muscle and athleticism. She glanced back at him and raised a brow at where his gaze had landed.

Gabe smiled, but it didn't reach his eyes. He'd been wrong. She'd changed a lot. There was a hardness about her now that hadn't been there before. When she'd first started with the CIA, there had been hope and an ideal of the greater good. Now there was just emptiness —a cold, green stare that didn't believe in anything—and it scared the hell out of him. Because it was no one's fault but his own.

"We've just crossed the border into Venezuela by my calculations," she said, slowing to a jog. "How much farther is your rendezvous point?"

"About another mile. Keep the sound of water to your immediate left." He put his hand on her arm before she could take off again. "Wait."

She stopped dead in her tracks, and Gabe could tell she was trying to hear what he had. They were silent for a few more seconds before the sound came again.

She blew out an annoyed breath. "It's the new guards. You always did have ears like a bat."

"What do you have on you?" he asked.

"My SIG and a hunting knife. How many do you think there are?"

"No more than a dozen. They're noisy bastards. And not too fast." He pulled his own pistol from the small of his back and checked the magazine. "I'll give you a boost." He replaced his weapon in his pants and laced his fingers together. He arched a brow as she looked back at him with irritation.

"I'm really tired of climbing trees." She exhaled and put her foot into his hands. He launched her up so she could reach the lowest branch, and she swung herself up with ease.

"Do you have good visibility?" Gabe asked.

"Yeah, I see them," she said. "You'll have to draw them close enough so I'm within range."

"Try not to hit me by mistake."

Her grin was sharp as she looked down at him. "Oh, it wouldn't be a mistake."

"That's what I'm afraid of." Gabe left her there to go meet trouble head-on.

He found cover behind a tree trunk the size of a small car and waited patiently. Heavy footsteps crunched over twigs, and he stuck out his foot as two of them passed by. One of the guards tripped and went sprawling to the ground, and Gabe struck out at the other with a palm to the chest, stopping his heart instantly. He broke the neck of the one who was already down before the man could rise off his knees.

Gabe ignored the steady stream of fire that came from behind him —despite her wanting to kill him, he trusted Grace to fight at his side during battle. It was after the battle that worried him.

He went searching for his next victim.

Only a few minutes passed before he stood in the middle of a ring of twelve guards—all of them dead. None of them had fired a shot. She was even better than he remembered.

Grace was waiting for him when he caught up to where he'd left her.

"Time's ticking," he said, looking at his watch.

They picked up the pace and ran the last mile in silence and slowed as they came to a winding dirt road with deeply rutted tire tracks, making footing tricky.

"Did we miss the pickup?" Grace asked.

A forest-green Humvee coated with a thick layer of dust came out of the trees behind them and pulled to a stop. Grace had her weapon out and her finger on the trigger.

"He's mine," Gabe said, opening the back door.

Grace slid across the hot leather seat.

The driver turned and looked at Gabe. Logan Grey had worked with him on other missions. He was a quiet man, tall and sinewy with muscle. He wore his dark-blond hair long, not as a fashion statement, but to help cover the terrible scars on the back of his neck. Logan was former MI6, but an almost fatal accident had gained him retirement before he was ready. Gabe hadn't hesitated at snatching Logan up to join the team. No one knew explosives better than Logan Grey.

"You cut it close, boss," Logan said. "In thirty seconds I wouldn't be here."

"Let's roll," Gabe said. "Be on the lookout for company."

Logan glanced once at Grace and then nodded, putting his submachine gun in his lap.

Gabe closed the window that divided the front and back seat so he and Grace had complete privacy.

"Who's your friend?" Grace asked.

"Logan Grey. Don't worry. He's heard all about you and still agreed to help me find you."

"I'm sure he's a real stand-up guy."

"He'll grow on you," Gabe said, keeping his gaze on the terrain around them, looking for threats. "So what do you think? It's just like old times. We always made a great team."

"Tell me what you want, and then let me go," she said. "I've got a tight schedule to keep."

"You don't have another job lined up once you deliver the flash drive to the South Koreans. Looks like you're a free agent." Gabe watched for a reaction, but she showed no surprise that he'd been keeping up with her movements. She waited him out with her silence and a hard look, and he decided to give in to the unspoken standoff... just this once.

"I've left the CIA," he told her.

"I heard. Congratulations. Let me go."

Gabe smiled and stretched out across the seat, crowding her with the length of his legs, but she didn't budge an inch. "Did you hear I'd joined the private sector and opened my own agency?"

She laughed, low and sexy, and the smoky sound swirled around him until he was dizzy with desire. "So, good boy Gabriel Brennan has decided to become a bad boy and go rogue. I assume the agency is displeased by your decision?"

"Not at all," he said, shrugging. "They know when something is out of their control. My agency is privately funded and our reputation is above reproach. Even the CIA recognizes the benefits unknown money can buy. Governments are still hampered by rules, for the most part. Sometimes there are jobs where the rules need to be broken. That's when they call me."

"Well, bully for you," she said. "You always did manage to get what you wanted. Everything Gabe Brennan touches turns to gold."

"Nothing could be further from the truth, and you know it," he said quietly. Gabe waited patiently for her to make eye contact. It didn't take her long. She'd never been a coward.

She tilted her chin defiantly. "I don't know anything about you. I never did. Our life together was a lie. I'm not even sure you know the real you."

He kept his face impassive, even though her words pierced his heart. "How long are you going to pretend she's not sitting here between us?"

"Don't mention her!" The quiver in her voice was quickly controlled. "I'll get out of this car and disappear off the face of the planet. If you want me to stay, then the past stays in the past. It's nonnegotiable."

"Fine," Gabe said. "Whatever you say."

The SUV slowed to a stop, and Gabe pushed the door open, not waiting to see if she'd follow. It was a stupid idea to think he could fix things—to heal the wounds that had been bleeding for the last two years.

Gabe's Gulfstream sat ready for takeoff on the hard-packed dirt the small Venezuelan city called an airport. He went up the stairs and then turned to face Grace, sure she'd still be in the car. But she stood at the bottom of the steps, her face carefully blank.

"You can either come with me or you can leave. The choice is yours," Gabe said without emotion, tossing her the flash drive.

She caught it one-handed and stared at him, studying him, trying to read every angle of the situation as she'd been trained to do at the agency. She finally nodded and started up the steps. "I'll come. A deal is a deal. And my word means something."

Gabe flinched before he could control it and let the pain roll through him. He had a feeling that before this job was over, she'd have one more reason to hate him.

AVAILABLE AT ALL RETAILERS

ACKNOWLEDGMENTS

Getting a book to publication takes an amazing team of people. I'm fortunate to have had these people in my corner for years.

To my editor—Imogen Howson for always making me better.

To my cover designer—Dar Albert for always blowing me away with your talent.

To my children—You're all so special. You have gifts and abilities beyond measure, and I'm excited to see what God has in store for each of you.

To Scott—thank you for answering a ridiculous amount of law enforcement questions and acting out weird scenarios with me. Any mistakes are mine alone.

ABOUT THE AUTHOR

Liliana Hart is a *New York Times*, *USA Today*, and Publisher's Weekly bestselling author of more than eighty titles. After starting her first novel her freshman year of college, she immediately became addicted to writing and knew she'd found what she was meant to do with her life. She has no idea why she majored in music.

Since publishing in June 2011, Liliana has sold more than ten-million books. All three of her series have made multiple appearances on the *New York Times* list.

Liliana can almost always be found at her computer writing, hauling five kids to various activities, or spending time with her husband. She calls Texas home.

If you enjoyed reading this, I would appreciate it if you would help others enjoy this book, too.

Recommend it. Please help other readers find this book by recommending it to friends, readers' groups and discussion boards.

Review it. Please tell other readers why you liked this book by reviewing.

Connect with me online:
www.lilianahart.com

facebook.com/LilianaHart
instagram.com/LilianaHart
bookbub.com/authors/liliana-hart

ALSO BY LILIANA HART

JJ Graves Mystery Series

Dirty Little Secrets

A Dirty Shame

Dirty Rotten Scoundrel

Down and Dirty

Dirty Deeds

Dirty Laundry

Dirty Money

A Dirty Job

Dirty Devil

Playing Dirty

Dirty Martini

Dirty Dozen

Dirty Minds

Dirty Weekend

Dirty Looks

Dirty Liars

Dirty Valentine

Addison Holmes Mystery Series

Whiskey Rebellion

Whiskey Sour

Whiskey For Breakfast

Whiskey, You're The Devil

Whiskey on the Rocks

Whiskey Tango Foxtrot

Whiskey and Gunpowder

Whiskey Lullaby

The Scarlet Chronicles

Bouncing Betty

Hand Grenade Helen

Front Line Francis

The Harley and Davidson Mystery Series

The Farmer's Slaughter

A Tisket a Casket

I Saw Mommy Killing Santa Claus

Get Your Murder Running

Deceased and Desist

Malice in Wonderland

Tequila Mockingbird

Gone With the Sin

Grime and Punishment

Blazing Rattles

A Salt and Battery

Curl Up and Dye

First Comes Death Then Comes Marriage

Box Set 1

Box Set 2

Box Set 3

The Gravediggers

The Darkest Corner

Gone to Dust

Say No More

Laurel Valley

Tribulation Pass

Redemption Road

Midnight Clear

Forgiveness River

Atonement Trail

www.ingramcontent.com/pod-product-compliance
Lightning Source LLC
Chambersburg PA
CBHW030858060726
47591CB00005B/1339